KV-637-930

BUGLES AT DAWN

Arrested as a young ensign after the eve of Waterloo, and interviewed by Wellington himself, John Bold flees to India where, in the 6th Bengal Infantry, he is confronted by a country where peace is an unnatural state as Mahratta chieftains plunder each other's territory. Riding high as commander of an irregular unit, John Bold is awarded a lieutenant's commission by Lord Hastings, Governor General. He christens his half-squadron native cavalry formation 'Bold's Horse' and spearheads the British break-up of Mahratta power while, despite all the protocol of British India, remaining his own man.

BUGLES AT DAWN

BUGLES AT DAWN

by

Charles Whiting

Magna Large Print Books
Long Preston, North Yorkshire,
BD23 4ND, England.

British Library Cataloguing in Publication Data.

Whiting, Charles
    Bugles at dawn.

A catalogue record of this book is
available from the British Library

ISBN   978-0-7505-2671-5

First published in Great Britain in 1990
by Century Hutchinson Ltd.

Copyright © Charles Whiting 1990

The right of Charles Whiting to be identified as the author of
this work has been asserted by him in accordance with the
Copyright, Designs and Patents Act, 1988

Published in Large Print 2007 by arrangement with
Eskdale Publishing

All Rights reserved. No part of this publication may be
reproduced, stored in a retrieval system, or transmitted in any
form or by any means, electronic, mechanical, photocopying,
recording or otherwise without the prior permission of the
Copyright owner.

COM RES 11/12.

Magna Large Print is an imprint of Library Magna Books Ltd.

Printed and bound in Great Britain by
T.J. (International) Ltd., Cornwall, PL28 8RW

And men in desert places, men... Abandoned, broken, sick with fears.

John Masefield

ONE: FLIGHT TO INDIA

1

Now it was almost evening.

Still the cannon on the ridge thundered. Over and over again the matches flared and the breeches of the cannon belched scarlet flame. But as the choking gunsmoke drifted across the front of the men waiting tensely on the ridge, it seemed that the battle for the centre was beginning to abate at last. Would it be their turn now?

All this long June Sunday, the line of Allied troops defending the ridge which barred the roads to Brussels had been holding off the French as they had come storming up the ridge, crying *'Vive l'Empereur!'*

First it had been the massed French cavalry, then their blue-coated infantry, and then infantry once again. Here and there the Allied line had broken. Once the Germans had begun pulling back in panic but had been beaten back to their positions by British dragoons wielding the flat of their sabres. Then the Belgians had collapsed altogether and had fled back to their capital ten kilometres away, bearing with them their tales of woe and defeat. Somehow Wellington had restored the line.

Now the weary troops, who had been marching and fighting for three long days on a few crusts of bread and a pannikin of soup, if they were lucky, kept looking at the darkening sky to the east. The French *had* to come soon; for they never attacked at night!

All along the ridge above Hougemont they sat in their squares, muskets at the ready. In the centre were their wounded, with the sweating surgeons, their shirts and breeches red with blood, working all-out while the orderlies plied the wounded with looted spirits, or laudanum. Wellington's veterans from the Peninsula did not seem to hear the cries of the wounded. They puffed phlegmatically at their little clay pipes or counted the silver francs they had already looted from the dead French to their front, sprawled out in the muddy grass like bundles of abandoned rags. But the veterans were few.

The men who made up Colonel Colborne's Fifty-second Regiment of Foot and their neighbours, General Maitland's Brigade of Guards, were mostly eighteen-year-olds bribed with the King's shilling and a few pints of ale by the recruiting sergeants to join the thinning ranks of Wellington's army. After twenty years of war against the French, fit men were in short supply. Most of the 'men' who would fight the last battle of this long bloody Sunday had been civilians only weeks before.

Ensign O'Hara frowned at the thought and looked at the heavily armed cavalrymen slumped in their saddles, sabres at the ready, just behind the Fifty-second's square. He knew why they were positioned there, staring warily at the infantry with red-rimmed eyes. Their principal task at the moment was not to fight the French. It was to beat back the infantrymen if they broke the square and fled. The Duke of Wellington knew just how thin his front was here at Hougemont and Napoleon still had his principal reserve – the Imperial Guard – uncommitted to the battle. When the Guard marched, it was muttered by the ashen-faced recruits, Old Boney always won. *Nothing* could withstand the charge of the Imperial Guard. *NOTHING!*

O'Hara's frown deepened at the thought. He had only been with the old Fifty-second three months, but he was immensely proud of the regiment in which his own father had served. It would be a terrible disgrace if it broke its square. He straightened his shoulders, trying to look manful and determined, his handsome face set. It was something he had learned from his dying father: 'Jean-Paul,' he had said in his soft Connemara accent, 'the men must fear ye more than the enemy... Make 'em fear ye and they'll follow ye to hell and back.' And he added cynically, 'especially if there's any prospect of loot, me boyo!'

Thrusting his sword across his shoulder, O'Hara started to pace his section of the square, an eighteen-year-old boy trying to bolster up the courage of other eighteen-year-old boys facing their first real action. Of course, he knew as an officer and gentleman he should feel no pity, no emotion, for these pale-faced youths. Soldiers had no rights; they were worse off than convicts. They had to obey, even when frightened out of their wits; because if they didn't, they would be lashed to a cannon wheel and flogged mercilessly. The Duke of Wellington was a remorseless advocate of the lash and the cat-o'-nine-tails.

But O'Hara knew that it was only starvation that had forced most of them into the army in the first place, especially the Irish recruits who made up most of the ranks of the Fifty-second. These Irish peasants turned soldier had lived off potatoes all year round, rarely seeing a piece of meat from one month to the other. Existing in their earth-floored hovels, eyes stung by the persistent peat-smoke, not even possessing a candle to lighten the fetid darkness, these Irish jackeens had been gulled into accepting King George's shilling so that the family would have one less mouth to feed.

The young ensign frowned again. When he did so, his dark handsome face, set against the curly jet hair he had inherited from his

French mother, looked much older. Already there was that droop of the lips which indicated a man who had been disappointed by life. But then, he told himself, he was little better off than those poor scared boys from the bogs. Was he not an orphan with not a penny to his name save his ensign's pay, with no prospects save those he might earn by military merit? He was in no position to buy another commission. Why, if Fate had it so, he could remain an ensign till he was sixty, not like those lordly Guards officers of Maitland's Brigade. All of them, with their splendid uniforms, gold-pommelled swords and affected airs, could afford to buy them a whole regiment if they so desired. Whereas he was just one jump ahead of the most lowly private in the whole of the Fifty-second Foot.

'I say, you there – fellah!' The voice was supercilious and instinctively O'Hara's skin crawled.

He turned round slowly, knuckles whitening on his sword hilt.

A pompous Guards officer, perhaps a couple of years older than himself, was staring at him, hands on hips, looking more like an angry housewife than a soldier.

'Yes?'

The Guards captain wet his lips. 'Pray have the goodness to say "Captain" when you address me, fellah,' he drawled, while behind him his fellow officers grinned at what they saw as the discomfiture of this young ensign from a lowly regiment of the line.

'*Captain*,' O'Hara said reluctantly, knowing the type: one of those puffed-up dandies who toadied to the Prince Regent and employed bullies to carry out their dirty work. The pudgy Guards captain with his gold epaulettes and ornate fur busby was one of that kind all right. 'What is it?'

The Guards officer was in no hurry. He took out a golden snuffbox, ran a line of the contents along his hand, then delicately breathed it in before sneezing in an affected manner and saying, 'Pray, sir, what are you doing walking in front of my part of the square, eh? You're a demned Fifty-Second fellah, aren't you? Just an ordinary infantry regiment. Can't you see that we are the Guards, what?'

His fellow officers laughed and one of them hooted, 'I say, Rodney, you are giving it him hot, eh?'

O'Hara coloured, although he felt nothing for the other officer but contempt. The gold braid and rich regimentals could not disguise a rich poseur whose father had probably bought him a captaincy for the summer campaign so that he could retire to Brighton for the winter season with the Prince Regent. He looked boldly at the Guards officers. 'I did not know, sir,' he snapped coldly, blue eyes sparkling dangerously, 'that it was not

16

allowed to walk the front of a Guards square. After all, we are *all* British officers, even if we are only members of a line regiment.'

Now it was the turn of the Guards officer to flush. 'What demned insolence!' he snorted, stamping his foot like a petulant child. 'Why, sir, if we were back in town I'd have my bullies deal with the–'

'*HURRAH ... HURRAH ... HURRAH!*' The burst of cheering, rippling along the lines cut into the Guardsman's outburst and the two of them turned to see the cause, as the Guards and then the infantry of the Fifty-second took off their bearskin and shakos and placed them on their bayonets.

A figure that O'Hara had only known from lampoons and caricatures was slowly trotting along the ridge line, followed by a handful of staff officers in cocked hats, some of them with bandages around their limbs and foreheads. There was no mistaking the lean figure of the Duke of Wellington, riding his chestnut Copenhagen. Although he wore civilian clothes – buckskin breeches, frock coat and blue cloak – the hook-nosed Allied commander was every bit a soldier: a man obviously used to giving orders – and having them obeyed.

He came level with the Guards officers. Hurriedly they raised their swords and saluted him. Casually he acknowledged them with his doffed hat and reined in his horse. He nodded to the Guards Captain and said with just a trace of the Irish brogue of his youth, 'Good evening to you, young Hartmann. Your father will be proud that you are with us this day, I do not doubt.'

'Thank you, Your Grace,' the other man fawned. 'Let us hope that we may meet them this evening before it is too late, and show them what the Guards are made of, sir.'

The Duke of Wellington looked down at the officer with hard, knowing eyes, as if not particularly impressed by what he had just heard. 'Never fear, Hartmann, you shall give them a taste of the steel before this day is out.'

Out of the corner of his eye, as he stood rigidly at the salute, O'Hara sensed that Captain Hartmann of the Second Foot Guards didn't quite like that reference to 'a taste of the steel'. For all his bluster, the fellow might well be a coward.

Next moment he dismissed the idle thought as the Duke raised himself in his stirrups and cried, 'Now listen you to me, all you brave fellows! Boney is almost defeated. All this day he has tried and tried again and in each case, other brave fellows like you have defeated him.' He searched their ranks with a gimlet eye, as if seeking weakness, while over at the French side the cannon started to thunder once more, muting the sudden rattle of the kettle drums sounding the *rappel*. O'Hara felt his blood thrill at the sound: the French were coming!

'Now it is in your hands, fellows. Boney will try again. There is no doubt of it.'

As if to confirm his words, from the other side of the ridge there came a great hurrah, followed by '*Vive l'Empereur ... Vive Napoleon!*' and then '*En avant ... en avant!*'

Wellington noted the cry, knowing that it was the Emperor of the French giving the final salute to his Imperial Guard before they advanced into battle. These were the magnificent veterans of the battles of Jena, Wagram and Austerlitz, who hitherto had never been conquered in combat. Now they were to meet his untried levees – youths from the industrial slums of the north and the bogs of Ireland.

His eye fell on the tall young ensign of the Fifty-second Regiment of Foot and liked well what it saw. Boys of that calibre never turned their heel upon an enemy. They would hold, he was sure of that. He raised his voice as the first balls from the French guns started to beat down once more on his ridge line and cried, 'Make ready, boys. *Here they come!*'

'Never fear, yer honour!' Private O'Holloran, the wit of the Fifty-second, called out as the ridge line started to disappear in a cloud of gunsmoke. 'Them frog-eaters'll nivver run the good old fifty-second off'n this hill.' Then his voice sank to a mournful

Church-of-England dirge: 'And may the Lord above make us thankful for what we are to receive... *Amen!*'

There was a burst of laughter and the Duke raised his plumed hat once more, as the sergeants started to bellow out their orders and the roll and tap of the kettle drums grew closer: '*Load ball... Fix bayonets... Load and ram ... cock yer locks...*'

In an instant all was controlled confusion, as the Guards and the men of the Fifty-second rose from the grass, broke their squares and under the orders of their officers, with the sergeants laying about them wherever they perceived tardiness, formed a triple line, the front rank kneeling, their muskets already raised, while the French cannon thundered. As they tensed, frozen into their positions on the ridge, with the fog of war weaving in and out of their ranks, they might have seemed to some casual observer like ghosts glimpsed through a drifting mist. Now even the cannonballs whizzing across the fields were forgotten, as the massive French force grew ever closer, their approach heralded by flaring trumpets, rattle of side drums and a steady tread.

A cannonball came hurtling, black and deadly, out of the smoke. It headed straight for the line of the Fifty-second. Instinctively a man here and there ducked as it whizzed overhead. 'For shame! For shame!' the others cried angrily at such conduct. They had been drilled never to duck and vented their anger on the momentary cowards. Despite his tension, O'Hara grinned softly. Trust the old Fifty-second, he told himself. It was a good regiment. There'd be no cowards in it by this evening. Then he concentrated his attention on his front. Old Boney never risked his last reserve, the Imperial Guard, unless he was absolutely sure of victory. What was to come would be a fight to the death.

The blare of the French trumpets and the urgent rattle of the kettle drums grew in volume as they sounded the *pas-de-charge*. Thousands of feet were just beyond the ridge now. They'd breast it at any moment. He tightened his grip on his sword and found that his palm was wet.

A salvo of grape struck the line of the Guards. Men went down screaming in a confused mass. '*Surgeon!*' someone yelled angrily and a moment later another voice, equally angry, bellowed, 'Damn you, you idle fellows, will you not dress your ranks – *this very instant!*'

O'Hara risked a quick look out of the corner of his eye. Already the young Guardsmen were shuffling their feet as if back in London on parade, dressing their ranks, filling the gaps left by the dead and wounded. He noted, too, that Hartmann had gone white under his busby. Suddenly he realized the man's fear, and looked away. The sight of a craven coward at this moment was not fitting.

Suddenly they were there! Thousands of them in tightly packed columns, their immaculate blue uniforms topped by massive fur bonnets. Each column was one hundred and twenty men broad, followed by rank after rank of gigantic guardsmen, urged on by officers who waved silver-bladed swords in Gallic excitement.

'Holy Mother o' God,' O'Holloran cried, 'did ye ever see the bleeding like? *They're all bloody giants!*'

'Silence in the ranks there!' Colonel Colborne called severely, his eyes fixed front, as the Imperial Guards stamped in their thousands up to the ridge, with the very ground seeming to tremble beneath them.

O'Hara swallowed hard, sudden doubt flashing. Would they be able to stop these victors of every battlefield in Europe?

Now the trumpets had ceased and the rattle of the kettle drums, too. The only sound was the heavy rhythmic tread of the Imperial Guard, each man in perfect alignment and step. O'Hara hardly dared breathe; the tension was too great. Something – *anything* – had to happen soon to break it.

Abruptly the Duke's voice was heard. 'They'll soon attempt to form a line for the charge, lads!' he called, standing up in his stirrups, tugging at the bit to keep Copenhagen from bolting. 'Maitland, it's your time.'

'Your Grace,' General Maitland called back, raising his sword in salute, whether to the French or the Duke no one ever knew.

The French halted some ninety yards away from the British line. In the front column their officers brought up their swords in salute to their enemies and gallantly kissed the blades. O'Hara watched fascinated.

'Stand to, you Guards,' the Duke yelled. 'Make ready!'

The young Guardsmen raised their muskets. *'Level!'* Maitland cried.

Each man squinted along the length of his musket, finger crooked around the trigger.

'Vive l'Empereur!' The massive cheer rose from ten thousand French throats.

Standing bolt upright in his stirrups in full view of the French sharpshooters, the Duke of Wellington waved his hat in a wide circle once and cried. *'FIRE!'*

2

The impact of that first volley was frightening. For one moment the whole battlefront disappeared in a cloud of gunsmoke – to clear an instant later. O'Hara gasped at the terrible havoc wrought by the Guards' salvo.

French soldiers had fallen everywhere, hundreds of them. At that range, even the worst shot among the Guards had been unable to miss. The dead lay in heaps or lined up in neat ranks just as they had in life, their powder-blue uniforms already turning scarlet, while the wounded and dying screamed for help and their mothers.

Behind him, O'Hara could sense the shock among his young soldiers. They had never seen anything like it. Perhaps five hundred men killed in a flash, slaughtered in the blink of an eye, and now piled up like butcher's meat.

To his left the Guards did not give the French a chance to recover. Feverishly as the kneeling front rank reloaded, whipping out fresh cartridges, biting off the paper end, spitting out the gunpowder, the second rank standing above them raised their muskets and aimed.

'*Fire!*' Maitland yelled. Two hundred and fifty muskets belched flame. Again that fire slammed into the stalled ranks of the Imperial Guard. The enemy, unable to take cover, went down screaming or cursing, the impact throwing them against their unhurt comrades behind, creating a human shock wave that rippled down the whole column.

French officers frantically waved their silver swords. NCOs struck savagely with their pikes or ramrods. *'En avant,'* they cried in rage. *'En avant, salauds!'*

But the Imperial Guard, never beaten in battle before, refused to move. Another volley smacked into them. The column reeled, the survivors swaying to and fro as if drunk.

Wellington laughed excitedly and raised himself in his stirrups to get a better view.

'M'lud, for pity's sake!' his staff cried, *'be careful!'* They knew the Duke in his civilian clothes was an obvious target for any French sharpshooter.

But the Duke had thrown all caution to the wind. He knew victory was almost his. If he broke the Imperial Guard, France would be defeated. 'We're seeing them off!' he cried in triumph. 'Go on, Colborne, go on. See them off with your gallant Fifty-Second... And you, sir, in command of the Second Guards. They won't stand. Don't give them a chance to rally, sir.'

O'Hara watched as the Colonel raised his sword. Suddenly his heart started to race. He swallowed and told himself it was the excitement, not fear. *They were going to attack, at last!*

Colborne flung a glance over his shoulder to check the two flag-bearers and their escorts were in place. They were. 'Lads,' he cried above the noise of the musketry and the pitiful cries coming from the French, 'we're going to give them a taste of steel.

Don't let the old regiment down, lads.' He raised his voice to a scream, his face flushed crimson. 'The Fifty-Second Regiment of Foot will advance!' He pointed his sword in the direction of the stalled French, who were at last beginning to fumble with their muskets, and take up position. '*ADVANCE!*'

As one the thousand men of the Fifty-second Regiment of Foot, bayonets lowered into a solid wall of steel, stepped forward, the boy drummer to the right of the line beating the pace on his kettle drum, the flags unfurled and waving in the slight breeze. To their left the Colonel in charge of the Second Guards shouted out his orders and immediately the Guards started forward, their officers to the front of the line, swords crossed over their chests, as was their custom.

It was a fine sight and O'Hara felt tears of emotion well up. What bold fellows they all were! He was proud to be one of this great company.

A charge of grape hissed into them. Someone screamed. O'Holloran cursed in Gaelic and clapped his hand to his shoulder to feel his own blood. He staggered and seemed about to fall out. Next moment he recovered and stepped on boldly with the rest.

'Brave fellow, O'Holloran!' O'Hara called.

''Tis nothing, yer honour,' the Irishman replied cheerfully. 'I've had worse scratches from the cat back in the Oud Sod, sir.'

O'Hara's smile lasted a second. A group of French cavalry was bearing down upon them. Chasseurs by the look of them, intent on giving support to the hard-hit Imperial Guard. They came leaning low over their mounts, swords already outstretched and in line with the horses' necks.

O'Hara gave his orders: 'Section – *halt!*' he cried above the thunder of the guns.

His section halted as one.

'Front rank – *kneel!*'

They did so like veterans.

Completely in charge of himself despite the danger and excitement, O'Hara waited till the men raised their muskets, then cried, 'Aim at the horses' guts! Don't worry about the riders – and wait till I give the order to fire!'

Now the French cavalry were almost upon them, the horses going all out as their riders applied the spurs.

Silently O'Hara, standing to the right of his section, counted off the distance: *Sixty … fifty yards … forty … thirty… IT WAS NOW OR NEVER!*

He brought his sword down sharply and yelled above the thunder of the racing hooves, *'FIRE!'*

The muskets exploded into action. At that range they couldn't miss. The Chasseurs simply disintegrated into a welter of blood, their mounts going down everywhere.

Hastily O'Hara yelled out his orders. The front rank rose to their feet. In quick time they hurried forward to keep up with the rest of the regiment, stepping over the gore regardless.

Now the Imperial Guard was finally beginning to recover. As Colbourne led his men in four ranks down the slope to the Frenchmen's left flank, they were forming a front, already raising their muskets to beat off the English attack. At the same time their Chasseurs and sharpshooters on foot were swarming out to the Guards' front in an attempt to delay the Fifty-second's progress.

A couple of French cavalry came riding full tilt at O'Hara's section. In the front rank O'Holloran raised his musket and fired. The leading rider screamed, his features sliding down his shattered face like molten wax. Next instant he slammed to the ground, dead. The second man jerked at the bit. His horse whinnied piteously and rose up on its haunches, great blobs of foam dripping from its muzzle. There it towered, as its rider brought down his sabre.

At the very last instant O'Hara jerked aside. The rider was caught off his stroke and O'Hara did not give him a second chance. He thrust his sword upwards viciously. The blade slid neatly into the Frenchman's unprotected stomach. He screamed shrilly as O'Hara withdrew the blood-red blade with a dreadful sucking sound. The horse bolted, dragging its dying rider, as O'Hara's men cheered and cried, 'Them froggies can't stand the cold steel, sir!'... 'See how–'

The rest of their words were drowned by the thunderclap of the first French volley. It hit the right flank of the Fifty-second Foot like a sledgehammer. Men went down screaming and choking in their own blood, with their comrades of the next rank stumbling and cursing over the fallen who writhed and twisted in their death agonies.

Colonel Colborne, the end of his sword snapped off by a French musket ball, waved the broken weapon angrily. *'Fire – damn ye!'* he cried urgently, as his line seemed to recoil, as if already preparing to break and run. *'FIRE!'* Behind him his sergeants lashed at the reluctant infantry with their pikestaffs, forcing them to stand straight and aim.

An ensign carrying the regimental colours darted forward, followed by his escort. 'Come on, lads!' he yelled in a high-pitched youth's voice, waving the heavy flag. 'Don't let the old regiment down–'

There was a scorching explosion. When the black smoke cleared, the ensign was no longer shouting. He was dead, stripped completely naked and charred by the explosion, his head rolling away quietly down the littered slope like a ball abandoned by some petulant child.

But his sacrifice was not in vain. The Fifty-second blasted a tremendous volley into the Imperial Guard – who went down like ninepins. Colonel Colborne did not give them a chance to recover. 'To the attack, lads!' he yelled above the din and ran forward, carrying the regiment with him. O'Hara waved his sword, carried away by the unreasoning bloodlust of battle, cursing obscenities he had not realized he knew. But to his left the nearest Guards, under the pudgy Captain Hartmann, had stalled. They were not keeping up with the advancing Fifty-second and even at this moment of crazed excitement, O'Hara knew that this presented danger. If the Imperial Guard rallied and attacked, they might well be able to turn the Fifty-second's flank and that could lead to disaster.

'Keep moving, sir … keep moving, sir!' he called desperately, his chest heaving with the effort of shouting above that chaotic noise. 'You must not pull behind, sir!'

But Captain Hartmann did not move. His horrified gaze was following the progress of that ball of flesh which had once been a human head, as it rolled and bounced down the slope. His face drained of all colour.

Suddenly O'Hara made up his mind. Running all out, he faced Hartmann. A slight trace of blood was trickling down the man's left cheek. 'I've been hit,' he quavered. 'I am not well.'

Behind him the young Guardsmen looked at him and then at each other and O'Hara didn't need a crystal ball to tell what they were thinking. Their officer was a craven coward. He had lost his nerve; he did not want to fight.

'It is the merest scratch, sir,' O'Hara gasped, seeing the gap between the two regiments growing by the instant. There was no time to lose. 'I'm sure you will be all right. But you must move, sir – *now!*'

Hartmann, his pudgy jowls shaking with fear, did not seem to hear. Once again he moaned weakly, 'I am hit … I can go on no longer.'

O'Hara's hot Irish temper flared. 'Shame on you, sir!' he snorted. 'You are risking the lives of my whole regiment. I order you to advance at once.'

Hartmann looked at him dully, as if seeing him for the first time. 'But I have just told you–'

Ensign O'Hara lost all control. He lashed out with his sword like an angry school-master at some schoolboy who had tried his patience too much and too long. The flat of the blade struck the coward's fat rump with a satisfying whack and he stumbled forward, as O'Hara raised the point parallel to the Guards officer's stomach and yelled furiously, 'Advance, damn you … or by God, I

swear I'll run you through here and now –
ADVANCE!'

The threat worked. Tears of self-pity
pouring down his ashen face, Captain Hartmann stumbled forward.

To the right the Fifty-second broke into a
run, cheering wildly. The Guards did the
same. And in that instant the Duke himself
came galloping up on his chestnut, for all this
day he had been present at every crucial
skirmish of the battle, losing all his gallopers
and many of his staff officers to enemy sharpshooters. It was the fact that he was always
prepared to risk his own life that endeared
him to the rank and file, although he had the
'scum', as he habitually referred to them,
flogged mercilessly for the slightest infringe-
ment.

For a long moment while the musket balls
whizzed back and forth, he stared down at
the handsome young ensign. Then he
nodded curtly, but whether that nod signified approval or disapproval O'Hara could
not fathom. But there was no mistaking
General Maitland's frosty look as he
cantered after the Iron Duke. He had obviously seen the incident with Captain
Hartmann and didn't approve. If Maitland
had his way, O'Hara was in for trouble.

But there was a battle still to be won.
Wellington knew that the Imperial Guard
had finally to be broken or even at this, the

eleventh hour, that old enemy of his, Napoleon, might still rally the French.

'Well done, Colborne,' he cried, riding towards the triumphant Fifty-second. 'Damned well done, sir! But go on, go on, sir. Don't give them a chance to rally. They won't stand, I tell you... *They won't stand!*' Almost as if he wanted to urge Colborne forward physically, he spurred Copenhagen, tossing his head with fright, right through the lines of the Fifty-second to within musket shot of the Imperial Guard.

That was too much for the survivors of the Guards and the Fifty-second, who gave a great cheer. Totally out of the control of their officers and sergeants now, they surged forward, eyes gleaming, teeth bared. Screaming obscenities, they fell upon the French.

In a flash they were in among the Imperial Guard, wielding bayonets tipped scarlet with enemy blood. They hacked, stabbed, sliced, giving no quarter, smashing the cruel butts of their muskets into the faces of the blue-clad giants, their own bodies shaking with the terrible violence of their rage. Everywhere the Frenchmen went down screaming, to be trampled under the feet of attackers who were so eager for blood they did not even stop to loot the dead and dying.

But now the French were beginning to surrender. Here and there whole groups of Napoleon's elite, never before defeated in battle, were throwing away their muskets and raising their hands in surrender, crying urgently, *'Pardon, m'sieu ... pardon!'* while to their rear, all order lost now, others started to flee the battlefield, throwing away their equipment in their unreasoning panic, even tugging off their boots and tossing them in the nearest ditch in the haste to escape this cruel slaughter.

Half an hour later, with a sickle moon already casting down its icy light on the terrible carnage, it was virtually all over. Old General Cambronne, tears trickling down into his dyed moustache, surrendered his sword tamely and the last two intact battalions of the Imperial Guard with it.

Above him on the hilltop which dominated the battlefield, his figure outlined a stark black by the moonlight, a weary Duke of Wellington raised his cocked hat in salute. 'Gentlemen,' he said in a tired voice, cracked and hoarse with a day long's shouting above the roar of the cannon, 'I may be wrong, but in my opinion we have given Old Boney the death blow. His army is destroyed... The men are deserting in parties, even his generals are withdrawing from him... I am now of the opinion he can no longer make any head against us.' He paused and looked sadly at the piles of dead, scattered as far as the eye could see, and sighed wearily. 'The men – poor fellows

– have done us proud, gentlemen.' He tugged at the bridle of his tired chestnut. 'Come, let us go home to Waterloo now. There is no more we can do here.'

His shoulders bowed beneath the blue cloak, almost as if *he* had been defeated instead of Napoleon, he started back for the village and his headquarters.

Ensign O'Hara watched them go as he leaned against the trunk of a leafless oak, suddenly assailed by an overwhelming emptiness as if a tap inside him had been abruptly opened and all the strength drained away. It had been a long, long day.

He sighed, watching the moon shine on that field of death, the silence broken only by the groans of the wounded who lay in helpless wretchedness beside their dead comrades, and by the clinker-hammers of the civilians who had swarmed on to the field of battle to chisel out the teeth of the dead.

O'Hara, too weary really to care, knew from his father's tales that the looters would not concern themselves only with the dead but would slit the throats of the wounded if the poor wretches attempted to stop them. But then, he told himself, it had always been thus over the centuries. To the victor belonged the spoils.

He yawned. He must find some place to lay his head this night. On the morrow, no doubt, the Duke would order the pursuit to drive Old Boney back into France. His stomach rumbled, but he was too shattered to attempt to find something to eat.

Jean-Paul O'Hara had fought his first battle. He would fight many more, but would never forget the Battle of Waterloo. For it would change his whole life, send him to exotic places and far climes and make for him strange adventures. But at this moment he was merely unutterably weary, a young man who had killed his first fellow creatures and now looked for somewhere to sleep.

3

''Twas no foight at all, bedad,' O'Holloran was saying merrily as light came back to the battlefield that Monday morning. His arm was in a dirty sling and a hunk of looted hard cheese was in his hand. 'Why our auld goat back in Kilkenny gave a divil more trouble, indeed.' He took another greedy bite.

O'Hara rubbed his unshaven chin and yawned; eyeing the battlefield once more, he was shocked by such massive carnage. The dead still lay where they had fallen, the blue coats of the French mingled inextricably with the red of the British, linked together like lovers in one last passionate embrace. Here and there came faint moans. There were so many wounded that the surgeons and their assistants had not been able to collect them all. Even now O'Hara could hear the grating of a surgeon's saw on some poor fellow's shattered bone and smell the sharp odour of boiling tar with which they would cauterize the massive wound left by the amputation. He frowned momentarily and ran his dirty hand thorough his tight black curls.

Somewhere in the lines of another regiment there came the sweet lift of a bugle sounding some call or other. His mood changed instantly, as it always did when he heard those calls carried on the still dawn air. 'Bugles in the dawn,' his father always maintained, often with sentimental tears, 'the finest sound a man can ever hear, Jean-Paul.'

And he agreed. But his father had not told him that call to action ended for many like this: mounds of shattered corpses, wounded left to die in their own gore while their marauding comrades stole their pitiful few possessions. He frowned pensively, his good mood destroyed, and even O'Holloran's new joke about the Frenchman and the pig could not quite restore it.

'Ensign O'Hara?'

He swung round, startled out of his reverie.

Colonel Colborne was standing there, his shako replaced by a bloodstained bandage round his head. He looked wan and his hand shook slightly. 'O'Hara, this officer wishes to speak to you.' He indicated the staff officer in a peaked cap standing next to him.

O'Hara recognized the officer as one of those who had accompanied the Duke of Wellington. He clicked to attention.

'O'Hara, that is your name, isn't it?' the staff officer said haughtily. 'Am I correct?'

'Yessir.'

'You were on the left flank of the Fifty-Second Regiment of Foot yesterday, were you not?'

'Yessir.' What the devil was going on?

At the staff officer's side Colonel Colborne frowned severely, as if he did not like whatever was going on one bit.

'I see.' He looked at Colonel Colborne expectantly.

'I say, Felton-Hervey,' the Colonel said, 'what is this? O'Hara is a fine young officer. I knew his dear departed father these twenty years. He served with me in the Peninsula. What—'

Felton-Hervey held up his hand for silence. 'Colonel Colborne, I am afraid, sir, this is a matter between this officer and His Grace. I am not allowed to speak about it. Now, O'Hara, are you ready?'

'You can borrow Captain Burrows' mount, O'Hara,' Colborne interjected.

O'Hara looked from the honest face of his CO to that of the staff officer, his mind racing wildly. 'Ready, sir,' he answered as firmly as he could manage.

They were flogging a private soldier outside the Duke's HQ in the little white peasant house in Waterloo's muddy, traffic-choked main street. As usual when there was no tripod available they had strapped him to a cart wheel, tying his wrists to it with his own crossbelts. Now a sweating provost sergeant was laying into the half-naked man with the cat-o'-nine-tails, ripping the young soldier's back to scarlet shreds with each fresh blow, while at his side a bored clerk counted off the strokes in a disinterested voice, as if he had done this a dozen times before.

Hurriedly the worried young ensign turned his gaze away. He did not like the traditional brutality of the British Army, although he knew it was necessary. The men, even the youngest among them, were a tough bunch who would rape and loot indiscriminately at the very first chance if they weren't kept in check. And, according to the Duke, the only way that that could be achieved was with the stick and lash.

'All right, Ensign,' Felton-Hervey rasped from the open door of the little house, 'His Grace will see you now.'

Squaring his shoulders and wishing he could have shaved, O'Hara hurried through into what had once been the kitchen, now crowded with senior officers, including

General Maitland of the Guards. Maitland shot O'Hara a black look, then continued with his conversation as the staff officer forced a path through the throng. Many of them were flushed and too animated as if they had been drinking to celebrate this great victory. Or perhaps it was the fever – half the army was suffering from the flux and high temperatures.

The Duke of Wellington was at a makeshift desk, parchments tied with blue ribbon rolled up neatly in front of him, quill pen in hand. In one corner a carpet-shrouded bundle lay on a camp bed. It was that of his quartermaster who had died of his wounds there that night, with the Duke sacrificing his own precious bed for his fellow officer.

For a while the Duke appeared not to notice their presence, but kept dipping the quill into the inkwell and signing the dispatches. O'Hara had time to observe his sharp lined face dominated by a great beak of a nose. This morning the strain of the last three days was all too obvious; the Duke looked a good ten years older than his forty-six.

Finally the Duke put down his quill and nodded quietly to Felton-Hervey. The aide opened the door. O'Hara caught a fragment of General Maitland snorting, 'The fellah's a blackguard, sir! Fancy a line officer striking one of my Guards officers. Where will it end, sir, I say?' and then the door closed.

The Duke surveyed the young officer with bright blue eyes for a moment and O'Hara was tempted to lower his own gaze under such intensity. The Duke's piercing look was calculated to frighten anyone. Suddenly he spoke, his voice hoarse but powerful and dominant: the voice which had in the last years imposed its will on the British Army and led it from defeat to victory.

'You are a very bold fellow, sir, a very bold one indeed. Do you not realize it is a serious military offence to strike a superior officer, sir?'

'Your Grace,' he stuttered, feeling himself go red.

'Yes, sir, you as a junior officer struck a senior officer, Captain Hartmann of the Second Guards. Indeed,' he added very severely, 'you did more. You sword-whipped him and there is no use denying it. I saw the incident with my own eyes. Now, sir, what have you to say for yourself?'

O'Hara hesitated.

The Duke tut-tutted impatiently. 'Well,' he demanded, eyes like gimlets, 'I am waiting.'

He stammered, 'I did strike Captain – er – Hartmann of the Second Guards and I know now it was wrong of me to do so. All I can say in my defence, Your Grace,' he ended a little lamely, suddenly fully aware of the gravity of his offence, 'is that I did so in the heat of the battle because I felt that his ... er ... reluctance to advance would endanger the left flank of the Fifty-Second.'

Again the Duke snapped, 'Do you realize that it is the most serious breach of discipline that an army can suffer when an inferior strikes a superior? The discipline of the whole formation can easily collapse thereafter.'

In misery Ensign O'Hara nodded and murmured, 'Yes, Your Grace.'

'Now if Captain Hartmann were prepared to duel with you, I should let him do so in an instant and the whole affair could be settled on the field of honour.' The Duke frowned suddenly and tugged at the end of his beaked nose. 'But he is not prepared to do so.' For a moment his voice took on a certain derisive note, as if he could not comprehend an officer who was not prepared to fight for his honour. 'So what am I going to do with you, sir? If you were a common soldier I would have you flogged like that screaming wretch out there.' Contemptuously he indicated the private tied to the cart wheel, his back torn to scarlet ribbons now. 'He took one hundred guineas from his own wounded officer. Most probably he would have slit the poor gentleman's throat afterwards if he had not been apprehended in time. I could even have you hanged. It wouldn't be the first time I have hanged a man under my command.'

'Yessir,' O'Hara answered, his head reeling now. Everyone in the army knew just how ruthless the Iron Duke could be. In his ten years of campaigning in India he had always maintained that instant savagery was the only way to subdue the natives who outnumbered his small European army a thousandfold, and he had slaughtered the Indians without mercy.

The Duke let his words sink in. There was a sudden silence in the room, broken only by the muted chatter of the officers next door and the fading screams of the soldier being flogged who was now relapsing into blessed unconsciousness. Wellington assessed O'Hara as if he was trying to see something in those features that only he could recognize and understand.

Abruptly he spoke. 'If Captain Hartmann's section of the Second Guards had hesitated much longer,' he said quietly, as if afraid he might be overheard in the outer room, 'the Imperial Guard might well have rallied and turned the left flank of the Fifty-Second Foot. If I had been in your place, O'Hara, as a hotblooded young man, I might have done the same as you. There is no place in the British army for cowards. Yesterday we had an officer who deserted his colours on the field of battle by pretending he had been stunned. Another actually fled the field on a

French cavalryman's horse. Totally dis-honourable and both officers are already on their way back to London in disgrace. They will be drummed out of the army, I can assure you, sir!'

O'Hara's heart leapt. *The Duke was taking his side!* There was hope after all.

The Commander-in-Chief noted the change in his expression and said harshly, 'Young man, don't raise you hopes too soon. For you have made a bitter enemy of a man of wealth and importance – too much im-portance in my humble opinion,' he added a little bitterly. 'The first Hartmanns came over with the first King George at the begin-ning of last century, and ever since have had great influence at court. The present Lord Hartmann, Captain Hartmann's father, has even succeeded in becoming an intimate friend of both the Duke of York *and* the Prince Regent.' He tapped the side of his long nose significantly.

O'Hara knew what the Duke meant. The two brothers, the Duke of York who com-manded the British Army, and the Prince Regent who ruled in place of his mad father, old George III, were deadly enemies. Lord Hartmann certainly had to be a man of great wealth and influence to remain friends with both of them.

'So, young man, what do you think would be the reaction of such – er – illustrious personages if I let you go unpunished for an offence against the son of their greatest crony, eh?' He glared fiercely at O'Hara.

'But Your Grace,' O'Hara protested hotly in the manner of young men who always believe that right and justice must triumph, 'you did say that Captain Hartmann's actions were those of a coward!'

'I did. But they were actions of a high-born coward with the greatest connections in the land, while you are a mere brave nobody.' He snapped his fingers and O'Hara started. Suddenly the Duke was all energy, his brain racing as it always did when he was planning some new action. 'We have to make a decision, do something before the Maitland clique in the Guards acts. Ensign O'Hara must disappear this very instant. You are a bold young fellow, so I now christen you *Bold* without benefit of bell, book and candle. Pray what is your first name?'

'Jean-Paul, sir. My mother was French–'

The Duke waved him to silence. 'John, you shall be. *John Bold,* yes I like the ring of it. John Bold – *nomen es omen,* as the Romans said.'

Hastily, while the young man's head spun at this sudden change of identity, the Duke picked up a fresh piece of parchment and scribbled furiously. 'I made my name and fortune, Bold, in the Indian sub-continent. Like so many other Englishmen, I went

there at the turn of the century, an unknown
… a poor man. I returned with money and
a name. You, with luck and your boldness,
might well do the same.'

Bold gaped. What did he know of India
save what little he had learned of that
remote continent in his dame school and his
father's tales of soldiering there before he
had been captured by the French?

'Now,' the Duke continued, 'I am writing
to the Marquis of Hastings, the Governor-
General and a friend of mine, recommend-
ing that John Bold who served under me
bravely here at Waterloo should be given a
commission in the John Company's – er, the
East India Company's – native infantry. That
won't cost you a penny piece, for there on
the other side of the world you do not have
to purchase your commission.' He gave a
crooked smile. 'If the plague does not carry
you off, the native wars will. There is always
a great need for white officers out there.'

'India … commission in the East India
Company…' Bold stuttered in confusion. 'I
am afraid I don't understand Your Grace…'

The Duke signed the parchment with a
great flourish, sanded his writing and rolled
the message before securing it with his
personal green ribbon. He looked up. 'Then
I'll make it perfectly clear to you, *Mister*
John Bold. Five minutes ago I made a certain Ensign Jean-Paul O'Hara disappear.

Now I'm going to do the same with John Bold. Once he leaves this room, all trace of him must vanish. He will be on his way to India and a new life.' He thrust back the simple wooden peasant chair and rose.

As Bold stiffened to attention, the Duke waved him to relax. 'You are no longer a soldier, sir, just a mere civil person, and civil persons do not stand to attention even for commanders-in-chief.' He forced a wintry grin. 'Now I am going to my privy to make water. There you see my cloak' – he indicated the blue cloak he habitually wore. 'You shall take off your shako now and don the cloak. It will cover your regimentals until you are able to possess yourself of civilian attire... Oh, yes' – he picked up a bag of coins – 'these are the hundred guineas that soldier out there stole. His poor unfortunate officer will need them no more – he died of his wounds during the night. Now they are yours.' He tossed them to a gaping John Bold who somehow managed to catch them. 'They will see you to India, if you are careful. Now I will make water while you escape, after stealing my cloak, through yon window.'

'But sir,' he said fervently, 'how can I thank you for what you have done for me. Sir? I don't–'

Wellington held up his hand for silence. 'You blotted your copybook because you felt you were doing the right thing. Unfor-

47

tunately you do not know the ways of the rich and powerful. For that you must pay the price of youthful stupidity.' The Duke's rasping voice softened a little. 'Nevertheless, you have my best wishes for the future. Good luck to you in India, John Bold. And now I must piss...'

Cautiously John Bold crouched and spied out the ground. Undoubtedly he would have no more than five minutes before the Duke raised the alarm and every man's hand would be against him. He must be out of this village before then. But which way? What would his pursuers expect a fugitive to do? Swiftly he had his answer. He'd be assumed to have taken the road to Nivelles, following the defeated French, hoping to find succour among them. It was the usual thing with deserters. Besides they might already know he was half French. So instead he would ride towards Brussels and somehow branch off to the east before he reached the capital, which would be full of Allied troops.

The clip-clop of hooves indicating a mount ridden at a sharp canter broke into his reverie. Coming up from the direction of Hougemont on a fine white Arab, lotioned, powdered and dressed in elegant regimentals, was the man who had caused his downfall and was now sending him into exile – Captain Hartmann of the Second Guards!

Bold's face contorted and flushed with sudden rage as his hand fell to his sword. But he controlled himself. He would not even have the chance to fell the scoundrel to the ground. Revenge must wait for another year. He watched Hartmann descend from his horse and enter the Duke's HQ, obviously to exact his pound of flesh.

John Bold waited no longer, but bolted for his horse. He was on his way into the unknown...

4

His parents, when they had been young and happy, untroubled by exile and the worries of money, must have ridden this same road, mused John Bold as he cantered along the dusty *pavé*, eastwards towards the hills on the horizon. With her help, Father had flown the notorious Revolutionary gaol, the Citadel at Verdun, the two of them posing as Flemish weavers returning home.

They had made a new life in a country foreign to them both, England. There his father, newly returned from years in India, had hoped to regain his broken health, while his wife, the last of the de la Mazieres, had waited for the counter-revolution which would restore her fortune. But their plans had come to naught. What use was a sick half-pay lieutenant of the Fifty-second Foot when England was not at war?

As he cantered along the dead-straight road that led to the Walloon township of Bande, Bold thought of his parents, living in the past with their impossible dreams.

'Why didn't ye know, my boyo, that the O'Briens, the O'Connors and the O'Haras are the last descendants of Old Ireland's Kings?' his father would chortle, face as red as his hair, when he had earned a few extra pence to enjoy a pannikin of cheap rum. 'Why, my spark, you might rightly have been on the throne of Ireland if things had been different.'

Not to be outdone, his mother, fingers blistered from making fine lace, her only skill, which she sold to the fine ladies of Brighton, would then launch into the history of the de la Mazieres of Lorraine and the great estates they had once owned before the Revolution. It was always *before* the Revolution before that scum, the *canaille*, had taken the house, the grounds, the farms – everything – away from them.

Two poor people, living for each other and finding that only the past gave any substance to their lives, the one outdoing the other with more outrageous lies. For as he saw it now, there had been no hope for them right from the start: a Catholic Irishman with no money to purchase a regiment and no hope of advancement in the service unless there were another war; and a spoiled French woman who barely spoke English. How could such a pair survive in the harsh Protestant climate of southern England?

Things had changed a little when Wellington had returned to England from India and begun recruiting a new army for the Peninsular campaign in Spain in 1805. By the time the Duke had landed with his new army at Mondego Bay to begin his long battle against the French in that country, Bold's father was a captain again in the Fifty-second and had begun sending money home. There had been bitter defeats and glorious victories, with Captain Patrick O'Hara, a true fighting Irishman, always at the forefront of battle – and the subsequent looting. Money and prize money had started to flow into the little cottage in the shadow of the ruined castle at Dover. For Bold's mother had insisted on living as close to France as possible so that when that 'foreign parvenu' Napoleon was defeated, they could return speedily to Lorraine and claim the estates of the de la Mazieres. But that wasn't to be. In 1812, three years ago when Bold had been a skinny boy running wild, his father had lost a leg in the assault on the great fortress at Badajoz. The brief good times were over, and his father returned home to die.

Six months later his mother had followed, more of a broken heart than any physical cause, as their old apothecary Joshua Atkins had told the sorrowing boy. But right to the end his mother had retained her French thriftiness. She had left behind two diamond brooches worked in the shape of the rose of Lorraine, the family crest. They were antique, the silver mounts tarnished, but the diamonds worth enough to buy an ensign commission in his father's old regiment, the Fifty-second Foot. It had been the natural choice of occupation for a half-educated boy with no parents, no fortune and no other future. He would devote his life to soldiering, come what may, just as his father had done and generations of O'Haras before him.

Now, Bold reflected bitterly as he trotted by another huge pile of abandoned French equipment – brass helmets, shakos, weapons, broken carts piled with loot, to be plundered by peasants from the local villages – his military career was over, at least in the British Army. Dressed in shabby civilian clothes purchased from a merchant en route, he was riding to an uncertain future on the other side of the world. He considered once again the rough plan he had worked out since fleeing the Duke's headquarters the day before. When his father had first sailed for India, Britain had been at peace with pre-revolutionary France, and travellers for that far country had first crossed France by coach, sailed from Marseilles to Egypt, then crossed the desert and taken another ship from the Persian Gulf to Bombay or Madras. The alternative was a long voyage with all its attendant perils – disease, pirates, storms, hunger – from Portsmouth right round the Cape and thence to India.

Now that France was enemy country, with Old Boney's beaten army retreating back to their own land, he would have to skirt her frontiers. As he saw it, the French would be withdrawing in a south-easterly direction towards Paris. Therefore he must travel *north-east* to the Rhenish provinces of Germany, now firmly in the possession of the Duke's allies, the Prussians.

Once safely there he could use the dead officer's guineas to purchase a coach ticket round the borders of France and into Italy. There at Bari or Genoa he would take ship for Egypt. With careful management of his money he would be able to reach Madras, present himself to the Governor-General and obtain a commission with the East India Company.

But first he must concentrate on getting out of the war zone. Bold was quite sure that the British Army was no longer interested in him – the Duke would see to that. But the French were different. He had heard what happened to a French army in defeat. Many of its soldiers broke away from the main body and became armed marauders, looting, raping and living off the land. In the end they turned into highwaymen and downright cut-throats.

There might be hundreds of such stragglers attempting to live in the woods which stretched for miles in this part of the country. If he were to survive, it would be by his wits and a strong right arm. The average French deserter would not hesitate to slay him for the sake of his horse alone. Unconsciously he touched the two light cavalry pistols, taken from a dead hussar, which now lay concealed in the furled horse blanket. A gentleman might display his sword without being taken for a soldier. But twin pistols would mark him as such. As it grew dark, the feel of their hidden strength gave him a sense of security. Their double barrels presented him with considerable fire power.

As his mount toiled up the steep height which led to the small township of Bande, Bold saw the dark heights beyond which marked the border between the Prussian Rhineland and the Dutch province of Belgium. On both sides thick pine forests marched up to the tops of the hills like spike-helmeted Prussian grenadiers. No smoke came from the chimneys of the dirty-white stone cottages he glimpsed now and again by the narrow road and it was as if he rode through a land which had gone to sleep.

He shivered slightly and felt the hairs at the back of his head rise. With a grunt he pulled the Duke's cloak tightly about his broad shoulders and resisted the temptation to look behind. He told himself he was behaving like a damned coward. Everything was quiet because the locals had already settled down for the night. In this part of the world, just as in Ireland, the peasants probably went to sleep with the chickens – thrifty good country folk who would not waste coin on tapers or candles. He rode on into the night shadows. There was no sound save that of his horse's hooves and its periodic snorts and head tossings.

Bold bit his lip with apprehension. His mount was too frisky, and he had to tug at the bit and give its flanks the spurs to keep it under control. Tired as the horse was, it sensed something that he couldn't. It was not just his imagination!

Carefully he looked left and right, where the trees were tightly packed right up to the heights. There was no way out there. He was confined, by the fact that he was mounted, to the narrow road.

Making a decision, he took the reins in his teeth and felt under the horse blanket with both hands for the comforting hardness of the cavalry pistols. Not taking his eyes off the darkening road for one instant, he cocked the pistols. Even muffled by the blanket, they made such a noise that he started.

'Damn fool!' he cursed himself softly.

Although he had been expecting something, it came as a shock when the first rider emerged from the trees to the right, perhaps a hundred yards away, and urged his horse up the grass embankment on to the road. There he paused and stared in Bold's direction.

A sickle moon had risen, and in its cold spectral light he could see the man, burly, wrapped in a rider's cloak and wearing what, for a moment at least, looked like a mask hiding his lower face. Then Bold recognized it: a moustache which had been set in hot tar to make a great splay of hair and give the face a frightening martial air. And the startled young man knew who affected to wear their moustachios in this fashion: the dragoons of Napoleon's *Grande Armée*. The man waiting silently for him, posted motionless like a black ghost, was a French cavalryman!

Bold reined his horse to a slow walk. They had been riding since dawn. The beast was very tired. But he hoped it would react to any demand for speed he might make on it.

Slowly the distance narrowed. The only

sound was the muted clip-clop of his horse's hooves on the silver cobbles and the occasional shiver of the other man's horse as it tossed its mane with apprehension. The blood coursed through his veins hotly. The hands which clutched the pistols were wet. His heart raced. He knew the symptoms, a combination of fear, tension and the urgent desire for violent action, *anything* which would break the heavy spell.

Now they were separated by about fifty yards. He was still out of accurate pistol range, and was not going to reveal his weapons until he was sure of hitting the stranger, waiting for him there motionlessly, menacingly.

There was a rustle of bushes to the other side of the road, followed by the snort of a horse taking the steep rise. Bold cursed under his breath. There was no mistaking the drawn sabre of the second rider, gleaming a cold deadly silver in the moonlight. He tightened his grip on the twin pistols. It wouldn't be long now. He rode on, his imagination racing as he tried to outthink the two of them.

'*Allez vite ... a l'attaque! ... allez, mer gars!*' The sudden command from within the bushes to the right cut into Bold's consciousness like a savage stab.

The two dragoons didn't hesitate. They dug their spurs into their mounts as one.

57

The heavy horses started forward. Waving their sabres they came straight at John Bold, yelling crazily in the French fashion.

Now he felt icy calm, in total control, just as he had been when the Imperial Guard had attacked at Waterloo in what now seemed another age. All decisions had been made for him. Now he must kill or die. He tugged the first pistol from underneath the blanket, reigning in his mount with a sharp tug from his teeth. Next moment he dug his knees in hard at the shivering horse. Everything now depended upon it remaining still. He dare not miss, for he would have no time to draw his sword.

Forty yards … thirty yards… The dragoons were galloping full out now and he could see them perfectly clear: the frightening moustaches, the gleam on their helmets, the flying dyed plumes – and those lethal sabres swishing the air to left and right, as if they were already lopping off heads.

Twenty-five yards away! He could wait no longer. He pulled the trigger in his right hand. The pistol bucked violently and he felt the peppery sting of the exploding powder in his face.

The dragoon on the right was hit right in the chest. He flung up his hands. His sabre clattered to the cobbles. He screamed like a woman in childbirth. Next moment he had been swept from the saddle. His horse fled by Bold at a tremendous rate.

He fired again. A sheet of angry purple flame and smoke obscured his vision for a moment, then he blinked his eyes free. *He had missed!* The second dragoon was still coming at him, sabre upraised, ready for the kill. He tensed his body for the killing blow, fumbling hopelessly with the other pistol, knowing that it was too late.

Nothing happened. In the very last moment, as he jerked his own trembling, terrified mount to one side, the other man thundered by and Bold saw that the whole right side of his face was gone, leaving a scarlet, dripping mass beneath the brass helmet. Within seconds the crazed horse, its dead rider held in the saddle by some weird trick, had disappeared.

For what seemed an age, though it might have been only a minute, John Bold slumped in his saddle, breathing hard, while his horse pawed the road impatiently. It wanted to be off, despite its weariness; it did not like the smell of the dead man.

Suddenly Bold remembered the voice which had ordered the attack. He drew his sword and searched the darkness tensely. But there was no one. Sheathing his sword and keeping one loaded pistol in his hand – just in case – he rode the rest of the way to the township of Bande, his mind full of the strange attack.

Why should deserters from the French Army be hanging around on a lonely forest road at this time of night? What kind of pickings could they expect there? Peasants did not travel at night, and in these war-torn times, neither did merchants and the like – if they were sensible and wanted to keep their money. Or had that deadly little ambush been arranged specifically for him?

It was only an hour later when he was safely seated near the great roaring open fire of the Lion d'Or, drinking a welcome tankard of mulled ale and waiting for food, that it struck him. The man who had cried from the dark forest *'go on, quick – attack!'* had given the orders in French with a cockney accent...

5

Aix-la-Chapelle, or Aachen, as the Germans called it, just over the Dutch border with the Prussian Rhineland, was in a state of complete confusion. For the last twenty years the old city, founded by the Romans, where once German emperors had been crowned, had been under French occupation. Not that most of the locals thought of it as an occupation. For the French had brought with them freedom from the yoke of the

Catholic Church and the feudal landowners who had treated their humble, meek peasants little better than serfs.

But now the Prussians had taken over. Although they spoke the same language as the citizens of the border city the victorious Prussians from the north were as foreign as the French; and now they were behaving like an occupation army. Everywhere, as John reined his horse to a walk, there were burly Prussian grenadiers in the narrow alleys and streets around the cathedral, using their long bayonets to rip down French street signs, pulling down the hated *tricolour* and trampling it underfoot, and plundering any of the little shops still foolish enough to display signs in French.

The locals watched in fearful silence. The citizens in their shabby coats and worn beaver hats and the country folk in white smocks and gaiters knew that the Prussians suspected them of having worked hand in glove with the French and having served in Napoleon's armies, which in truth a lot of the younger ones had. Now they realized the Prussians were going to make them pay for their real or suspected treachery. It would be 1792 once more when the ragged drunken revolutionary army of the new Republic of France had come swarming across the border like locusts. For a while they were going to have to suffer.

But it was no concern of his. He must find food and lodging for the night. Then on the morrow he would sell his horse and discover how the coach ran to far-off Bavaria in the south, where he would cross the border into Italy.

He penetrated deeper into the streets huddled against the great Romanesque cathedral, their houses leaning against its massive walls as if in need of protection. Barefoot urchins ran errands. Men hawked stone pots from carts pulled by dogs. A knife-grinder was busy at his wheel, watched by a crowd of gawping yokels. Housewives gossiped as they carried buckets of water from the street wells on yokes. A few raddled whores leaned from upper windows, their hair unkempt under dirty lace caps, breasts bulging from filthy fichus. It could have been any big city, yet to John there was an underlying tension about the scene.

Suddenly the succulent odour of roasting meat assailed his nostrils. He stopped and felt his lips begin to water. For the last three months since the campaign in the Low Countries against Napoleon had commenced he had been living off 'choke-dog' hardtack, and the usual British soldier's rations of oatmeal and peas. Even in Bande the fare had been poor, a thick porridge garnished with slabs of salt bacon. Now the thought of a real roast and what went with it made his stomach rumble in anticipation.

He paused in front of the establishment from which the smell was coming. It was not an ordinary alehouse but a real coaching inn, with the bugle-horn of the post engraved on its façade above the sign which announced this was the *Gasthaus zur Alten Post* – the Old Post Tavern. He nodded his approval. Such places, in contrast to the rough and ready alehouses where one slept in the barn or on the rough benches after the other customers had departed, would be expensive. But he felt he deserved the luxury. Besides, here he might not only dine and sleep, but also find out about the coaches.

Half an hour later, his horse stabled and fed, his few bits of baggage stowed away by the ostler's assistant in a low-ceilinged room dominated by a double bed with a stuffed goose-feather coverlet, he sat expectantly in the dining room. At his side was the huge green-tiled *Kachelofen* which reached to the ceiling, adding its heat to the open fire at the other end of the room, where a cook in a dirty apron tended the roast on his spit and constantly stirred various copper pots and kettles.

'*Guten Abend, junger Herr.*' With a curtsey the serving wench, a pretty young thing with flaxen hair in a braid around her head, said, 'And what are the young gentleman's wishes?'

John grinned roguishly. She was a ripe young pigeon and he knew what some of his fellow officers back in the Fifty-second Foot would have answered. Speaking slowly in the Lorraine *patois* he had learned at his mother's knee, he said, 'Some of that roast, *Jungfrau*, and what goes with it ... and, yes, some bread and ale.' Again she bobbed a curtsey, giving him a flash of her pretty blue eyes, and he told himself that title of '*Jungfrau*' – maiden – was merely a courtesy. With her figure and the kind of look she had just given him, he doubted if she would have preserved her virginity long in a place like this.

Five minutes later she was back with a wooden platter, piled high with slices of the sour roast – beef marinated in herbs and vinegar – plus *sauerkraut* and the steaming small dumplings of the area, filled with chopped liver.

From the zinc-covered bar, already awash with beer suds, she watched him enjoying his food. What an attractive young man he was, she told herself, despite the fact he was a foreigner...

It was when she brought the *Kompott,* a mixture of currants and dried apricots covered with a thick layer of cream, that he discovered the reason for the stifling heat. Although Aachen lay high above sea level and was usually subjected to cold northern breezes, it was June and what landlord would waste money on heat at this time of year?

'It's yon blackamoors,' the girl whispered as she answered his question. 'There in the *separée.*' She nodded to the almost closed-off wooden alcove in the corner. 'They say in Africa they run around naked.' She giggled suddenly and covered her mouth, as if she had said something shameful. 'They need the heat. That is why the landlord has fired the oven so. I 'spect they pay him well.'

Replete with good food, he looked casually at the *separée.* Her 'Blackamoors' were undoubtedly Indians of some sort, for above the partition he could see the silken domes of turbans and the gleam of what he took to be pearls, holding them in place; while beneath there were curved sandals of expensive leather, worked in intricate designs. He grinned to himself. The serving wench probably had never heard of India.

Idly as he picked at his *Kompott,* knowing that he had eaten too much already, he wondered what these rich Indians were doing in this remote German city. Once as a boy he had gone to London with his father and had seen a group of them with some rich nabobs, just returned from making their fortune with the East India Company, all of them wrapped in silks and expensive furs. How alien they had looked: all dark flashing eyes, hooked noses and sensual, rapacious mouths. They seemed to him to belong to a civilization, if that was the word for it, which was totally remote and foreign.

The trouble in the inn started some half an hour later jut as he was about to finish his ale. The place had filled up, mostly with civilians, drinking the potent local apple wine, but there was a handful of Prussian light infantrymen in green uniforms with dark facings, who were soon flushed with beer and schnapps. There were five of them, lean tall young fellows with short blond hair and extravagant moustaches, waxed and turned upwards in the French fashion. Five insecure young men, wishing to attract attention to themselves and doing it in the only way they knew how. By being loud and unpleasant.

It began with the serving wenches. It was the usual business. The hands grabbing and pinching, the arms encircling their waists, trying to force the sweating, red-faced girls on to their laps, the lips sucking the backs of their hands with a loud smacking noise like an obscene kiss. John had seen it all before: British soldiers were no different.

But he felt sorry for the wench who had served him. The older ones were used to that sort of thing and were quick to escape, shrugging off the infantrymen's crude advances with a bold look and a contemptuous comment. But she was obviously new, and her plump cheeks grew progressively redder every time she was subjected to their crude advances.

One of the Prussians, the tallest of them, a surly-looking fellow with hard eyes, roused Bold's ire, though he told himself the plight of an anonymous girl meant nothing to him. He teased the flushed girl with importunings and finally when she bent low to place a tray heavy with beer steins on the table, he thrust a big paw into her fichu and grasped one of her breasts, forced upwards by the tight embroidered waister, and seizing the nipple between his lips pressed his teeth cruelly into the red-tipped flesh.

The civilians gasped. The cook dropped his ladle into the big pot. At the bar, the landlord clenched his fists with impotent rage. The girl dragged herself free, her face suddenly white with shock. Abruptly a heavy silence fell upon the crowded room as she started to sob softly, and cover her blue-veined breast.

The Prussian with the dangerous blue eyes looked around the room calmly, seeming to savour the sudden stillness. Slowly he drew his bayonet from the scabbard at his side and challengingly placed the naked blade on the table in front of him.

Bold knew he was a fool to interfere. He was a foreigner in a strange country and Marshal Bluecher's Prussians were hard ruthless men. Why make it his cause? But he felt that black Irish temper which had impelled him to strike the cowardly Guards captain on the field of Waterloo, rising once more. As he pushed back his chair it made a loud scraping sound and all eyes turned on him. The shamed wench raised her tear-stained face in some kind of warning. But John had no eyes for her. His gaze was fixed on the Prussian.

John Bold drew back his clenched fist deliberately so that all could see. Next moment he smashed it into the Prussian's face with all his strength. The man flew from his chair and crashed back against the wall, looking suddenly foolish and not at all dangerous as he slumped there dazed, blood seeping from a split lip.

There was an angry murmur from his comrades. They looked up at the tall young Irishman threateningly. But he knew the type. Without a ringleader they were all cowards, waiting for one of the others to take the initiative, and in the end doing nothing when faced with determination. He dropped his hand to the hilt of his sword. Through gritted teeth he hissed, 'Well, you Prussian scum, do you want any further trouble, *Saukerls?*'

The threat worked. The murmurings ceased. They dropped their gaze, as if suddenly ashamed. The man with the bleeding lip wiped the blood from it with the back of his hand and then stared at the blood as if he couldn't quite believe it was his own.

John knew he had won. There would be no further trouble from the Prussian light infantrymen. He dropped his grip on the sword, turned to the girl who was now looking up at him with eyes full of admiration and said softly, 'Adjust your dress and go about your business. These swine won't bother you any more.'

It was then that the partition cutting off the *chamber separée* from the taproom opened. A woman, dwarfed by two other Indians with fierce martial faces, their hands on curved swords, stood there gazing at him with huge dark hungry eyes. Like the men she was dressed in rich flowing silks but her head was uncovered, her jet-black, glistening hair pulled tightly back, a line of red lead marking the parting, with another red circular mark on the perfect forehead. She smelt of sandalwood, jasmine – and naked sex. In all his life, John Bold had never met a more exotic and provocative woman. Those burning black eyes, made even larger by the kohl which outlined them, and that carmine, avid mouth exuded naked sensuality. The Prussians completely forgotten, John felt himself flush with desire, his lips suddenly dry. He licked them with his tongue and almost immediately they were dry again.

The Indian woman smiled softly. Slowly,

never taking her eyes off his face for a moment, she brought her palms together in front of her face, moved them up to her forehead and then down again in a gesture which John would one day find out was called the *namaste*. 'You are very brave, Englishman,' she said in a voice which was just as sensual and provocative as her appearance. 'Very brave,' she repeated, seeming to linger upon the words, her pink tongue slipping slowly between small, perfectly white teeth and caressing her own lips with sensual slowness. He felt his heart pound.

Suddenly she dismissed him. *'Chalo!'* she commanded imperiously. The two Indian men ranged themselves at her sides and without looking left or right like some regal procession they swept through the awed room to disappear up the stairs, leaving John Bold to stare after them like some gawping yokel. Thus it was that he was hardly conscious of the other member of the party from the *separée:* a runtish white man who sidled out of the inn along the wall, like some human rat afraid to come out of the shadows. By the time John had become aware of him, he was gone, out into the night. A little dazed by it all, John finished the last of his tankard and followed him across the room to the accompaniment of friendly nods from the locals and a whispered 'Thank you, sir, God bless you, sir and rest you well,' from the innkeeper. John returned the thanks and then with the aid of a taper proffered by the serving wench, who gazed at him with obvious devotion, he made his way up the narrow stairs, telling himself he would sleep like a log.

But that was not to be. Five minutes or so after the bugles of the Prussian garrison had sounded the curfew for the good citizens of Aachen, who were still under military law, there was a soft tapping at the door of his room.

'*Ja?*' he called sleepily.

With a soft creak the door opened and in the flickering light of the yellow taper he saw it was the girl he had rescued from the Prussians. Now she was dressed in her shift, with a shawl flung round her shoulders.

'What–' he began, startled.

Hurriedly she held her finger to her lips before closing the door and turning the key softly. A moment later she was snuggling into his bed and wriggling her plump body, her breasts like warm soft melons rubbing up against his naked chest, already gasping in pleasurable anticipation...

6

When he awoke she was already gone although it was still dark. But *das Gasthaus zur Alten Post* was beginning to stir. There was the rattle of pots from below and the squeaking of the water pump. From the coaching yard he could hear the hoarse soft talk of the ostlers and the lazy clip-clop of sleepy horses being led out of their stables.

He yawned pleasurably, feeling satiated and happy, though stiff. The serving wench. – Bettina was her name – had certainly been no virgin, though she was no raddled doxy either. She had been pathetically eager to please in a clumsy sort of country girl manner. The night had flown. He doubted that he had slept more than two hours.

He had lost his own virginity at sixteen to one of the fine ladies who had come to Dover for the sea bathing. She had patted his head affectionately afterwards and given him half a guinea by way of a reward. He smiled at the memory.

Suddenly seized by a raging thirst, he swung out of the big trestle bed and padded across the cold floor to the water ewer. Perhaps the sour roast had been too well spiced. He found the pewter beaker, fumbling a little for it in the darkness, and was just about to fill it with water when his gaze was attracted to the parting in the curtain of the room directly opposite.

He swallowed hard, the water forgotten instantly, tumescent almost at once, overcome by overwhelming lust by what he saw there through the crack. It was the Indian woman who had looked at him so provocatively. A maid had obviously just bathed her. Now she fluttered around the totally naked woman, patting her beautiful body with a white towel which flashed against the smooth dark brown of her skin.

The woman was obviously enjoying it. She arched her head, teeth bared and gleaming, her full breasts rising almost unbearably, the nipples big, taut and erect. He gazed at her open-mouthed and erect, knowing it was not the gentlemanly thing to do, but unable to tear himself away. She was small, but her breasts were full and geometrically circular, unlike those of a European woman. She had a tiny eighteen-inch waist which accentuated plump hips and the gentle swell of her belly. The space between her thighs was shaven clean of hair so that the deep cleft appeared childlike and surprising and strangely erotic.

Now the busy twittering little maid had finished her towelling. Taking warmed oil in both hands she smoothed it across her mistress' body, starting with the breasts, gently kneading them in turn, running her cunning little fingers about the nipples so that the gasping, shocked watcher in the dark imagined the naked woman shivering with the joy of it all.

John felt himself choking, strangled, his breath coming in short hectic gasps. There was no doubt about it, the Indian woman was enjoying the tiny hands of her maid as she rubbed now her thighs, taking long sensuous strokes, smiling up at her mistress the whole while. The woman's breast heaved. Her mouth had fallen slack. Her eyes were closed and John, his heart pounding like a trip-hammer, fancied she was emitting small groans.

Suddenly the candle was extinguished and the room and its scene of strange foreign depravity vanished, leaving him leaning weakly against the window, pressing his burning forehead against its coldness, trying to restore his crazed senses...

When he came down for breakfast they had gone. Their horses had been saddled and their private coach had vanished from the yard, although it was still barely light.

'They paid well for blackamoors,' the innkeeper said jovially as he ushered John to a place close to the crackling log fire. 'I always thought they ran around Africa as naked as the day they were born, living off berries and bits of dead monkeys.' He shook his white head in bewilderment. 'The gazettes must have lied.'

Five minutes later Bettina came across, bearing his breakfast and a mug of weak ale, her gaze knowing, silently pursing her lips in a kiss when she thought the innkeeper was not watching.

'Did you see them go – the blackamoors?' he asked.

She nodded and said enthusiastically, 'The woman, she gave me a silver taler, just for carrying her case to the coach. Why in her own country, she must be a princess at least.'

He smiled at her enthusiasm and said, 'And what did you say to her?'

'Nothing. For she could not speak our tongue like you – *John*,' she whispered his name lovingly.

'Bettina, you lazy slut,' the innkeeper called, 'come on over here and get some work done, and let the good gentleman get on with his food.'

She mouthed another silent kiss and fled back to her work, leaving him to muse about the Indian woman. If she could not speak German, how had she known he was an Englishman? She had spoken to him in his own language.

He frowned and ate the hard black bread and cheese reflectively. Since he'd sword-whipped that damned fellow Hartmann, his

75

life had become very complicated. An attempt had been made on his life at the command of someone who spoke French with a cockney accent. Now there was this strange, provocative Indian woman with her even stranger sexual tastes, who seemed to know something about him. Was it just chance that she had spent the night in the same inn? And what about the furtive little white man who had been closeted with her in the *chambre séparée*? What role did he play?

In the end, he gave up. John Bold was not given to introspective; he was a man of action. As the sun started to filter through the leaded windows he told himself it was time to be moving. Whatever was going on, he had to get on with the business of finding out how to reach the Italian border. The sooner he arrived in India the better. His money wouldn't last for ever. Besides, perhaps out there he might once again meet that intriguing and highly desirable woman...

The morning passed swiftly. He discovered in the old city that there was an establishment which had complete control of the coaching links throughout what had once been the Holy Roman Empire of Germany – *Das Heilige Römische Reich*, which flourished between the eleventh and early nineteenth centuries. Back in the depths of the Middle Ages the German Roman Emperor had granted the right to a minor German nobleman, the Count of Thurn and Taxis, to carry passengers and post throughout the three hundred-odd states which made up that Empire. Even after the dissolution of the Empire at Napoleon's command, the family still possessed that sole right. For varying sums of money to be paid in Prussian silver talers, Rhenish crowns and Bavarian gold crowns, he could travel from border to border of these various German states until he reached his destination. So the rest of his morning was spent with the moneychangers, mostly bearded Jews in ragged black kaftans, who seemingly lived in fear of their lives in stinking hovels within the walled ghetto, which they could not leave without permission.

He was returning to the inn when the runt he had seen with the Indians sidled up to him. Eyes everywhere, he said out of the side of his mouth, 'Englishman, you are a soldier, yes?' His English was strange and heavily accented, as if he might be a native German speaker, but understandable all right.

John stopped and looked down at him, not liking what he saw. The man had the shifty appearance of a common cutpurse. He would not trust him as far as he could throw him. 'Why do you ask?' he said coldly.

The runt rubbed his dirty hands together and wheedled, 'A fine figure like yours, young sir, could only belong to a soldier.'

'All right then I am – *was* – an officer in

the British Army,' he snapped. 'What is it to you?'

'Well, sir' – the shifty dark eyes flashed a swift look up and down the alley, the dirty paws shuffled together – 'I know some person who could put a soldier willing to serve in foreign climes in the way of some good money, sir.'

Later, much later, John Bold wished he had posed the questions on the tip of his tongue at that moment – 'who' and 'where'? But he only snapped angrily, 'Be off with you, fellow! I want nothing to do with the like of you!'

The runt flinched and scuttled off, ratlike, as abruptly as he had appeared. John Bold was left more puzzled than ever.

Bettina met him at the inn door when he returned, as if she had been waiting to catch him. *'John!'* she whispered, pronouncing his name in the German fashion, 'in here, please.' She pushed him into a little side room, which smelled strongly of urine – the corner was stacked with the white chamber pots that were sent up nightly to the bed-rooms. After the Prussians sounded the curfew, even the outside privy was out of bounds.

'What is it?' he asked, seeing the alarm on the girl's open face and the concern in her eyes.

She closed the door and pressed herself

against it, almost as if she thought someone might attempt to throw it open by force. 'A man has been asking about you. He gave me this. She opened her palm neatly to reveal and old-fashioned gold Louis d'Or. 'He wanted me to open the door of your room so he could see inside.'

John listened to the urgent flow of words with growing bewilderment. He didn't like it one bit. 'Slowly. *Doucement!*' he said, taking her by her bare arms and pressing her firmly. The girl was bordering on hysterics. 'Let us take the man first. What kind of a man was he?'

She shrugged helplessly, her pretty bottom lip trembling, close to tears. 'Please don't be angry with me, John. I see so many people here.'

'I am not angry. I just want you to answer my questions slowly and sensibly. Now what kind of a man was he – this fellow with his gold piece?'

She swallowed hard, trying to pull herself together. 'A little man ... about forty... A foreigner. French ... at least that was the language he spoke.' Again she shrugged a little helplessly. 'But then here in Aachen, all the foreigners who cross the border speak French even if they are not so. I let him give me the coin, John – I hope you are not offended, but Herr Schroeder pays so little and my mother in Stolberg... I took him up to your room, to the door, and then I pretended my key was the wrong one and wouldn't fit the door.'

'Then what happened?'

'Nothing. He went away and that was that.' She shrugged her shoulders and he caught a glimpse of delightful white orbs beneath her fichu, and felt a sudden sensation of lust.

'I shall see you tonight in my room,' he whispered as she opened the door.

Already the innkeeper was beginning his usual litany of curses which always commenced whenever the girl disappeared for more than a minute. *'Bettina ... Bettina, wo bist du, du faules Frauenzimmer? ... Bettina!'*

Bettina knew that this was the last night they would spend together. She knew, too, that all her life would be like this – a succession of travelling gentlemen who bedded her and then departed. Serving wenches were to be ogled, pinched and squeezed, perhaps slept with, but not married. That would offend the morality of good, solid Catholic Aachen.

So she came to be loved, carried to his bed easily, laughing softly so that Herr Shroeder wouldn't hear – a simple country child with full women's breasts and desires. She arched under his body, her knees splayed, fingers pressing greedily into his back as he thrust and thrust hard for the strong cushion of her thighs with animal brutality, her breath coming in short gasps, rising by the instant in intensity.

In ecstasy, she screamed, body arched, trying to devour him with her sex, and wanting this moment to go on forever. But already he had collapsed upon her like a dead weight, all strength drained, his heart beating as if it might burst from his breast-cage at any second.

Down in the darkness of the courtyard, unworried about the curfew, the listener in the shadows smiled and licked his thick lips. 'Like a bleeding fiddler's elbow,' he whispered huskily, recognizing the sound for what it was. 'Like a bleeding fiddler's elbow. Lucky dog!' He could imagine the two of them, the doxy with her plump white legs still sticking up in the air and the young buck plastered all over her, gasping for breath and feeling his spigot wilting by the instant and wishing fervently that this was not the way of men. 'But it is, old son,' he whispered, talking to himself in the fashion of lonely men always on the fringes of things, watching and waiting.

Soon he'd better be on his way. He would not like to chance trying to bribe Prussian Army patrols twice of an evening. The Prussian bleeders weren't as easily greased as were the frogs, all of whom could be bought.

Then from above came the sound of weep-ing, soft and muffled, as if stifled by a handkerchief, the way women wept when they knew it was all over... He recognized the sound well enough and thought he knew the cause. The young buck had rogered her, now he was telling her how much he loved her, but he had to leave in the morning. Even while he'd be telling her, he'd have his hand on spigot, playing with it, trying to get it to stand to attention again.

The listener in the dark tugged the end of his nose cynically. 'Weep for him, my plump stupid pigeon, *weep for him*... Soon I'll give you something to weep your bleeding heart out for, you silly cow!' He smiled evilly in the darkness, then raised his hand as if in salute. 'Good night, Mr Jean-Paul *bleeding* O'Hara. Better enjoy the doxy this night, for likely it's your last...' His accents were purest cockney. A moment later he had vanished into the night.

7

Lightning slashed the night sky in jagged stabs. Thunder rolled back and forth in the tight valley of the Rhine as the summer storm raged. But the eight wet-glistening horses, pulling the coach with the post-horn emblem of the Thurn and Taxis on the door, were undeterred. Steadily they pulled the old coach up the steep incline.

To the driver's front, as he squatted muffled in scarves and blankets, loomed yet another of those medieval castles which dominated virtually every twist and turn of Father Rhine. Inside, next to John Bold, a Frankfurt corn merchant, Frankel, shivered and pulled his cloak tighter. 'Mary, Jesus, Joseph, a louse runs right across my liver when I see such places! God only hopes that we will not have to stay there longer than an hour while they change the nags.'

Opposite him a pale-faced woman who looked like a nun crossed herself. Holding her rosary to her lips she mumbled prayers rapidly to herself, as if the Devil himself were waiting to snatch her to perdition.

John grinned wearily. Whatever happened he would be glad to stretch his legs. It had been a long journey since their last stop at Remagen on the Rhine. He could do with something hot to drink, too; the coach was now damnably cold. But he did agree with his fellow travellers. The castle did have something a little eerie about it, like one of those mythical castles of 'auld Ireland' his father used to tell of, filled with hobgoblins and the 'little folk'.

The pace eased slightly as the driver picked his way down a long drive. Bold craned his head to see the place. The arched windows, long bereft of glass, stared down at him like eyes, while the portcullis through which they would soon pass became for an instant a gaping toothless mouth. There appeared to be no lights anywhere and he guessed that the place had been long abandoned by the nobility, to be bought cheaply by the von Thurns and Taxis to serve as a staging post on the long journey from Aachen to Frankfurt.

The coach pulled up under a signboard showing four headless men in black, carrying a coffin in funereal solemnity to a crooked tombstone. The legend painted in weathered lettering read *Zum Ende der Reise* – Journey's End.

'God in heaven, what a name for an inn!' Frankel muttered indignantly.

The woman clicked her beads even more rapidly – the Devil was almost upon her now.

'*Alle raus, Herrschaften,*' the coachman called. 'We stay an hour. Must look after the horses.'

The three of them descended, John gallantly offering his hand to the woman, who disdained it hurriedly, as if his touch might be the first step to the violation of her middle-aged virginity.

The smell of warm food drew them to the open door where they paused in consternation, peering the length of a huge grey room. A one-time castle refectory, now much decayed, it was both dank and dusty.

John shuddered a little and Frankel snarled, 'Like a damn ghost story! Where is that coachman? What–' He gulped and whispered hoarsely, 'What in three devils' name is that for a creature?'

'Guten Abend, Herrschaften,' the crippled man facing them said in a strangely slurred way. His left arm hung loose and he trailed one leg, but it was his face that horrified the travellers. It was smooth and round, as white as the full moon and hairless, with thick lips pulled back in a fixed ghastly leer. John recognized that horrible look. He had once known a woman who had contracted the disease all too common to match-factory workers – lockjaw.

With difficulty, slurring his words and leering horribly, the hostelier completed his welcome and indicated with his good arm to a grim-faced woman who had now appeared at the far end of the room. 'She will feed you.'

John took a grip of himself. The whole place stank of age and decay – *and evil!* But they would not be here longer than it took to change the horses.

They seated themselves at a long rough trestle table and the woman brought the food in silence, with a look of sullen resentment.

John dug into the food, but soon found his appetite had been killed by the sinister atmosphere. All three sat in silence, only toying with their food, waiting on the coachman's reappearance. Eventually the man sidled in uneasily and gave Lockjaw, as John was now calling the hostelier to himself, a nod before addressing the three travellers. Later John would reflect that he had avoided looking at them directly as he spoke.

'Rear axle's gone, *Herrschaften*,' he announced baldly. 'Thought it was going all the way from Remagen...'

'And what does that mean, eh?' Frankel demanded.

The coachman swallowed hard. 'Sorry, sir, but it means you'll have to stay here the night.'

'The night!' the merchant exploded, jowls wobbling with rage. 'Can't you repair it?'

'It's a job for a wheelwright, sir,' the coachman quavered.

The landlord hissed in that strange way of his, 'And no wheelwright would come out from the village at this time of night.'

The fat merchant frowned and the woman began to tell her beads once again.

'Is there anywhere to sleep here then?' Frankel asked, the bluster gone from his fruity voice now. 'I know you'll have fleas and bedbugs, but we can't wait up all night in this–' He glanced around the gloomy brooding walls and shivered unconsciously.

'No fleas, no bedbugs, sir,' Lockjaw answered. 'Just plain but clean country beds, sir, with sheets made of fine Krefeld linen. Can I have the honour of showing you the rooms?' he waited expectantly.

Frankel puffed out his cheeks uncertainly and looked at John a little helplessly. 'What do you think, Englishman?'

John hesitated. He didn't like the place or its inhabitants one bit. But what was the alternative? He shrugged finally and said with obvious reluctance, 'I don't suppose we can do anything else till morning, Herr Frankel.'

Tamely they followed the man up the winding oaken staircase deeper into the interior of the grey ruin, his flickering candles casting weird, eerie shadows on the rough walls.

John's room was freezingly cold and as bare as he had expected. Under the mullioned window, which rattled and shook with the fury of wind and rain, there was a massive carved oak chest, while a great four-poster bed occupied the centre of the room, its puffed-up pillows and goose-feather mattress fresh and clean. There would be no fleas or bedbugs as Herr Frankel had feared. He shivered and laughed the next instant at his own childish fears. Still, just before he removed his boots – with a sigh of relief – he did go to the door and turn the great iron key in the lock. Then he sat down on the bed. God, how tired he was!...

It was Waterloo all over again. In all his

years he would relive that great battle time and again. The shock at the first sight of the Imperial Guard as they breasted the rise at Hougemont, the trumpets blaring, the officers shouting, the kettle drums urgently beating. Now in the dream, however, the Imperial Guard were really giants, towering into the evening sky, as the redcoats stared up at them like Lilliputians at Gulliver. Again there was a sense of being rooted to the ground as the blue-clad ranks of giants advanced upon them without sound, their bayonets gleaming. Suddenly the heavy silence was broken as the cannon roared into life.

He sat up in the great bed with a start, heart beating wildly. For a moment he could not make out where he was. Then he blinked and realized he had been wakened by thunder, echoing and re-echoing the length of the narrow valley of the Rhine. But then he heard something else – closer, smaller. He seemed to sit motionless in the bed for an eternity, though in reality it was only a minute, hardly daring to breathe, every sense acute as he tried to assess the sound – manmade or a product of the storm?

He slipped from the bed, his celtic sixth sense warning that, whatever the source of the sound, danger was near. Someone who wished him harm. He was sure of that. At Bande they had actually attempted to kill him and at Aachen he had sensed that

88

another try to do the same would have taken place if he had not left in time. But who was after him? How could they move so swiftly from one city to another and from one country to another? If they were out there, how could they know about his movements with such rapidity? It was all very puzzling, frustrating, frightening.

He yawned and shivered. He really ought to sleep. On the morrow, once they reached Frankfurt, he would take the very next coach out to Munich. Yet some hidden caution warned him about sleeping in the huge four-poster. It would be tempting the fates. He bit his bottom lip thoughtfully, then he made his decision and moved. First the door and then the bed.

Five minutes later the body huddled beneath the mountainous goose-feather quilt as if inside a protective cocoon was completely still, as if its owner had not one single care in the world...

8

John woke with a start.

Perhaps it was that the noise of the storm had been replaced by a heavy, brooding stillness. He raised himself cautiously from the cover of his cloak, his hand on the butt of his pistol. The night was *too* quiet.

He was wondering if he was imagining things when he felt the slight tremor of rain-cooled air fan his left cheek. He turned his head cautiously, every sense tingling. The tremor of air grew to a draught. A door was open stealthily – the one to the next room, which he had thought locked on the other side. He noted, even at the height of his tension, that it had been well oiled. Unlike all the others in this grey pile it made no sound. The trap had been set in advance. Now they – he knew not who – were about to spring it.

Slowly, with infinite caution, a shadow detached itself from the darker shadows near the bed.

John dare hardly breathe. The intruder's right hand was raised and clutching something. Very gently, John eased off the pistol hammer.

The dark figure with the raised hand was almost at the bed now. Something *had* to happen soon. John's whole body screamed out for action to break this unbearable suspense.

He felt a fresh tremor of disturbed air, and caught his gasp of surprise just in time. Another, smaller, figure slipped into the bedroom and watched the first intruder creep closer to the great bed and its motionless figure.

For what seemed an age John was paralysed – not with terror but with a seeming inability to forward this murderous scene to an end, though his body cried out for action. Soon he would have to participate – become an actor in this treacherous little drama being played out in the dark bedroom – yet he seemed unable to move.

Suddenly, startlingly, the smaller figure at the door brought his own hand down sharply, as the other hovered over the bed, knife raised high. *It was the signal!*

With a harsh intake of breath the would-be assassin thrust his blade downwards and immediately over-balanced as his knife met no more resistance than a pillow.

John sprang from the floor in the corner, firing from the hip. The pistol erupted flame.

There was a shrill scream. The attacker was propelled away from the bed as if slammed by an invisible fist. With a smack that must have broken bones he careered into the wall and then slowly slithered down it, half his head missing, the blood spurting from the great gaping wound in red profusion.

The smaller figure was attempting to bolt through the door. John flung the pistol and caught the man on his right shoulder. He staggered and went down on his knee. John didn't give him time to recover but dived on top.

Furiously, desperately, the little man

91

writhed and twisted. John's nostrils were assailed by the overpowering stink of unwashed flesh. Grimly he hung on, avoiding an attempt to knee him in the groin. Then the man seemed to go limp, and John relaxed his grasp for a moment. The little man shot up his right hand, two fingers outstretched. For an instant he managed to get them in John's nostrils. But before he could extend any further and rip them up and outwards to tear open John's nose, the latter slammed his left hand down hard.

The butt of the palm struck the intruder squarely on the bridge of his nose. Something cracked sharply like a dry twig underfoot. John's palm was flooded with hot sticky blood and the little man, ceasing his wild attempts to break free, said thickly, his throat full of the blood he was being forced to swallow, 'All right, Capt'n ... you've got me ... I'll give up!'

Warily, trying to control his own crazy breathing and overcome his excitement at the fact that the runt had spoken English, the English of the gutters of Spitalfields, John sought and found the pistol. Still holding the other man down, he cocked the second barrel and, levelling the pistol at him, stood carefully.

'In a second,' he said as coldly and masterfully as he could, 'I'm going to tell you to get to your feet, you rogue. When you do so, go to the table over there and light the taper. But do so carefully, for I swear I'll blow the back of your head off too, if you attempt the slightest mischief. Move – *now!*'

The little man stumbled to his feet, still holding his broken nose. 'I'll behave mesen, Capt'n... Don't worry. You have nothing to fear from me, sir.'

'Get on with it!'

The man fumbled for the matches and there was a spurt of blue flame. John saw a cunning little peaked face, a long crooked nose already beginning to swell, and sharp but terrified brown eyes. A moment later the taper spread its wavering yellow light.

'Come here,' John commanded, not shifting his eyes for a moment. Injured as he was, his hand filled with blood held to his nose, the man looked as if his brain was racing at top speed.

The man came forward reluctantly, eyes fixed on the pistol. 'I'm all right, Capt'n,' he said, 'not an ounce of 'arm left in me.'

'Put your arms up – and turn round.'

With a little sigh, the other man did as he was commanded.

Swiftly, with his left hand, John patted the fellow's skinny body, disliking the touching intensely, for he smelled as if he hadn't washed for months. The pistol he found first. It was one of those little ladies' pistols, with an ivory butt, which had become fashionable since the Revolution, when rich ladies had begun to fear for their lives at the hands of the mob. It was concealed in the left tail of the man's coat. The knife came next, in a sheath strapped to his inner thigh, with a hole in his trouser pocket so that he had easy access to the razor-sharp blade. The bag of gold coins was hidden next to his skinny chest and John indicated that the runt should unbutton his moleskin waistcoat to free it and hand it over. He did so with a sad shake of his head and a muttered curse, as if life was simply too much for him.

'Blood money!' John said, balancing the bag in his hand, 'blood money no doubt, eh, you rogue?' He judged that the leather bag contained at least a hundred pieces of gold. It would take an ordinary decent working man years to acquire that.

'It was the first half of my payment, sir. You can have it, Capt'n, and gladly. I didn't like the business from the very start, as true as my name is Jem Jones.'

John looked at him scornfully. 'Yes – another lie, I'll be bound. Now you can lower your hands, and stop that blood dropping from your damned nose. But I assure you I will pistol you the very instant you act foolishly.'

John reasoned that the coachman and Lockjaw were in on the plot. But the great oaken main door behind him was securely bolted and he now wedged a chair beneath the handle of the other door. Anyone trying to get in would have their work cut out for them.

'And who was going to pay the second half of this blood money?'

Jem Jones, as he called himself, pretended to fuss with his nose and avoided John's challenging look.

He jerked up the pistol threateningly, feeling complete master of the situation, although from far off he could hear the sound of hesitant feet. Probably the coachman and Lockjaw were coming to see if the dastardly assassination attempt had succeeded. 'Someone paid you to kill me,' he barked, eyes hard and fierce. 'Come on, man, I want the truth. *Who was it?* Speak out!'

Jem Jones could see that he wasn't joking. The fellow might be slightly damp behind the lugs, but he looked prepared to shoot. 'You'll spare me, Capt'n?' he quavered.

'If you tell the truth.'

'Right, sir … right, sir.' He saw John's knuckles whiten as he exerted pressure on the trigger. 'I'll tell you… It was Captain Hartmann, or better his governor, Lord Hartmann.'

John almost dropped his guard for a moment, the pistol wavered in his grasp. Then he caught himself. 'You mean the Hartmann family paid you to kill me?'

'Yes.'

'At Bande back there ... and now here?'

Jem nodded mutely, as if he thought it better at precisely this moment to keep his mouth shut for a while.

'But how could they?' John gasped after a few moments. 'This ... er ... Lord Hartmann was in London and you were over here... A galloper would take days to cover such distances...'

Jem Jones grinned at having surprised his bold young captor. 'Ain't ye never heard of the new telegraph and Mr Reuter o' Aachen?'

John shook his head, his turn now to be dumb.

'Lawd, sir, this Mr Reuter, he's begun sending dispatches with the telegraph all over the place. London, Paris, Brussels, Aachen – all over, quicker than you can blink an eye. Marvellous, ain't it?' he added quite cheerfully.

With such a devilish machine, John told himself, Lord Hartmann and his bully boys could pursue him everywhere. In every great city he could hire other rogues like Jem Jones and let him get on with the dirty business of murder; while the real killer played cards with the Prince Regent or sauntered the promenade at Brighton with Beau Brummel. John Bold would be safe nowhere.

Down the corridor the cautious footsteps were coming closer. He could just imagine the two of them, pressing themselves against the wall as they advanced through the silent shadows, alert for the signal that the deed had been done and they could have their reward.

Then the footsteps ceased. They were undecided. He had time. 'Listen!' he whispered urgently, formulating his plan as he spoke, 'do you wish to live to collect the second part of the blood money you will undoubtedly receive from the Hartmanns when you report my death?'

Jem Jones nodded, licking his thick lips. Suddenly his eyes were cunning, calculating, greedy. There was going to be something in this for him after all. 'Yer, Capt'n,' he whispered back slowly. 'But how do you mean?' He realized that for all his youth, John Bold knew what he was about. The fact gladdened his evil black heart. In the past amateurs and innocents had been the ruination of many of his plans. He'd sooner deal with a villain any day. 'What now, Capt'n?' he asked.

John didn't answer directly. 'Grab my cloak and cover the body. Those two outside must think it's me.'

Jem Jones' dark eyes gleamed with admiration. He did as ordered whilst John stowed his few valuables about his person – telling himself he could make up for what he was being forced to leave behind with the money taken from Jem Jones. Lord Hartmann would unwittingly provide for his needs in Frankfurt. Finished, he pulled off the little silver ring from his right hand.

'This is the coat of arms of the de la Mazieres – my mother's family,' he explained hastily. 'Don't steal it. It is going to be your proof that you have dealt with me. *Remember Hartmann's second payment?*'

Jem Jones looked up at him approvingly. 'You're a schemer after me own bleeding heart, Capt'n,' he said warmly, and then as the tall young man crossed to the window, ready to drop out into the wet darkness, 'Well, sir, shall I let them in? With this busted conk of mine, I'll need someone to give me a hand with the shovels.'

John, with his right leg already cocked over the sill, turned and queried, 'With the shovels?'

'Why bless yer, Capt'n, yes. Can't expect me to bury a big, heavy feller like the late John Bold by mesen, can yer now?' He gave an enormous wink and for a fleeting moment John almost liked him.

Next instant he was dropping into the darkness … and the unknown…

TWO: AMBUSH

1

India!

The glare from the red ball of the sun cut his eye like a knife as he peered through the telescope at the land beyond the white race of the surf just off Madras. No breeze blew. The air from the land was furnace hot so that his shirt stuck to his lean back in black sweaty patches. But despite the heat John Bold felt a mounting, wild excitement he'd never experienced before. This was where his fate would be decided. India would become his destiny!

As the East Indiaman reefed its sails and they glided deeper into the bay he could see through the bright circle of glass that the shore was crowded with half-naked brown men. They squatted on their haunches, wilting in the afternoon heat, spitting regular streams of red saliva to the baked earth. Naked children splashed listlessly in the muddy green water without the energetic screams of European children; while their mothers and sisters glided back and forth, wrapped in bright gowns, bearing pots upon their heads, moving with a barefoot sensuous grace that was totally foreign to him.

The bosun bellowed his orders and the

fiddler, squatting barefoot on the top cap-stan, started to scrape his old fiddle for the benefit of the sweating sailors. On the shore, a totally naked old man with a fringe of white beard, squatted motionlessly on a kind of raised platform, legs crossed, hands limp at his sides, staring into nothingness, while a young attendant painted strange white marks on his emaciated black body. John guessed he would be a holy man, and refocused the instrument on a line of carriages and horsemen waiting in the shade for the passengers to be borne ashore. From the old India hands on board during his month-long voyage he knew who they were. They would be the friends and relatives of passengers, of course, but most of them would be lonely men – merchants, officials of the East India Company and officers – waiting for the 'fishing fleet' to arrive: women from England sent out to India to 'catch' some rich nabob. For women – white women, at least – were a scarce commodity in British India, and nabobs, tired of their dusky mistresses, were prepared to pay a good price for a white woman, however ugly. John lowered the telescope, his nostrils already assailed by the smell of this strange new country: a heady mix of garlic, coriander, dung and sweat. Now he was finally here after the terrible voyage from the Persian Gulf, sharing one latrine with a hundred men and women, with nets rigged above the upper deck to prevent heat-crazed passengers throwing themselves into the Red Sea, and all the time struggling to keep fit and passably clean, proof against typhoid, scurvy and scabies which were rampant on the vessels on the India route.

When he had joined the ship he had considered himself as sailing into exile, banned to a strange and utterly foreign land due to no fault of his own. Now at his first glimpse he already felt India's magic and his heart raced at the thought of what lay before him.

The sub-continent, he knew already, was King George's territory in name only. In reality the country belonged to the East India Company, known as the John Company, divided into the three presidencies of Madras, Bengal and Bombay. Here a governor could tell a new arrival, 'I expect *my* will to be your rule, not the laws of London which are simply a heap of nonsense. *My* orders must be obeyed as if they were English statute law!'

The John Company traded as it wished – minting money, making laws, executing criminal and civil justice. It kept the peace or made war, as it desired. Its head, the Governor General, lorded over the fates of nearly a hundred million people, ten times the population of the old country, with almost unlimited power.

For here everything depended upon trade

and profit. Men came to India to make money, *fast,* before the myriad tropical diseases or the riotous life in the white cantonments caught up with them. By forty, the average nabob, as they were called contemptuously back home, wanted to be on his way back to England, taking with him a vast fortune with which to buy a landed estate, a seat in Parliament, and in due course a title. India for the white man simply meant profit.

With corn on the Indian market at fivepence a bushel to be sold at Liverpool's docks for three shillings and tenpence, it was not surprising that everyone was motivated solely by money. Junior officers of the John Company, even ministers of the church, took part in commerce and made a fortune – if they survived.

The thought made John pensive as the other passengers now began to come on deck. The land intrigued him, but also inspired a certain dread. He knew already that the heat was almost intolerable for a white man. The sun's glare, reflected off the white-painted shanties lining the shore, stabbed to the very eyeball. The palms, motionless, were stirred not by the faintest breeze. The shadows offered no coolness and flies hummed everywhere.

White people did not go out in the midday heat. Their womenfolk lay naked on rumpled beds in shuttered rooms, while from another, native servants worked the overhead punkah with their toes; while the men slumped sullenly and half drunk in rattan chairs, drinking one whisky-soda after another. All waited for the evening when the million invisible cicadas filled the cooler air with their monotonous chirping and at last the European quarters would begin to stir, the promenades and assemblies commence and life seem a little more bearable.

He tugged his nose and his fingers were wet with sweat. His lean face hardened. The idle chatter of the nabobs, breaking reputations with their backbiting, always concerned with the overwhelming need to make money, would not be his life. He needed adventure. He would join one of the Company's three armies, and do what he had always wanted – to thrill to the sweet sound of those bugles in the morning.

At the bow the East Indiaman's swivel cannon thundered, as if to emphasize his sudden warlike mood, saluting St George's Fort opposite. The passengers clapped and John turned to take a last look at them.

There was the fishing fleet, all giggles and hands clasped to their gaping mouths, a plain bunch for the most part, some of them women who would never see thirty again. Then there were returning nabobs, fat and puce-faced; officers from the Company coming back from leave, splendid in their exotic regimentals, their faces either bright red or a deep yellow, the result of persistent fevers; and a handful of awed, scared sixteen-year-olds, Company clerks trained at Haileybury, all hoping that one day they might be a second Clive of India. Finally there were the Frenchmen.

They were in civilian clothes now since Napoleon had been finally defeated and exiled, but there was no mistaking that air of authority about them or the sabre scars which marked their faces, especially that of Nom de Dieu, as the English on board had called him – behind his back!

Nom de Dieu, who uttered the curse at least once a minute, might well, with his flowing dyed moustache and carefully curled hair, have been one of those *beau sabreurs* who had ridden with Murat. He did everything with Gallic élan and dash; and he walked with a bow-legged swagger which marked him indelibly as an ex-cavalryman.

John wondered why so many Frenchmen were coming to India. The Company wouldn't employ their recent enemies and all the French colonies in India had been captured from Napoleon three or four years ago.

The anchor rattled down in a rusty clatter and his attention was caught by the shouts of the naked brown boatmen in the horde of ramshackle *masula* boats expertly braving the heavy-running surf, and now offering their services to the passengers. For at Madras there was no way of unloading a large vessel save by transferring to these rough boats, powered by skinny yet muscular natives.

Lugging his total possessions, limited to one shabby carpet bag, he found himself in the middle of a gaggle of women from the fishing fleet wanting to get ashore. The waiting men were eager to eye the new arrivals, and it would not be the first time that marriage proposals had been made there and then.

One woman stood out from the rest, and John eyed Georgina Lanham with respectful admiration. He had seen her the day he had joined the ship. Thereafter she had been struck down by the ague and he had not seen her until now.

He had been immediately stirred by the beauty of her oval face, surrounded by a mass of golden ringlets dangling in carefully contrived disorder. She stood out like a beacon among the other women. Her figure, too, was superior. They were either too thin or too fat, all angles or flat curves in their cheap cotton gowns. She was dressed in a sheer green silk robe which revealed slender legs, and the burgeoning breasts forced upwards from the tight waist seemed to be about to spring from the deep décolletage of her Empire-line at any moment. As she bent low to reveal a generous cleavage he felt a dry longing in his throat and his heart hammered. It was like being on the battlefield once more.

But the beautiful Miss Lanham was too concerned with lifting the hem of her gown and getting safely down to the bobbing boat to notice him, crying to the nearest boatman when he was too slow to help her, *Mail, mail somalo ... ek dum!*' in a sharp voice which was obviously used to giving orders – and having them obeyed!

John took pleasure in her use of the native language. She had obviously been here before, and so was not one of the fishing fleet. Perhaps he might cultivate Miss Lanham, however haughty and distant she might seem at this moment.

Their boat pushed off, the skinny natives standing upright, faces glazed with sweat as they battled the current. The roar of the surf grew ever louder, the men rowed harder, then they were in that fierce maelstrom, their long narrow craft shooting up and down the white fury of the waves. Women screamed and men clung on grim-faced. Frantically the natives controlled the craft as the water attempted to seize and sink them. John was deafened by the roar, the spume stinging his face and making him blink. But Miss Lanham seemed totally unaffected. She made a pretty picture, defiance written all over her, golden curls streaming and the spray-dampened silk clinging, revealing every lush curve. He fell in love with her at that instant!

John felt carried away by the heady sexual excitement of riding through the surf and the sight of that beautiful nubile body. In this hot climate it would be easy to be rash, carried away by the warm sensuality of it all. Again she bent and he almost caught sight of her nipples. He was overcome by longing.

They were almost through, gliding in on the crest of a wave as high as a house, heading for the still water beyond, where a crowd of young men on horseback and in elegant carriages were laughing and clapping their hands at the spectacle.

Now the craft drifted in calm water while the crew leaned gasping on their paddles. Young men were already beginning to wade waist-deep into the water to offer their services. 'Can I help you, ma'am?... Over here, miss, if you wish aid... I say, you with the black ringlets, can I be of assistance?' they cried, while the ugly ducklings of the fishing fleet simpered and cooed, like great heiresses with beauty and private fortune instead of poor country parsons' daughters sent to India as a last desperate resort.

Miss Lanham looked at them in disdain, then turned her gaze on John, seeing him for the first time. What she saw pleased her: a tall young man with jet-black side-whiskers curling up against high un-English cheekbones. But if the face was hard, the mouth was sensitive, almost sensual. The curved lips sent a delicious but improper shudder down the length of her body and between her legs. This was no company clerk, she saw approvingly, no powdered foppinjay of the kind she had met in the two years she had spent in Miss Marbles' Academy for Young Ladies in the village of Croydon 'finishing' her education. This was a man.

'And you, sir,' she asked boldly, challengingly, 'what are you about?'

'About?'

'Yes, sir. Am I to be forced to tolerate the attentions of those half-witted Mary Anns in the water yonder?'

His blush deepened. It was the first time he had heard a woman use the term for men who were not really men.

'Or should I use the services of these niggahs?' Contemptuously she indicated the boatmen, holding out their hands for further tips. 'Would you trust a white woman to those blackamoors, sir?'

'Why no, Miss Lanham.' He dropped his bag and held out his hands.

'Fie, sir, not that way,' she chided. 'You cannot carry me in your arms. It will only wet my skirt.'

'How then, Miss Lanham?'

'Piggyback, sir, just as in the nursery.' She smiled, showing pearl-like teeth.

When he bent awkwardly in the small craft, she didn't hesitate to draw up her skirt – giving him a glimpse of plump white thighs above her stockings. Then he felt the firm flesh of her legs encircle his neck tightly, sending currents of excitement tingling down his spine. His heart throbbing crazily, he slid into the muddy water up to his waist.

She chuckled, urging him on with a 'Giddiup, old Dobbin ... come on now, show your paces!'

She pressed her legs close to him and he felt himself become hard, thanking God that the muddy water hid the tumescence which bulged the tight buckskin of his breeches. God, her nearness, the smell of her body – a mixture of cologne and animal sensuality – was almost intolerable.

'*Allo, mon brave,* you make the little gallop, *hein?*' It was the big French cavalryman, Nom de Dieu. He was blundering through the water with one of the fishing fleet on his broad shoulders. His hands, however, were not secured around her ankles, but hidden well beneath her skirt and by the radiance on the woman's face, John could well imagine what they were doing. The Frenchman winked knowingly at John and chortled, '*Quelle vie, hein!*'

A minute later John reached the burning white sand and hastily bent to let her dismount. She did so carelessly and again he caught a flash of the flesh above her stockings.

'Thank you, kind sir,' she said, looking down at his soaked trousers boldly and seeing what she shouldn't have. 'I hope you did not get too wet on my behalf?' Now her green eyes were wide and excited.

'No, not at all,' he stammered, embarrassed and excited. 'In this heat they will soon dry.'

'Yes, I am sure of that. Perhaps you would tell me your name now?'

He told her.

As a native servant hurried towards them across the sand, she stretched out her hand for him to take. 'With such a name, perhaps you will be *bold* enough to call on me when you have the time?'

'Why ... yes,' he stuttered, taking the hand for an instant. Then the servant was escorting her to the waiting coach, leaving him feeling drained and very alone in this alien world...

2

'*Impossible!*' Colonel Monroe, the Military Secretary snapped testily, 'Quite impossible for me to do a thing for you at this moment, my dear Bold.' With a hand that shook he took another sip of whisky-soda, his face a choleric red, as if he were in a rage. He wasn't. His colour was due to twenty years of the tropics and the heavy drinking that went with it.

In the two days that he had spent in Madras, trying to see the Governor General's Military Secretary, John had encountered quite a few employees of the John Company with the same choleric red faces. 'Touch of the liver, my boy,' one of them had assured him yesterday. 'Nothing to be frightened of.'

'You see, Bold,' Colonel Monroe continued, as above them the punkah fan stirred the stifling air of the office, 'it is entirely up to My Lord Hastings who he commissions as an officer in the Company's armies in India. It is his desire and command to see each one personally before he does so. As you perhaps know, he leads his own campaigns in the field and he prefers to know *personally* the kind of officer who serves under him. It is very important when they are in the command of native troops.'

'I see, sir,' John began, 'but I am in a diff–'

'*Punkah wallah!*' the Colonel, whose belly bulged beneath his light blue uniform, cut in with raised voice, 'What are you about, you lazy dog? *Jildy!*'

The cry had the desired effect and the half-naked old man, hidden in a side cupboard, the rope that agitated the overhead

113

fan attached to his right foot, started to move the fetid air a little more speedily.

Monroe mopped his balding head with a large silk handkerchief and breathed, 'I do declare, I shall never get used to this demned heat!'

John nodded – his own clothes were sticking unpleasantly. But it didn't seem to affect the natives too much, though their pace had slackened. Through the open window he could see them thronging the street. It was vibrant with their noise: the tinkling bells, the wails of the *gurus,* as he had already learned to call the near-naked holy men, the cries of the shopkeepers, the screeching wooden wheels of the ox-drawn *tongas.*

What a mass they were, as they plodded or pushed their way through the stinking filth of the cobbles which were dyed red with betel juice spit and prowled by skeletal dogs. And the stench was indescribable: a pungent mixture of curry, drying hides, boiling ghee, urine and cowdung.

John forgot the heat and stench. He had only ten guineas left. He had reckoned on being commissioned straight away. Now it seemed he must find Lord Hastings as soon as possible.

'If Lord Hastings isn't here in Madras, sir, where is he?' The urgency in his voice was all too obvious. 'How can I reach him, sir? I have little fortune and no friends here.' He thought of Miss Lanham, who he had glimpsed, surrounded by admiring young men on horseback, the previous day. But she would be in no position, he guessed, to help him.

With a sigh Colonel Monroe waddled over to the wall map of India and pointed a beringed finger at it. 'He is here – at Musulipatan, some fifty miles north, just off the coast. He is visiting Mr Lanham, the Collector.'

John's mind raced. Could he be related to *his* Miss Lanham?

'A capital fellow,' Monroe was saying, 'though sorely tried by these demned raids. There are the bane of our life here in Madras. Hardly had we seen off the froggies than they started. I don't doubt they'll turn into a full-scale war before the year is out. That is why Lord Hastings had gone up country personally to assess the position.' Monroe forced a smile, though his faded, red-rimmed eyes did not light up. 'You are new to the country, my boy, and you come to us with an excellent reference from the great Duke, so let me tell you a few things that you fellahs from home will not know.' He patted the map again. His rings sparkled with diamonds and John told himself that Colonel Monroe had obviously done well out of India. 'We've been in India for over a hundred years now – the John Company, I mean – working mainly

115

from our three ports of entry, Madras and Calcutta here and here. And Bombay – here – on the west coast.'

John listened attentively, for like most young men he knew nothing of England's greatest possession save the tall tales he had heard from his father.

'Over the years these three territories have expanded into the interior, by means of treaty – and occasionally war, that is why the Company keeps an army. We expanded thus because we needed a hinterland for trade, one ruled by princes friendly to the Company. It was strictly a matter of commerce.' He raised his voice again: *'Punkah wallah!'*

In the closet the old man stirred and the fan began to move again as Colonel Monroe swept his hand across Central India. 'Now, however, due in part to those demned froggies, a great confederation has been formed against us right across the country. They are a bunch of niggah princes who are too big for their boots. They bar our further progress north and undoubtedly they will have to be dealt with in due course. The Mahratta Confederacy they call themselves – the niggahs have a taste for grand-sounding titles.' He sniffed and took a drink. John nodded his understanding.

'As yet,' Colonel Monroe continued, 'the princes have not declared their hand. Our victory over Napoleon means we have more troops at our disposal and they have been impressed by it, too. But while we have been dealing with Old Boney they have been encouraging those demned cowardly black Pindarees to raid our territories, especially here in the east. Why, the demned fellahs are becoming more impertinent by the month!' His fat cheeks flushed puce, as if he were personally insulted by whoever the Pindarees were.

'May I ask who these raiders are, sir – an Indian tribe, perhaps?'

Monroe shook his head. 'No, they are neither a race nor a caste. They are a collection of no-good bandits, footpads and cut-throats from all races and castes and demned religions, assimilated by one common pursuit – *outrage and robbery!* They aren't encumbered by tents or baggage as are our troops,' he continued. 'Each one of the mounted cut-throats carries a few cakes of unleavened niggah bread for himself and his mount. For the rest, they live off the land. Each raiding party consists of one to three thousand chargers advancing across country some forty or fifty miles a day – much, much faster than we can do. They head straight for their target and make a sweep for all the property and booty they can find. Then they rape and pillage and then they're off back to their mountain fortress before we can organize a force to tackle the rogues.

117

'Three years ago they raided the Morzapur district in the area of Ganes which belongs to the Company. Last year they actually plundered part of the Madras Presidency and this year they're up to their demned tricks again. Demnit, sir!' he snorted, 'we cannot allow this sort of thing to continue. We must finally bring stability to Central India. The people demand it from us. Stability!'

We must bring stability to Central India! How often in the years to come would John Bold hear that phrase. In due course 'stability' would be achieved, brought about by bribery or outright war, with the result that this or that part of India would be annexed to the British crown and the Company's profits would grow.

But in the winter of 1815 John Bold was still young and naïve, and could share Monroe's indignation. 'But have they not a base camp?' he asked.

'No, that's the demned trouble,' Monroe answered, taking a sip from his Waterford glass. 'Their booty and families are scattered over a wide area in the mountains or in fortresses peculiar to themselves, or those with whom they consort. And by that I mean those niggah princes, who supposedly are *our friends!*' He snorted indignantly and yelled, '*Punkah wallah!*

'Nowhere do they present a firm front where we can attack and defeat them decisively. The defeat of a raiding party, the destruction of a cantonment or the temporary occupation of a mountain refuge produces no effect beyond the ruin of an individual freebooter.'

'But do they not have a leader, sir?'

'Oh, leaders enough they have,' Monroe replied. *'Lubbers* they are called and their forays are called *lubburiahs.'*

Yet another new word, John told himself. For already he had come to realize that Company officers spoke their own language, heavily larded with Indian words. A *gharri* was a chaise, *tats* were horses, a bathroom was a *ghustkana.*

'As far as we know they have no senior chief, though the bazaars do speak of such a man,' he conceded slowly, 'that is if one believes that kind of *gup* – gossip. They say there's some sort of big niggah – Chuto or Cheetoo by name – who's their great leader. There was some talk of him nine years back but none of our people ever saw him, if he actually existed.'

'Strike off the head and the body dies of its own accord,' John murmured, as if to himself.

'What did you say, Bold?'

'Nothing much, sir, just thinking out loud.' He raised his voice and attempted to change the subject. 'Now sir, if Lord Hastings is up country with Collector Lanham, when and how can I present my compliments to His Lordship, sir? My resources are strained, I do confess.'

Monroe eyed him sympathetically. 'All our resources were strained when we came out here first as young men. Even Lord Hastings came to India in order to recoup his crippled finances – and he would be the first man to admit it. Money – or the lack of it – brought us here in the first place. Though in your case I don't quite know.'

He frowned at the note the Duke of Wellington had given Bold, a little puzzled. Then: 'All right, my boy,' he said. 'Tomorrow morning at first light, a convoy of *daks* and the like is setting off for Musulipatan. Its purpose is twofold. It will ensure that Miss Lanham reaches her father, the Collector, safely...'

John's heart leapt.

'The second reason is to ensure that a consignment of muskets and powder reaches the same place, equally safely. Lord Hastings is currently discussing with the Collector the possibility of raising another regiment of native infantry. Things are coming to a head and we must be prepared.'

'And I, sir? Where am I to fit in?'

'Oh, yes. There will be an escort under the command of Captain de Courcy of the Bengal Light Cavalry – a good fellah, though not given to a great deal of talk.'

Colonel Monroe waddled to his desk and scribbled a note which he gave to John. 'A message to Captain de Courcy requesting him to loan you a horse and to have the goodness to take you with him as an extra rider.' He beamed at a surprised John as the latter stuttered his thanks.

'It is the least I can do for a protégé of the great Duke, my boy,' he said heartily and then raising his voice, cried, '*Syce,* attend this gentleman at the door. You will take him to the Honourable Captain of the Bengal Light Cavalry, *ek dum!*'

An Indian in the livery of the East India Company and the strange baggy riding trousers called jodhpurs, appeared at the window.

'My groom,' Colonel Monroe explained, 'lazy fellah like all the niggahs, but a damned good horseman. He'll see that you get a good mount. Well, young Bold, no doubt in due course, if the pox or ague don't get you first, we'll make a Company general of ye yet!'

And with that he dismissed a somewhat startled John, who had not expected his fortune would take this surprising turn so suddenly.

The *syce* was leading the way to the barracks of the Bengal Light Cavalry when they heard a clatter of hooves and an instant later a mass of some twenty horses or more, packed tightly together, thundered round the corner.

They pressed against the wall as the riders swept by, each rider sitting in the saddle with a casual, expert ease that John could not hope to emulate in a million years.

It was the Frenchmen from the ship. As they scattered the Indians before them, not even deigning to notice the panicked rabble, John was quite sure that they had once ridden for Napoleon. There was no mistaking that bold French swagger. The question sprang to his mind: *But for whom did they ride now?*

At their head rode Nom de Dieu. He spotted John in the white dust raised by the thundering hooves and recognized him, but did not speak. The old soldier's smile of their days on the ship was gone – replaced by a direct, challenging look, as if he were staring down at the new enemy.

3

Dawn.

From the sea a gentle cool breeze wafted inland and the palm fronds trembled. The only smells were of freshly brewed coffee and the *sowars'* chapattis. In the horse lines of the Bengal Light Cavalry a boisterous horse snickered. All was calm and unchaotic, that time before the teeming noisy crowds assembled, which John would come to love.

Captain de Courcy, a large, moustached young man with thinning hair, came out of the cantonment, leading his grey.

He nodded to the waiting civilian in his off-hand manner and twisting his cheroot to the side of his mouth, grunted, 'Morning, Bold.'

'Morning, Captain de Courcy,' John replied, thinking that de Courcy was not the most ideal travelling companion, but he certainly looked like a good man to have at one's side in time of trouble.

'You armed, Bold?'

'Yes, Captain.'

De Courcy nodded his approval. 'Good, I've only got a native *rissaldar* with me. No white officers. You might come in useful.'

'Do you think there might be trouble, Captain?' John asked eagerly, with the enthusiasm of youth.

De Courcy looked at him coldly and shrugged. 'Never can tell these days,' he grunted. 'Never stopped since the froggies started the whole damned thing.' He ran his hand the length of his moustache, his face stony and revealing little. 'The guns and powder,' he said, indicating the donkeys which were beginning to emerge from the native barracks, urged on by their drivers, 'will form up in the middle of the column. They'll be best protected there.'

The *rissaldar,* a native officer, an old man with white hair, but with a tough lined face dominated by a great beak of a nose, pushed his way with his horse to where de Courcy was waiting, saluted and reported in his own tongue.

De Courcy returned the salute and said to John, 'Miss Lanham's *palkee* is on its way.'

As he spoke a strange boxlike contraption, looking like a seventeenth-century sedan chair and borne on the shoulders of four nearly naked natives, came swaying round the corner.

'Funny-looking thing,' John commented, his heart beating a little faster at her nearness.

'Damned nuisance!' de Courcy cursed and flung his cheroot into the dust. 'Far too slow. But that's the way the memsahibs always travel around here. Can't have them riding on horses showing all their underpinnings to the natives. So they travel like some niggah ranee, with a change of bearers every eight miles.'

'I see,' John replied, his gaze concentrated on the swaying carriage.

Suddenly, surprisingly, the taciturn Captain de Courcy said softly, *'Who danced with whom and who is like to wed and who is hanged and who is brought to bed.'* His voice was full of malice and John, abruptly a little angry, felt sure the doggerel was aimed at the approaching Miss Lanham. He ought not to sneer at her in that manner. Surely she was not like one of the fishing fleet, ready to throw herself at anything in trousers and with money in the bank?

As she passed, her face pale and her beautiful eyes still heavy with sleep, he swept off his hat and bowed low. She deigned not to notice. He frowned and told himself it was too early in the morning. As the day progressed and she woke up, she would undoubtedly noticed him. Hadn't she specifically asked him to call upon her?

De Courcy replaced his shako, saw the look on John's face and said, the sneer vanished from his voice now, 'A heart-breaker, Bold. Pay need to my words!' Before John could speak he had spurred his horse away.

Two hours later they were on the march north, with the heat increasing by the moment. Strung out in a long slow column, with the sea to their right and the jungle to their left, they sweated through their uniforms.

There was no road, just a kind of broad sandy path, and the sound of hooves was deadened by the thick white dust which rose about them like a London fog. But the lush green jungle was loud with noise: the incessant, nerve-racking noise of the jungle. Monkeys gibbered crazily, animals roared and the copper bird kept up his *dong-ding, dong-ding* like the persistent blast of massed muskets.

Yet despite the heat and monotony the men were on their guard constantly. Every so often de Courcy would rise in his stirrups and rein in his horse in order to peer to the end of the column, as if he half expected some fiend to be creeping up on them.

John felt his gaze straying repeatedly to the curtained palanquin in the centre of the column, but all he saw was a shadowy outline behind the muslin.

Was she a tease, he considered? Like some of those well-born county girls he had known back in England, happy to play with an ensign of some looks, but intent on marrying some rich colonel with his own regiment in his pocket? And what had de Courcy meant by that little piece of bad verse?

They made their first halt when the sun was at its zenith. The *sowars* were too weary even to eat their chapattis, and contented themselves with hefty swigs from their water flasks and slumping in whatever shade they could find. De Courcy dismounted for a few moments only, before getting back into the saddle and scanning their surroundings, hand never far from his sabre. John saw the anxiety on his brick-red face and forced himself up to cross to where de Courcy kept solitary guard.

'What worries you, Captain?' he said directly.

'The Pindarees attacked a village not ten miles from here last week,' de Courcy answered grudgingly, as if he felt he was saying too much.

'And you think–'

'I think nothing, Mr Bold,' de Courcy cut him off sharply. 'I just prepare.'

They were on the march again when, about three that terrible, long, burning afternoon, they spotted the black vultures hovering in the hard blue sky to their front. John urged his horse up to de Courcy. 'Could they mean trouble?'

De Courcy shaded his eyes. 'Possibly,' he answered, and ordered the column to stop. Then together with John and his bugler-galloper, he went to the head of the column, where the *rissaldar* was waiting, his sabre already drawn, face fiercer than ever.

De Courcy nodded to him, as if in approval, and trotted on. Now they could see that the obscene, bald-headed birds were coming down. Out of the side of his mouth, gaze fixed firmly on his front, de Courcy said, 'Looks as if they've spotted a meal. Filthy brutes!' His mount flared its nostrils and tossed its mane, obviously made uneasy by the birds.

'Cruel country this, Bold,' de Courcy rasped. 'Vulture symbolizes it. The cruelty-killings… They're the *mehtars*, you know, the sweepers of this whole blood-stained community.' He frowned and spat in disdain. Next moment they rounded the bend and saw them.

The bugler waved and clapped loudly. The vultures rose lazily, flapping their huge wings, their beaks crimson with blood, and started to circle, cawing in hoarse protest.

John gasped and tugged at his reins, suddenly sick. Their prey was the remains of what had once been a woman. Her stomach had already gone, a gaping red cavern from which the entrails hung out like a grey-purple snake, and her neck had been pecked clean of flesh. The eyes had been ripped out, too. But a woman she was definitely. Hesitantly, but knowing he had to do it, he urged his shying horse up to where de Courcy and the bugler, who had gone a strange shade of green, was staring down at the remains.

'Half breed,' de Courcy pronounced. 'Perhaps one of those French by-blows from the time when they occupied this part of the coast.'

John nodded numbly, unable to speak as he stared down aghast.

Both her breasts had been hacked off. Then she had been flayed by the steel-topped *lathis*, which John had already seen the Company's police wielding on reluctant natives outside the compounds. Afterwards her legs had been prised open and she had been subjected to the final indignity before death had granted her the blessed boon of oblivion. Her murderers had stuffed a huge green plantain banana into her vagina, from which it now protruded with obscene cruelty.

John fought his nausea, forcing back the sour green bile which threatened to choke him. 'Who ... in God's name,' he finally managed to gasp thickly, 'could do such a thing?'

De Courcy said nothing. But John could see that he was now staring beyond the poor murdered woman, to the hoof-marks of unshod horses in the dust – lots of them. The creatures who had committed this foul atrocity, he told himself, burning with rage now, were not simply locals, crazed with the dope they sometimes smoked, but men of substance: men who owned horses. *Pindarees?*

De Courcy shrugged. 'Perhaps.'

'But why?' he cried angrily, as the bugler now called for the rest of the column to close up.

'A half breed, wasn't she?' de Courcy said, as if that in itself was explanation enough.

A few moments later the column began to wend its way past the corpse, the soldiers shivering a little as they saw it. Miss Lanham's attendant, a pretty little thing of fifteen, cried out loud as they came level and flung up her sari to hide her face. But Miss Lanham's face did not change when she looked down from her swaying perch. Beneath the swimming green surface of her eyes there was no emotion.

That night de Courcy and John yawned a little, enjoying the pleasant cool of the evening on the beach, a soft wind stirring the ocean gently, as the men ate their first real meal of the day. A hundred yards away, Miss Lanham and her maid squatted native-fashion and ate by themselves.

'This is a bad country,' de Courcy said lazily, relaxed for the first time and sipping his *chota peg* as he sprawled on the cool sand. A little moodily he stared into the campfire. 'There are perhaps a hundred million natives under the Company's control, speaking six-hundred-odd languages and dialects, so they say, but I doubt if any one of them in whatever language can describe what motivates this damned place! There is no rhyme or reason to the whole country!' He took another sip of his whisky. 'Some of 'em have religions which forbid them to kill an ant even. Yet they will slaughter their neighbours if they are of a different faith or lower caste without batting an eyelid. You can go into some of their villages to find the natives starving, with literally not a crust of bread to eat. Yet their sacred cows wander around untouched. They honour their dead excessively, yet some of them put their dead out on the rooftops *naked* to be picked clean by those damned vultures!' He shook his head, while John stared into the flames, awed. This, indeed, was a strange country.

'Thank God,' de Courcy said suddenly with unusual vehemence for him, 'I'm coming to the end of my time here. I've made a couple of *lakhs* of rupees. They'll see me out comfortably and I shall be leaving with a whole skin and with my health not totally ruined.' He leaned forward and nodded towards Miss Lanham and her maid. 'Take her father's district, for instance,' he said. 'Early this year one of Collector Lanham's district officers was stabbed to death by one of his Muslem servants, a man who had worked for him for years and whom he had treated well – at least for a niggah. Why? I shall tell you. The native had noticed that the district officer had started to sleep with his feet in the direction of Mecca – quite unwittingly, naturally. But the man took it as a deadly insult to his religion, which had to be avenged by death.'

John breathed out hard. God, he told himself, his mind still full of the horrors of the afternoon, how much he had to learn about this great continent!

De Courcy chuckled drily, an unusual sound coming from him, and continued, 'So you know what Collector Lanham did? You see the Collector is chief judge and magistrate, as well as the Company's agent for pulling in taxes. Well, after they'd hanged the Muslem, he ordered the cadaver to be sewn up in a pigskin. That meant, as the Muslem's think the hog unclean, that he would be disdained in his heathen paradise. That sort of settled his hash in the hereafter, what, Bold?'

'Is Mr Lanham a hard man?' John ventured.

De Courcy did not respond. He was beginning to relapse into his normal sombre self, but he did glance to Georgina Lanham, and John sensed that de Courcy bore a grudge against her; knew more about that beautiful girl than he would say.

He yawned and de Courcy finished off the rest of his drink. 'Crack o' dawn,' he said, 'g'night.' So saying he rolled himself in his blanket and seemed to go to sleep almost immediately.

In time John slept too.

4

Reveille startled him, cutting into a drugged sleep. Wearily rubbing his eyes, John sat up in his makeshift *charpoy*, as he had already learned to call his bed. Cursed by the fierce-faced *rissaldar* the first three mules, their muskets and powder unloaded, were straggling out of the little camp with their *syces,* heading for the nearest village to buy fodder for the day for the horses.

The troopers, too, were already up, shivering in the dawn cool, hawking and spitting with great energy, running water through their nostrils to clean them out, making stomach-churning gurgling noises as they did so. John thought lazily it might well have been a spital back home, filled with consumption patients in the last throes of that terrible, wasting disease.

'Chofa harzi, sahib,' a soft voice said.

It was one of the troopers, bearing a tray on which rested a piece of cold chapatti, filled with something or other, and a mug of steaming tea that gave off the odour of wood smoke. Gratefully John accepted the 'little breakfast', savouring the last few minutes of ease before another blazing hot day commenced.

It was while he was crouching, sipping his hot tea alone, that he saw Georgina Lanham coming across the strand, attended by her little native girl carrying a canvas bucket. Miss Lanham was dressed like a native herself, in a green *saree,* and towelling her blonde ringlets. Obviously she had been down to the ocean to bathe. The *saree* clung to her beautiful body, revealing every soft curve, the swelling roundness of the breasts, the nipples erect against the thin material with the coldness of the water.

'Good morning, Mr Bold,' she said, greeting him properly for the first time since they had set out. 'I trust you slept well?' She paused above him for a moment, towelling her hair deliberately. From the ocean the breeze moulded the green gown even more tightly around her still-damp body, emphasizing her mound of Venus. He felt a sudden urge of desire.

'Good morning,' de Courcy's voice, unnecessarily harsh and urgent, broke in. He touched his hand to his shako to Miss Lanham, face revealing nothing. 'Morning, Bold,' he addressed John. 'Start to look lively. I'll need you at the rear today. I want the *rissalder* up front with me.'

Miss Lanham lowered her towel and looking disdainfully at the stern-faced cavalry officer, said mysteriously (at least to John), 'Are we getting cold feet – *again* – Captain de Courcy?'

'Not at all, Miss Lanham. Just a necessary precaution. Now then, Bold, hurry up with that tea.' And with that he cantered off to where his men were beginning to form up, leaving John to wait awkwardly for Miss Lanham to leave before he could emerge from the blankets.

By midday John realized that de Courcy was expecting trouble at any moment. Now whenever the column halted for the hourly five-minute break, he posted sentries all along the trail, once even ordering his bugler to shin up a tall palm to spy into the bright green jungle. The *rissaldar* reappeared, too, with the three mules, but they had found no fodder, and de Courcy and his native officer had a hurried whispered conversation, their faces grave. But it was not only the obvious precautions which made Bold aware that something was amiss. It was the jungle. The hot dry air that shimmered above it in blue waves seemed to exude menace. Even the usual irritating chatter of the monkeys had died away.

When it did happen, it was sudden. Next to de Courcy at the front of the long column, the bugler had just begun to sound the next rest, when he started to slip side-ways from his horse.

The scarlet which spread rapidly across the small of the bugler's silver-grey back told all. Urgently de Courcy rose in his stirrups and cried, 'Dismount … for God's sake – *dismount!*'

Almost immediately the orders were inter-rupted by the fierce war cries of horsemen who burst from the trees, sabres flashing.

De Courcy fired his pistol, and the first of the charging horsemen shrieked and dropped from the saddle, to be trampled on by the mounts behind.

Now the troopers had their horses lying on the ground, and were dropping behind them, already aiming their Eliott carbines. A ragged volley struck the attackers. They went down everywhere, crying *'Maro feringhee!'* De Courcy, cavorting round on his foam-flecked, terrified horse, cried in the same tongue, *'Pindaree ... don't snatch... Pick your man ... aim for his guts..!'*

The troopers steadied. They knew the drill well enough, and were battle-experienced soldiers. As the *rissalder*, sabre drawn, stood up in full view of the enemy, they began to fire in regular volleys. Fire, twist on their backs to bite the end paper from the next cartridge while enemy balls whizzed over their heads and their panicky steeds twitched wildly, empty the black gunpowder into the carbine, ram home, squirm round, aim and fire again. Now their whole front was thick with smoke as the attackers milled round, taking casualties all the time, shrieking their heathen cries, looking for a break in the foreigners' line, making little wild dashes forward only to be mown down in that merciless fire.

John, to the rear of the stalled column, heard the outbreak of firing and after the first moment of shock felt absolutely calm. Under his command he had five troopers, and three *syces* with supply mules. None of his troopers understood more than a few words of English, but they were all veterans and they acted automatically, without orders, tugging down their animals at the edge of the trail and levelling their carbines at the jungle.

But the Pindarees' attack came from a totally unexpected quarter. Bunched together tightly, thrusting their bare knees into their comrades' horses to keep them out of the way, tossing their sabres from left hand to right in order to confuse the defenders, they came pelting hell-for-leather down the trail to the rear. As his troopers scrambled to turn and face up to this crazy charge, John urged his own horse forward, already slashing mightily to left and right, screaming wild obscenities.

With a crash that jarred his bones he smashed his horse into a white Arab. The Arab reared up, flailing with its forelegs, its rider caught off guard. John didn't give him a chance to recover but thrust home his blade. It scraped along the man's ribs in a way that made John grit his teeth, before sliding into the soft flesh.

The Pindaree screamed shrilly. Swiftly John pulled out his sword, the blade suddenly a gleaming red. The Pindaree flew backwards, waving his hands in a crazy hurrah, and slammed to the ground.

John urged his mount on, slashing to left and right, cutting his way into the stalled, confused mêlée while the troopers began to fire, picking off the attackers on the flanks. The Pindarees thrashed about, waving their sabres and yelling threats, but the steam had gone out of the attack. The men to John's front, as he hacked away at a circle of dark, hawklike faces, had the same vacant look which he had seen on the Imperial Guard after that first tremendous volley at Waterloo.

Slowly, jabbing their naked heels into their horses, bits held rigidly tight to make their horses move backwards so that they were still facing John and his troopers, they began to retreat. At first slowly, defiantly – but as the thunder of hooves up the trail indicated that Captain de Courcy was sending rein-forcements, more quickly – until finally with a great yell they broke and raced back pell-mell the way they had come.

But John knew he and his men would not withstand another charge. There were too few of them. Making his way over the dead, his horse picking up its feet in a kind of nervous tripping dance, he signalled his men to remount. They needed no urging. John gave the nearest donkey a great slap across the rump and they were off, a ragged volley of fire from the jungle speeding them on their way. Five minutes later they had rejoined the main party, accompanied by the gasping troopers de Courcy had dispatched to assist him, and John Bold knew that they were lost, if the Pindarees attacked again.

A good half of de Courcy's men lay sprawled dead or dying on the trampled trail, while their wounded mounts, long streamers of blood trickling down their heaving flanks, hobbled around, neighing and whinnying piteously, or licked the faces of their dead masters, as if the beasts felt this might bring them to life again. De Courcy had only just avoided being completely overrun.

For a moment or two, in the tension which follows a battle, John felt at a loss. What was he supposed to do? He glanced over to Miss Lanham's shattered conveyance. She knelt there in the dust next to it, staring down at her little maid. A ball had smashed into the centre of her face, causing a great gaping wound. Now she squirmed and writhed in the dust, choking in her own blood, her dark hands grabbing at handfuls of dirt in her death throes; while Miss Lanham stared at her in silence.

There was no fear on her face and in her right hand she clutched a small lady's pistol, as if she were determined to use it when the time came. John nodded his approval. This was no silly hysterical female, calling for her sal volatile salts at the first sight of a pinprick of blood. Georgina Lanham was as brave and as fearless as any man present here this bloody day.

De Courcy came cantering up, his shako gone and his right cheek cleft by a vicious sabre blow. But he seemed unaware of the terrible wound. He sheathed his own sabre, blood-red to the hilt, and cried in sudden alarm, 'Georgina, are you hurt?' There was genuine concern in his voice and it was only later that John was to realize that he had used her Christian name.

She shook her head and stood up as if to show him that it was not her blood splattered over the green *saree*. At her feet the girl suddenly arched her spine, her hands clawing as if she were climbing an invisible ladder. Next moment she fell back dead.

De Courcy sighed, as if with relief, and forgot Miss Lanham. 'Listen, Bold,' he said urgently. 'I cannot let the muskets and powder fall into their damned thieving hands. There is no hope of saving them, so I'm going to blow up the lot. You are leaving with Georg–' he corrected himself hastily – 'with Miss Lanham.'

The yellow bone-dry grass caught fire immediately. John and the girl sprang back, surprised by the sudden intensity of the flames as they hurried, sparked off by the trail of gunpowder, to where the gunpowder kegs and muskets were stacked. In a very few moments, John told himself, as balls hissed through the air lethally all around, there was going to be one devil of an explosion.

'Are you ready?' he cried to her above the

thunder of the muskets. She gave a final wrench at the bottom half of her *saree* and ripped it off, revealing shapely legs. 'I can run better this way,' she explained, her voice unflustered and steady as if she did this sort of thing every day.

He nodded. The plan de Courcy had worked out for them was simple enough. They were to make a dash on foot for the shelter of the jungle when the gunpowder exploded. The Pindarees would not follow them into the thick jungle where their horses would be useless. 'And they never would abandon their chargers. The horses are their working capital,' as de Courcy had explained. 'To soldier – and loot – they need a mount.' There they would hide as long as it took de Courcy to extricate what was left of the column from the trap.

John flashed a glance up the trail. The fiery-faced *rissaldar,* supporting himself against a bullet-chipped palm, blood jetting from a wounded shoulder, was directing the fire of the main body of survivors. But the Pindarees were becoming bolder, making little sorties, charging along the trail, yelling their war cries, swinging their sabres, bent low over their mounts, only to wither away under the concentrated fire of the troopers. But the outnumbered defence couldn't last much longer. Even de Courcy had taken up a musket.

5

'Ready, Miss Lanham?'
'Ready!'
'Now!'

Then they were running all out for the cover of the thick undergrowth. A cry of rage rose from the Pindarees. Balls began to cut the air around them and stitch spurts of earth at their feet.

De Courcy, kneeling now, blood spurting from a fresh wound in his side, yelled an urgent order. A ragged volley slammed into a group of Pindarees galloping towards the two fugitives. They were blasted out of their saddles and hurtled to the earth in a mess of flying limbs and dying horses. But there were others, already dragging their mounts round to intercept the runners. They came springing over their dead and dying comrades, scimitars flashing.

Then it came. Beneath their flying feet the very earth shook. Behind them a great sheet of flame split the sky as the mass of gunpowder went up. John yelled with pain. It felt as if a horse had kicked him between the shoulders. He was hurtled forward, dragging Georgina Lanham with him, and flung into the jungle...

John's lips formed a silent *'Quiet!'*

Georgina, her face lathered with dirt and sweat, hair lank, *saree* ripped by thorns, obeyed instantly. They had been on the run all afternoon in that murderous heat. For a while they had moved parallel to the track. But constant forays by the Pindarees hunting them had forced them deeper and deeper into the jungle. But even here they weren't safe. Local men, forced by the Pindarees, would be looking for them.

But now John had had enough of the jungle. He had decided on a bold new plan: to do the unexpected and move back to the track where they might find horses and flee post-haste to the safety of Collector Lanham's fort.

But still nature seemed against them. To their front, in a glade just off the track, were just the two horses they needed for their flight, tethered to saplings. For a bold and brave young man it would not be difficult to take them, save for one thing. The glade was bathed in the beautiful but lethal yellow light of the tropical moon; and the two Pindarees who owned the horses, which at this moment John desired with an almost physical longing, were definitely *not* asleep.

They squatted on their haunches, chatting in the desultory manner of men forced to stay awake at night. They were obviously guards. John bit his bottom lip and considered the problem.

After a while he crooked his finger and she silently came closer. He felt the softness of her breast and scented the exciting odour of woman as he placed his mouth tight to her ear. Exhausted as he was, he still controlled himself with difficulty. 'I shall kill them,' he whispered. 'But I can't use my pistol, that's for an emergency.'

'I understand,' she whispered, her breath warming his cheek like a kiss. As if by accident her hand fell on to his thigh. He drew back hastily and the hand fell away. But he heard her give a little sigh. She had felt him.

Time passed tensely. Slowly, painfully slowly, the yellow moon started to drift behind scudding cloud. Darkness began to descend upon the glade. The idle chatter died away. One of the Pindarees walked over to his mount, swung into the saddle and unslung his carbine. Perhaps his chieftain had given him a previous order to patrol the trail at this time. At all events, he started to walk the horse away from the glade.

John sucked his teeth. That left only one horse for the two of them. But it also left only one Pindaree to tackle. He counted ten. The horseman had vanished, there was no time to be wasted. He crawled forward, carefully parting the shrubs and thinking their leaves made a devil of a noise.

She followed on hands and knees, the tiny lady's pistol grasped in her dirty hand, face as determined as his. For Georgina Lanham was no shrinking violet – she intended to survive, and if she had to kill to do so, why not? The hammer of the pistol was ready cocked.

Only a matter of yards from the unsuspecting Pindaree, John wiped his hands dry of sweat on his ragged buckskins. He wanted a firm grip on the creature's skinny throat right from the start; he could not afford a cry for help. The damned Pindarees were everywhere.

He launched himself and his hands found and tightened around the brown throat, exerting every bit of his strength. The Pindaree writhed, clawed and kneed viciously for the crotch. John dodged expertly, hopping as if on the dance floor. His breath coming in frantic, hectic sobs, he pressed and pressed.

The man's struggles weakened. His eyes bulged. The veins on his face stood out like writhing purple snakes. Suddenly he went limp, but John did not yet relax his murderous pressure. He hung on, his fingers biting deep into the neck, now swollen and engorged with blood. The man's tongue hung out of his gaping mouth like a piece of purple leather.

After what seemed an age John let go, gently lowering his victim to the ground.

Nothing happened. The man made no move. He was dead all right, his *dhoti* polluted and stinking with his own body wastes.

John leaned against a tree for a moment, his hands shaking.

'Good,' she breathed, her eyes shining, 'you did it, John!' It was the first time she had used his name.

He did not seem to hear, but stood with chest heaving as if he had just run a great race. Then he blinked and her beautiful face came into focus. 'Yes ... Georgina,' he gasped. 'Come, we must–'

Coming round the bend in the trail was the other Pindaree and it was quite clear that he had seen them, for his carbine was already at his shoulder.

John acted instinctively. It was a basic reaction, engendered by fear. He dived forward, grabbed the man's leg and gave a tremendous tug. The Pindaree came sliding down from the rearing horse's back, right on top of John and still holding the carbine.

In a flash he had twisted away from the Englishman and had risen to his knees, bringing up the little cavalry carbine. John could see the triumph in the hawklike brown face as the trigger finger tightened. '*Maro Feringhee*,' the man snarled, lips twisted in a cold sneer, '*kill the Engl–*'

The crack came with startling suddenness. The man reared up, spine arched, face raised to heaven as if pleading for mercy. But there was no mercy this cruel night. Slowly, very slowly, he crumbled. The carbine tumbled from nerveless fingers. In absolute total silence, a trickle of bright blood running from his gaping twisted mouth, he sank to his knees, and now John saw Georgina.

She stood there, upper body at an angle, right arm level and outstretched, as if she were on some English shooting range, a thin wisp of smoke coming from the muzzle of her deadly little pistol.

With a slight thud, the Pindaree hit the ground. John stirred him with his foot, but he was dead all right. Her bullet had put a scarlet hole in his back.

Quietly and with no apparent emotion, she said, 'The sound of that shot will have carried for miles. It's best we move quickly, John.'

He nodded numbly. Together, like two grey sleepwalkers, they crossed the glade to the horses...

It was a strange night of alarms and sudden scares. The Pindaree encampment and piquets were everywhere along the trail north, some in groups which seemed to number hundreds. More than once the fugitives nearly blundered into them, sleeping along the track or guarding it, and it was only because John had insisted they muffle their horses' hooves with cloths taken from the dead men that they were able to withdraw unheard.

As they progressed north in this slow and hazardous manner, it became clear to John that de Courcy's party had been wiped out, and that the rider who had been sent to contact Hastings had obviously not made it. That meant there was nothing but unfriendly territory between them and the Collector's fort. Now the ocean's horizon began to colour a sinister blood red, and John knew their time was running out...

As if she could read his thoughts, Georgina broke the heavy silence, her voice husky and strained. 'The ocean. That has got to be the only way, John.'

'You mean some sort of boat?'

'Yes, it doesn't even need to have a sail. The prevailing wind here runs from south to north. All we need is a paddle to steer with.'

He laughed hollowly. 'All we need, Georgina, is a *boat!* But where do we find it?'

'One of the fishing villages hereabouts. They have boats and I have money still to buy one.'

'But the Pindarees will be occupying those villages, too.'

She reined in her tired Arab and said, 'Yes, but they can't be alert all the time. And if we can't buy a boat, then we must steal one.'

'You're right, Georgina. These horses are fast, but they haven't much stamina.' He considered a moment. Between them they had three pistols and he knew now that she was resolute and would use hers in an emergency. They might frighten off a small party of the marauders, but hadn't a chance against a larger number. A boat was the only way out. He made up his mind. 'Let us find a fishing village by dawn. We can hide through the day and–'

Suddenly he nudged her mount off the track with an urgent, 'Quick, there are riders coming!' They smashed their way deeper into the jungle and dismounted to clap their hands over the muzzles of their abruptly nervous steeds.

The first riders into view were Pindarees, laden with loot, their carbines slung over their shoulders as if they were finished with marauding and were heading back to their mountain fastnesses.

Behind them came Nom de Dieu and his Frenchmen. When they were past, John and Georgina slowly relaxed their grip on the horses' muzzles. She looked at him in bewilderment. 'They were the French ... from the boat?' she said slowly, reflectively, as if shocked to see these European gentlemen and ex-officers riding with the Pindarees.

Numbly he nodded his agreement.

'But what...' She stopped, for it was clear that John Bold was as puzzled as herself.

6

An hour later they were approaching the first fishing village warily, leading their weary mounts through the edge of the jungle, taking no chances. All the Pindarees may not have ridden north, as those with Nom de Dieu had done.

They could see grey wisps of smoke ascending lazily into the hard blue sky from some of the crude thatched huts resting on piles. Here and there, black skinny chickens and old dogs nosed and picked beneath the huts, but they could not see any people, nor any indication of whether the village was occupied by Pindarees.

John nudged a very weary Georgina. 'Look,' he whispered hoarsely, 'to the right of that bigger hut.'

She thrust back her unkempt blonde hair and stared. Some fifty yards away from the waves curling, then breaking with a soft hiss on the gleaming white coral sand, was a primitive boat: a hollowed-out tree trunk, supported by two rickety outriggers for stability, with a large carved prow representing some mythical sea creature.

'Not too difficult to manage,' he whispered. 'With a bit of luck we could push it into the sea in, at the most, five minutes.'

'Yes,' she agreed. 'The wood of those craft is exceedingly light – and there's a steering paddle too. To the right, in the sand. The only question now is whether those wretched Pindarees still hold the place.'

In answer there was a sudden sharp whinnying which indicated a horse, hidden somewhere from their view by the huts.

The happiness of their discovery vanished from John's face. 'They're there all right,' he said sourly. 'I doubt if fishermen would have a horse.'

'Yes,' she answered. 'But you had anticipated that, John, hadn't you? We must hide until we find a chance to steal the craft. Let us go.'

They found a thick clump of bamboo cane close to a stretch of marshy ground, flecked here and there with white salt licks, as if the swamp had been caused by flooding from the sea, and John hacked a tight burrow into the bamboo with his sword. Fortunately the sun had driven off the flies and mosquitoes, but it was terribly hot and sticky. They lay on the soft earth watching the village, their throats as parched and dry as cracked leather. They had not had a drink since the previous evening. Still they felt fit enough and confident, as they surveyed the village. It was obvious from their actions that the

151

inhabitants of the hamlet were terrified of the Pindarees occupying the place. Emaciated, half-naked brown men crouched fearfully in the shadows, while their womenfolk, clothes across their faces, went about their tasks in a hurried, nervous manner. Their fear was tangible. The two hidden observers could smell it on the very air.

A heavily bearded swaggering Pindaree, hand clutched to the sabre at his waist, came into view, shouting arrogantly for food. A frightened fisherman, bowing and scraping, promptly brought a steaming bowl of rice and fish.

Over the next hour they saw a good dozen Pindarees, one of them dragging a poor half-naked girl who didn't look a day over twelve. She was sobbing quietly, her spirit completely broken.

'Now we know,' John said thickly. 'We're easily outnumbered.'

'Yes, but we have surprise on our side!'

He nodded and wondered. If the Pindarees started to drink after sunset, indulging in the potent rice wine of the area, then their reactions would be slowed down. The noise of a boat being pushed through the sand might take some time to register on their addled brains...

At last it was night. One moment the sun had been burning in all its terrible brightness, the next it had slipped over the horizon

and darkness came with the startling suddenness of the tropics. They left the bamboos
and skirted the hamlet, blundering through
the fetid stench of the mangrove swamp.
Overwhelming thirst tormented them, and
John knew they must drink soon.

Slowly they approached the still ocean, the
water shimmering under the tropical moon,
the noises of the village becoming steadily
louder: the tired barking of the lean dogs,
the scrape of a pan, an axe chopping wood,
the raucous sound of someone already in his
cups.

Another thirty minutes passed. Now they
were crossing under a dark lofty tunnel of
trees, with slippery mud underfoot. To their
front a gentle mist was rising. There seemed
something alive and malignant about it, like
some evil creature watching their every
movement.

In the ever-increasing gloom they began to
tread more uncertainly, not sure that the
curling shapes at their feet were tree roots or
snakes. But all the same they progressed ever
closer to the hamlet, hearing now by the
steady beat of a drum. Perhaps the Pindarees
were having some kind of celebration.

They came out of the jungle. Before them,
wreathed in a low mist, lay the strand. But
above them the yellow moon still shone.
John cursed. Why couldn't nature favour
them for once? Nearby the drum continued

its monotonous, nerve-racking beat.

He almost stumbled over the water trough in the low mist. It was a crudely hollowed-out tree trunk, supported on stones – and it was filled with liquid!

Cautiously he dipped his hands in it. She crouched next to him, her gaze fixed firmly on the flickering cherry-red fires of the village. He tasted, and his heart leapt. It was pure rain water, sweet and blessedly cruel. *'Water!'* he croaked.

Together they gulped it down in great choking sups, lifting their heads whenever there was a strange sound, their foreheads matted with wet hair, the precious liquid running down their chins.

By the instant John felt fresh energy pulse through his dehydrated body. Suddenly he felt strong, confident of success.

But what did those damned drums mean? Squatting there, water still dripping down his chin, he peered at a slow procession of horsemen – moving out of the fishing village now. He gasped with shock, for in the ruddy wavering firelight he glimpsed a horrible, shrivelled thing hanging from one of the saddles, bobbing up and down obscenely, long black curls trailing down to the sawn-off neck.

Next to him, Georgina recoiled and her hands flew to her mouth to stifle a scream. *'Robert!'* she gasped.

John gritted his teeth, fighting off nausea. It was ... it was the head of Captain Robert de Courcy!

As the riders passed, the shocked fugitives, hidden in the undergrowth only a few yards away, caught a glimpse of an imperious proud face, hook-nosed and arrogant, surmounted by a great silk turban adorned with pearls. John had the impression of some great chief – perhaps one of those *lubbars,* as Colonel Monroe had called them – leading his warriors home. Then they were gone, and the drums ceased beating one by one, perhaps signalling the end of the Pindarees' lethal foray into the Madras Presidency, only a handful staying behind to cover their withdrawal.

John pressed her arm tightly. For the first time he sensed that her nerve had almost broken at the sight of that severed head. With more confidence than he felt, he whispered, 'It's all right, Georgina ... all right,' and stroked her arm soothingly. 'They've had their fill of looting now. Those over there are just a rearguard. Look, they're going back to their carousing.' He indicated the half dozen Pindarees returning to the huts or squatting down again by the fires. 'It's time we set about our task.'

'Yes,' she said, recovering herself, her voice firm and clear. 'We must be gone.'

Hand in hand they went to the boat. It was

not tethered down in any way, and moved easily on the dry sand. Wasting no time, they slid it down to the waves. John's triumphant grin was shattered by an alarm call from the hamlet.

Acting as one, they gave a final heave, the boat was afloat, and they tumbled in. John grabbed the paddle, thrusting it into the water from side to side, trying to control their direction. A musket ball screamed past his bowed head.

'*Malo Feringhee* – kill the English!' The Pindarees pelted across the sand. Another ball passed close and struck the water in an angry splutter.

'My God, John!' she screamed.

Already the first of their pursuers was in the water, ready to strike the killing blow.

Desperately he steered the light craft's prow into the spluttering surf which seemed determined not to allow them to pass. Striking from left to right, his lungs wheezing like bellows, he thrust his paddle into the waves. Behind him the splashing of the Pindaree came ever closer.

'*Pistol*,' he choked to her. '*Pistol!*'

But she seemed frozen, the little pistol held uselessly in a limp hand, eyes wide, wild and staring, as the man raised his great curved sword to cleave the white man's skull into two, black face set in a look of animal joy, dark eyes crazed with *bhang*.

'Sh–' John's impassioned last plea was drowned by the surge of water, as it suddenly took hold of the prow and raised it high. The attacker was caught completely by surprise. The great blade fell. But not on John. Instead their pursuer howled with absolute agony as he stumbled and the sword burrowed deep into his own vitals.

He staggered back, both hands trying to pluck the killing blade from his belly. But already it was too late. As he died on his feet and his fellows fired fruitlessly, the current caught the little fishing boat and swept it out to sea at a tremendous rate. They had done it!

7

The bright ball of the sun hung like a burning glass above the limitless sea. There were no enemies now, save nature itself.

John licked cracked lips rimmed with salt. There was no longer any need to wield the steering paddle. The current was taking them directly towards a thin pencil of land.

He glanced at Georgina who was clawing out handfuls of seawater and wetting her makeshift headgear with them. She was clearly at the end of her tether, her spirit almost broken. His heart went out to her.

It was night when the current brought the boat to the shore. Not knowing where they were, with barely the strength to move, they fell into gentle wavelets and crawled up the sand. They slept.

The old man with the skinny brown frame and fringe of white beard watched them as they came awake there in the fringe of palms by the shore, their rags steaming in the heat of the new sun. Then he stepped forward timidly, bowed, and said something in his own tongue.

Georgina started, but seeing the old man was harmless, replied in the native language.

'What does he want?' John asked, but before she could interpret, the old man indicated that they should follow him.

John felt too drained of energy to care much. If the old man was leading them into a trap, then so be it. He followed in a kind of weak-kneed coma. Georgina did the same, her face drained.

Their guide moved quickly as he led them through rotting mangroves to a clearing with the typical circle of thatched huts on stilts of a fishing village.

Again the old man bowed and indicated they should clamber up a rickety bamboo ladder into the nearest hut. They obeyed tamely, fighting for breath, for they were exhausted by the short trek. The hut was empty save for some crude rush mats and a few gourds hanging from the roof. They collapsed on the mats, overcome by weariness, but suddenly feeling secure. It was not a trap after all.

The man smiled down at them as a loving father might at his weary children who had returned home after a day at play. Then he lit the coconut oil lamp with flint and tinder and went out.

A few minutes later two young women in *sarees*, smiling and giggling, appeared. The one, with a small pearl let into her left nostril, bore on her shoulder a huge jar of clear well water; the other on her hip a dish of steaming rice and fish. They bowed and set their vessels down.

Greedily the two fugitives gulped the fresh water in great sobbing gasps before tackling the food, which the women ladled out into rough gourds. Not a word was spoken. They ate like animals, shovelling the hot food into their mouths with dirty fingers, while the women, their great dark eyes outlined by *kohl*, stared as if amazed at such prodigious appetites. Moments after they had finished, feeling content and replete for the first time in days, they fell asleep, her hand in his. Gently the girls covered them and left them there together like new lovers...

It was a long sleep, deep and untroubled. Once John awoke briefly to the soft pad-pad of bare feet and the hoarse barking of a pariah dog. He had the vague impression that the women were in the hut again, but it was just an impression. In her sleep Georgina turned and pressed her body closer to his. He sighed and fell asleep once more, a gentle luxurious warmth coursing through his tired body.

When he awoke again she was sitting up, trying to comb her hair and listening to the old man, who squatted on his haunches, his frame outlined by bright moonlight. With him was a boy, his bright intelligent face wreathed in smiles, his jet-black hair gleaming with coconut oil.

Georgina nodded at the boy. 'He is the old man's – the headman's – youngest son. He can't speak...'

As if to confirm her words, the boy opened his mouth to reveal, among bright white teeth, the ragged stump of his tongue.

John shook his head. He would never become accustomed to the cruelty of this place. 'Who did it?'

'The Pindarees. That is why the father is helping us. Sabu here is to take a message to my father.'

'But we have only their word for it, Georgina,' John objected. 'Perhaps they're fattening us up for the kill? What if the boy is being sent off to betray us to the Pindarees?'

She considered. The unwritten law of India forbade any villager, however poor, to refuse food and shelter to a starving stranger. Yet equally there was no law forbidding him from slitting his guest's throat afterwards or betraying him to his enemies. 'But why should he have rescued us in the first place?' she countered. 'He could have left us to die of thirst.'

He shrugged and accepted the logic of her reasoning as the two young women reappeared once more, bearing rice and a sauce of fishpaste and durians. For the time being he would question nothing, but let fate take its course. Suddenly hungry once more, he began to stuff the hot rice into his mouth.

8

Days passed. The boy without a tongue had been entrusted with one of Georgina's rings and a note to her father, but neither the headman nor Georgina knew how long it would take him to reach Musulipatan. So they idled the days away, regaining their strength and trying to make themselves presentable for the day when the Collector arrived. The women took their tattered clothing away, replacing his with a *choti* and loose vest, in which he felt patently absurd, and hers with the deep green *saree* of the harvest time, which set off her figure and hair to perfection. While the women washed and patched the rags, the men reinforced their worn shoes with stout bark; for they would never kill one of the humped sacred cows, however short of leather they might be.

At night, replete with yet another huge meal of rice and fish, sat at opposite sides of their hut (for after that first night of lying exhausted together, virtually in each other's arms, he kept his distance strictly), she regaled him with tales of her life with the Collector at Musulipatan.

She told him that India was a land of nicknames. The English of the Madras Presidency were called Mulls, after the hot pepper mulligatawny soup that everyone there ate; while those from Bombay were known as the Ducks because their favourite dish was supposedly Bombay duck, a strong-smelling dried fish. Those from Bengal, on the other hand, were named not after food but from their usual manner of summoning their servants with the words 'Koi hoi'– 'Is there anyone there?' So they had become nicknamed, *qui-his*.

But from whatever presidency they hailed, all the English kept a host of servants. Even the poorest European could not manage without a bearer, who rubbed him down after dinner and carried his money; a butler; a cook (who had unfortunate habits such as using his bare feet as a toast rack and straining the soup through an old sock); a scullion; a *scye* for his horses; and above all a sweeper who emptied the privy and ranked with the water-carrier as the lowest of the low, being 'untouchable.'

'But how am I expected – on an ensign's or lieutenant's pay – to keep that number of servants, Georgina?' he had protested good-humouredly. 'My salary – surely – will not be that large?'

'No, it won't. You will be a captain in the Company's army at twenty-nine, a major at forty-four and with luck a lieutenant-colonel at fifty-four. Those are the averages. You see, there are few chances of advancement and salary in the Army. Naturally your duties as a soldier will not be arduous. Some black rascal will shave and feed you tea an hour before daylight. He'll dress you. If there's a parade, he'll pack you in your uniform and you'll ride a couple of hundred yards across the drill square, shout a few orders to your company and then you'll go back to your quarters to resume your nap.'

He laughed hollowly at her account of the military existence and said, 'I take it, Georgina, you hold little regard for the military?'

She shook her beautiful blonde head. 'No,

163

I don't. In time of war, they're useful. In peace they're unnecessary lazy fobs, given to drink and loose women.'

She must have seen the sudden look on his face, for she added hastily, 'But India offers other chances for bold young men. One doesn't have to be like Robert...' She hesitated, as if another memory had come to mind.

'De Courcy?' he prompted.

'Yes,' she snapped, 'Robert de Courcy, ending his life like that for a pittance, with his head cut off! Careers can be made here, John.' She leaned forward intently and laid her hand on his knee, eyes angry and burning. 'Look at My Lord Hastings. He was a ruined man when he came out here, his fortune gone. Yet today he's the most powerful man in the land, with a title and a fortune to take back home with him when...' Her words trailed away and she said slowly, the sudden fire gone from her voice, 'You're not interested in such things, John, are you?'

'No, Georgina, I don't want money really, nor power. I was born to be a soldier and undoubtedly,' he laughed, 'I shall die one when my time comes.'

'Then more fool you!' she snorted, and relapsed into a sulky silence as if it were purposeless to spend words on such an unambitious fool...

On the night of the fourth day jingling bells

164

and soft insistent drums summoned them to a village wedding. The women wore bright *sarees*, their hair sleeked with palm oil and smelling of sandalwood; the men, shaven for once, sported intricate ceremonial turbans.

The bride and groom sat on high-back chairs, the girl of only fourteen with down-cast eyes and breasts firm beneath her thin *saree*, the boy proud yet embarrassed. A line of well-wishers formed up to deliver presents on cushions as if the couple were royalty.

Now the fires were stoked higher. In their ruddy fantastic light the bridegroom rose, every inch a king though in reality he was a young fisherman. He raised the girl from her throne, gently, smiling down at her shy face before loosing her *saree*. Now he undid his own gown and wrapped the loose folds around her, too.

John felt his heart beat more quickly and cast a look out of the corner of his eye at Georgina. Her gaze was fixed hypnotically on the couple under that one garment, as the material moved, indicating what the new bridegroom was doing to his bride. Slowly her bottom lip, wet with saliva, drooped, and he was sure he heard a faint moan of pleasure.

Three dancing girls came writhing into the circle of light as a kind of violin joined the drums, etching unreal arabesques on the night air. They were obviously village girls,

165

not much older than the bride. Ankle bells clinked in time to the music as they danced, their hands fanning the sky, taut breasts, nipples erect, bulging in tight-fitting bodices.

John caught his breath. The girls arched their bodies, legs spread in total provocation, as if they were already spreadeagled on a soft broad bed, impatient to be raped. He broke out in a sweat. God, it was too much to bear!

One of the girls brushed by him and he caught the musky woman smell of raw sex. For a moment her hand caressed his cheek daintily, a finger tracing a course along his burning flesh. He choked. Next to him Georgina did not take her fascinated gaze from what was happening beneath the robe.

The fiddle scraped. The drums continued their hypnotic beat. The dancing girls whirled, stamping their bare feet, twirling skirts revealing naked flesh. Now the men were gulping the warm raw rice wine from their gourds, their dark eyes aflame, riveted. Even the children had grown silent, awed by the strange spectacle. The very air was alive with sex.

Now the wedding couple, still locked under the gown, headed for the gaily decorated hut where they would spend their first night of love. Immediately they had vanished, the crazed revelry began. Old men, women, children commenced gyrating to the beat of the drum, working themselves up to a frenzy, eyes blank, teeth flashing, saliva dripping from slack open mouths.

John decided to leave before the orgies began. In Madras he had seen some of their obscene templed friezes and reckoned they were capable of any obscenity. 'Georgina,' he hissed, pressing her arm, 'we must go.'

She did not respond. Her gaze was still riveted, her beautiful face somehow slack, as one of the dancers stripped off her skirt, twisting her naked lower body in slow ecstasy, a secret little smile on her girl's face.

'Georgina!' he commanded brutally and dug his fingers into her bare arm cruelly, 'You must come with me – *now!*'

'What … oh yes, John,' she stammered.

He propelled her through the frenzied throng, reeking now of sweat, oil and sex, already beginning to fumble with each other in crazed abandon like the spreadeagled women he had seen on their stone temple carving, grasped by grinning, fat, many-handed gods. It was no use going back to their hut, it was too close to this scene of total abandon. They must wait outside the village until it was over.

Slowly and in silence, minds still racing with the excitement, they walked along the white beach where combers slithered back and forth in timeless harmony. The village sounds grew fainter and fainter, yet still both their young hearts continued to beat to the heady intoxicating rhythm. They walked as if mesmerized; as if they might never stop.

There was a wordless communication between them, a warm longing and desire, an aching overwhelming feeling that something – *anything* – had to happen soon. *It had to!*

She stopped and sat down, her arms around her knees, which were tightly pressed together, and stared out at the yellow sea stretching to a purple horizon studded with a myriad silver stars. He sat down beside her. He did not speak. He could not. She turned. Suddenly she gasped as if she were unable to breathe. She flung herself on him. Instinctively his arms tightened around her. His lips pressed themselves on her burning lips. There was pure joy and relief in her body as she opened her mouth. She went soft and relaxed and fell backwards on to the sand, carrying him with her.

Her legs parted. His hand slid inside her *saree*. She gasped with pleasure, her body trembling with anticipation. He cupped the beautiful right breast which he had desired ever since that day at Madras with the fishing fleet. He touched the trembling rigid nipple. She quivered all over. Her tongue slid into his open mouth, warm and liquid, and her hand fell to his thigh. After a moment it moved to the swelling. He choked with pleasure. Suddenly he began to pant like a dog on rut. He must have her soon!

Later they lay naked in the sand. Once she had broken loose from his hot grasp and run laughing into the water. He had followed. Gracefully, deftly they had swum together, feeling each other in the warm gleaming wavelets. She had stood up and he had dived between her legs. They had laughed uproariously. Now they lay clutching each other, his body brought close to hers so that she could feel the burning urgent tautness, his hands still damp from the water, touching, searching, caressing her everywhere.

In sudden anger, he called, 'Do you want it? *Do you?*' Why he was so angry he did not know.

'Oh yes ... but wait ... oh, wait – *please!*' she moaned, her voice brittle and feverish, almost as if she were in pain. 'You must ... wait for me...'

'*I can't!*' he hissed back frantically. 'Not much more ... I can't!' Desperately he clutched her burning body to him, digging his fingers savagely into her flesh. He fumbled momentarily and then forced open her thighs with the hardness of his right knee, feeling her moist and hot against his skin. '*You must do it!*' he moaned, unable to control himself any longer. '*Do it ... now!*'

Abruptly she slipped out of his grasp. Caught off balance, he fell back on the sand, panting wildly. Next instant she had positioned herself above his loins.

Dizzy with desire, straining upwards for that final release, he waited.

She didn't take long, for now she was to have what she had desired all along. Legs splayed apart, face distorted with unbridled passion like that of a demented woman, she thrust herself upon him. Spine arched, head flung back, hair flying wildly, she rode that pillar of hard burning flesh, mistress of love, taking her pleasure as she had always done – *alone!*

9

The rescue expedition arrived at nine the next morning. First came the lumbering elephants, with Sabu perched on the first one. Urged on by bad-tempered *mahouts*, they bore the expedition's brass six-pounder cannon manned by European gunners, scouring the countryside for any sign of the Pindarees. Behind the elephants came the Company's cavalry, and a squadron of British cavalry sent by Hastings personally at the Collector's insistence. Finally there were the civilians, mostly officials but as heavily armed as the soldiers, within their centre the Collector Lanham himself. For Mr Thomas Lanham had a great sense of his own worth. He was not going to risk his very valuable person to some marauding heathen blackamoor.

John recognized him at once as Georgina's father. He had the same pale oval face and light green eyes. But the body had run grossly to fat and the challenging boldness of his daughter's face had been replaced by a look of pudgy, self-important avarice. Collector Lanham, John decided on the spot, as he grasped Georgina's hand tightly, looked exactly how a collector of taxes should look.

While Sabu rushed to his father, clutching the golden guinea that Lord Hastings had given him personally, and the troops fanned out to both sides of the village as if they half expected a trap, Lanham, secure behind his screen of civilian volunteers, waited. He appeared nervous, playing repeatedly with his golden fob watch and at the same time constantly dabbing his bald head with a flowered silk handkerchief like a man whose time was precious.

A captain of the European cavalry, dashing with his sabretache and shako, dolman hung from his right shoulder, galloped up and reported to Lanham, gleaming sabre raised to his forehead in salute. Obviously he was reporting that the village was safe; there were no Pindarees in the neighbourhood.

'Thank you, Captain... 'Bout time, sir. Now where is my daughter, sir?'

'Here... Here, here, Father!' Georgina cried. She pulled free from John's possessive grip and sprang up and down so that her father could see her above the heads of the natives like some little girl about to be given a treat.

The Collector smiled when he saw his daughter. But his eyes did not light up. John, suddenly apprehensive at the prospect of meeting the father of the girl he had made love to the night before, felt that he had probably never really smiled in all his life. Lanham jerked at the bit and his heavy mare ambled forward, the villagers parting to both sides obediently. He never even noticed.

He reined in his horse and stared down at his daughter, seeing everything, including the handsome young man with the hard face of an adventurer standing next to her protectively, as if he might already be her husband. Lanham was a man well acquainted with the drawing of accounts, especially when he could do so in his own favour. Now he realized almost immediately there was a debit here somehow – and he didn't like that realization one bit.

Ponderously he dismounted and embraced his daughter, though not taking his gaze off the young man with her for a moment; while his entourage clapped politely as if this was some kind of theatrical performance.

Still clutching his daughter in pudgy white

hands, he looked over her shoulder and said coldly, 'And who are you, sir, pray?'

Before he could answer she pulled herself back and said, 'This is John Bold, Father. We were the only two survivors from the column led by Captain de Courcy.'

Lanham sniffed, as if he felt only disdain for the dead captain, and said, 'You were of some assistance to my daughter no doubt, Mr Bold?'

'He *saved my life*, Father!' she said energetically.

'I see,' he said, as if making a calculation of what this might mean to him in hard pounds, shillings and pence. He put out his flabby hand. 'I am deeply indebted to you, sir,' he said without enthusiasm.

John took the hand. It was soft, damp, and unpleasant, and he repressed the sudden desire to wipe his palm on the seat of his trousers, muttering that it had 'Been a great honour to serve Georgina – er – Miss Lanham.'

Lanham, always alert for the slightest error as a good collector should be, noted that 'Georgina' and told himself Mr John Bold would need watching. Then he dismissed him. He and his daughter started towards the headman's hut, deep in conversation.

Leaving John standing in the hot sun and suddenly feeling very alone. Fate, he suspected, was about to deal yet another blow…

THREE: BOLD'S HORSE

1

Lord Hastings, his staff and the Collector breakfasted lazily and at length, as was the Company officials' wont. They had risen at dawn while it was still cool, worked a couple of hours, and then ridden.

Above them the punkah billowed like an ill-reefed sail as they slumped round the polished table, eating their way through a menu of curried rice, fried fish, mutton chops in gravy, omelettes, preserves, coffee and tea, taking time out between each course for a puff or two at the hookahs which stood at the side of each dignitary; while silent black servants in crisp white glided in and out like dusky ghosts, taking away and placing down silver and gilded dishes.

Watching them from his hard seat on the settle in a far corner of the big room, his place untouched by the efforts of the punkah-wallah, John Bold focused his attention on the man sitting to the left of the Collector – The Governor General himself, Lord Hastings. He was a small dark man, hiding his balding head under the beaver he wore even at table, for he still retained the habits he had acquired, before he had been ruined, as one of the Prince Regent's bucks. In those days back in Brighton the Prince and his cronies had always worn their hats to dine, to spite the Prince's father, George III, who had striven to retain the proprieties, even in his madness. Surveying Hastings now and feeling the sweat trickle unpleasantly down the small of his back, John thought there was definitely something simian about the Governor General. With the dark shadow of beard across his broad face (although his Indian servant would have shaved him in his sleep only a couple of hours before) and his jug-handle ears, he really looked like a monkey. His gait, too, hanging-armed and awkward, had something of the primate.

Yet despite his appearance and his old reputation as a rake-hell, Hastings had made a success of his office. Nor was he a coward like his former patron, the Prince Regent. He had not left the fighting, which had taken up much of his time in these last few years, to the professional soldiers. He had ventured personally into the field as commander-in-chief in every campaign that the Company's armies had undertaken. The Collector, John thought ruefully, was different. He had probably never smelled powder in all his life.

It was seven days now since they had finally reached Musulipatan and it had become clear to John that the Collector disliked him.

Admittedly he had invited John to his large mansion one evening, but the rooms had been filled with local notables, dressed in the height of London fashion (for Indian tailors and seamstresses were swift at copying), and he had felt awkward and out of place in the poor suit of 'ducks', which was all he had been able to afford with the last of his money.

It had been obvious, too, that the Collector was determined to keep him away from Georgina. That night he had surrounded her with young officers and those Company employees known to the locals as 'three hundred pound a year' men: their widows would automatically receive that sum for the rest of their lives. 'Dead or alive, *he's worth three hundred!*' it was trumpeted of such men, who were generally regarded as the best catch one of the fishing fleet could make.

That night he had got her briefly on to the verandah of the bungalow, as these one-storey houses were called. Hidden from sight within by the *chupper,* a large screen of thatch used to prevent the monsoon rains from soaking the walls, he had pleaded, 'But why do you spurn me so, Georgina – after what we have been to one another?'

She snapped back, 'It's no use being angry with me, John Bold. It's not my fault. My father, the Collector' – later he would reflect that she often referred to her father by his title – 'is very conscious of his position. And since Mama is gone, I must act as hostess. That is all.' She hesitated. 'But you must understand that he means well for me.'

'And what is that supposed to mean? Come on,' he demanded with the fierce impatience of youth as she hesitated.

'Well, if you must know, John, he wants me to marry well and live in style.'

Savagely he pulled her to him, feeling her body soft and desirable beneath the loose silk of her gown, and tried to kiss her, hissing, 'You will marry me – and damn living in style!'

But she twisted her face aside, as if his kiss was repugnant to her, and fled back into the big room.

But now that episode was temporarily forgotten – his immediate concern was his commission. For the last two days he had been signing chits for his board and lodgings. Now he was penniless in a foreign land. He needed money desperately and the only way he knew of getting it was to become a soldier again.

This whole week he had waited on the hard settle, while the great man had breakfasted, trying to catch the Governor General's eye. Without success. He had noticed the Collector glancing at him covertly, though he had made no attempt to present John or bring him to the great man's notice. Now he was almost in despair.

He was bored, too. He was sick of the garrison with its scandal and small talk. In England people talked about things. Here they talked endlessly and maliciously about *people*. What Mr This said to Miss That and what they did – the endless trivial gossip about marriages and non-marriages and will-be-marriages and ought-to-be marriages ... ladies flirting, reunions, clothes and the latest *burrakana* – big dinner. How he longed for the open air and the simplicity of the soldier's life!

Outside, a servant commenced attaching a thermanticote to the window. It was a huge wooden contraption, hollow and circular, containing four fans and covered with grass mats soaked in water. When the fans turned, a stream of cooler air, made fragrant by the grass, would enter the room and enable the company to smoke their bubble pipes and digest their enormous meal in some comfort. John shifted stickily. He hoped the servants would start the fans working soon. It was damnably hot for December!

Lord Hastings had just chortled, 'I do declare that Madame Chuman has eleven-pence of the shilling of Hindoo blood floating in her veins,' when the big machine went into action and cooler air flooded the room. There was polite applause from the others, and in that instant the Collector crooked his finger at John.

He found himself stumbling to his feet, mind racing, wondering why the Collector should be helping him.

'John Bold,' the Collector announced, his bulging eyes as cold as ever.

'Ah,' Lord Hastings said, his black eyes twinkling a little roguishly, 'the young man who rescued the beautiful Miss Lanham, I presume.' Hastings lingered significantly on that 'rescued' and John felt himself going red. It seemed to imply that he had done more with Georgina than rescue her.

'I have read the note from His Grace the Duke of Wellington,' the Governor General continued, taking a pull from his hookah, sending huge bubbles coursing through the scented water. 'He recommends you most highly, indeed, Bold, and after this business of yours with the Pindarees I haven't the slightest hesitation in accepting his recommendation. You will receive a lieutenant's commission in the Company's service. In the Bengal Light Cavalry, to be precise.'

'Thank you, My Lord,' John stammered, wondering: Why the cavalry? The white arm, as it was called, was usually reserved for rich fools.

'You will be gazetted with effect from to-morrow. My aide-de-camp Major Tomkins will explain everything to you, Bold.' He indicated a large, efficient-looking officer at the far end of the long table. 'Later.

'But let me say a few words to you, Bold, before you go off.' He breathed out, his black-button eyes suddenly hard, as if he were thinking of something not particularly pleasant. 'You must understand, Bold, that we English have ceased to be the wonder to the natives that we once were. More and more they are beginning to inquire why they were subdued by us in the first place. What particular strengths do we possess to enable us to come to this remote place and conquer so many? And such doubters are being actively supported by the Mahratta Confederacy.'

'Yessir,' John said automatically, wondering why the great man was bothering to tell this to a junior officer.

'Now, Bold, during the time of Napoleon we veered on the side of leniency to the Mahratta princes to our north – since we hadn't the strength to do anything else. But now the time is rapidly coming when we will have to show those heathens who is master in Central India.' Hastings' voice was hard and determined, and John could see now how he had risen to his present status. He was a man who would brook no nonsense, who could impose his will on virtually anyone.

'The trial of strength with those Hindoo princes is not far off, Bold. Let me explain. Tomkins!'

His aide-de-camp rose rapidly, dabbing the

omelette from his dyed-black moustache with a snowy napkin the size of a small tablecloth.

Hastily the servants removed the dishes from in front of the Governor General, and Tomkins spread out a map of Central India.

'Here is the Deccan,' the Governor General announced, running a hairy paw over the centre of India, 'and here is Berar, now ruled by Apa Sahib, supposedly our ally. In reality he is a blackguard, sir, capable of any trickery... Now at present we have six battalions of native infantry in and around Apa Sahib's capital – here at Nagpore – at the disposal of our Resident, a Mr Jenkins – good, capable fellow, don't you agree, Collector?'

Lanham nodded his agreement, his green eyes as wintry as ever. John felt that he was all the same very interested in what was being said, although such matters were not his concern.

'There at Berar, at least in its capital, we have a slight hold, but *here* further north at Burrapore we have no presence whatsoever. Bold' – Hastings lowered his voice significantly – 'there Apa Sahib and the other Mahratta princes are actively encouraging the ruler of this tiny princedom to feed the Pindarees southwards through Berar and on to Company territory. Why? To test our strength, naturally, and our resolution.'

John nodded his understanding. 'You

mean, sir that if that means of feeding the Pindarees into the Company's territory,' he ventured hesitantly, acutely aware of all these important gentlemen, listening, 'was stopped, the Pindaree menace would be over?'

Hastings didn't answer directly, but said, 'I am in the process of raising great armies.' He raised his voice so that everyone could hear him, almost as if he might be speaking in the House of Lords. 'I want the Grand Army of Bengal to number forty thousand fighting men. The Army of the Deccan will supply another seventy thousand while the Presidency of Bombay will field a similar large number. When they are all raised, gentlemen, then we will march and crush the Mahratta Confederacy for good!' He slammed the table so that the plates rattled.

The Collector frowned. Perhaps he was calculating the cost to him of any broken dishes.

'But first, we must halt the depredations of the Pindarees. I cannot have them sending thousands of riders south while the territories are denuded of their fighting men in this coming battle with the princes.' He looked directly at John.

'But in order to block that funnel through Burrapore and Berar, I need intelligence about the Ranee of Burrapore.' There was an intake of breath from the old India hands, and Hastings nodded. 'You know well who I mean, gentlemen, that heathen woman who has been likened to a blend of whore, tigress and Machiavellian prince ... a dangerous combination indeed.'

There was a chorus of 'hear-hears' from his listeners.

Hastings looked at John. 'You, my dear young man, are going to supply me with that intelligence.'

In his surprise, John blurted out, '*I* sir?'

Hastings nodded, and there was no mistaking the smile of smug satisfaction on Lanham's pudgy face. He had known all along about his commission and the job that went with it.

John went out into the glare of the December morning with Major Tomkins, his mind whirling. Why had the Governor General honoured him so surprisingly with a commission – *and a mission?* And what had motivated the Collector, for John was sure that Lanham was behind this sudden change in his fortune.

The two of them pushed through the usual mêlée, deafened by the chatter of the Indians, who seemed to talk all the time, unless they were asleep. Graceful women carried water jugs on their heads and naked infants on their hips. *Bhisties* – water collectors – were filling their leathern bags from the filthy tidal wash of the river, ignoring the dead Brahmins, dogs and other appalling debris bobbing in the sluggish current. And all the while the *palankeen* bearers shouted for custom and slapped the sides of their empty boxes. All was noise, heat, dust and confusion. It was the face of eternal India.

Once clear of the main streets, heading for the blinding glare of the whitewashed fort, Major Tomkins said with a kindly smile, 'You've been here a bit, Bold, but you're still a griff, you know.'

'A what, sir?'

'A griff or griffin – that's what we call a newcomer, still wet behind the ears.'

'Oh, I see, sir.' Now it was John's turn to smile. He was beginning to like Major Tomkins, who was unlike most of the Company's pompous and overbearing officers and officials. But then Major Tomkins had been in the King's service before coming out with Lord Hastings.

'Well, Griff, let me tell you a few things. You can see that My Lord Hastings is in earnest when he says we are preparing for war.' With his gold-topped cane he indicated the skyline where a long column of native infantry was practising forming a square and then reverting back to a marching column. It was the standard formation for withstanding an attack by cavalry. 'We're recruiting at a tremendous rate – but trained men are hard to find. So your command – a half squadron of native cavalry – will be raw. You will have to train them in double-quick time.'

'But I was in the Foot, sir,' John objected, whilst inwardly rejoicing at the thought of a half squadron. 'I know virtually nothing about cavalry, save that I faced them at Waterloo.'

'Not so important. I've made provision for the training. It will be sufficient if your men can handle a sword, carbine and horse. Your job will be intelligence. And by the beginning of the new year My Lord Hastings will want you riding to Nagpore to start your mission into Burrapore.'

'I see, sir. And this Ranee. Is she–'

'A she-devil,' Tomkins cut him short hastily. 'We have heard stories of her, Bold. Just make sure that you never fall into that creature's hands.'

Their ears were assailed by the wail of a native fiddle and beat of drums. They were passing a rough stage on which squatted a pretty young woman in a vermilion *saree*, surrounded by berouged children in cheap finery, watched by a crowd of gawping, barefoot peasants.

'Princess Sita waiting for the Lord Rama to rescue her,' Tomkins explained, a cynical smile on his tough face. 'It's part of their mythology. Unfortunately the actor who plays Lord Rama won't appear today – it's tradition – and she will wait there till the morrow. And those chuckle-headed peasants will wait with her, gawping all the time. Funny country. Imagine Mrs Siddons waiting on the stage of Drury Lane all night.' He shook his head in wonder. 'But then,' he added with a sidewards look, 'this business of rescuing damsels in distress is always fraught with complications, what, Bold?'

John was a griff, but he was no fool. He realized that there had been some talk about him and Georgina. Did that explain the Collector's attitude and his obvious relief that he was being sent away?

At the fort's entrance, standing next to the sentries in their red coats and drill trousers, an undersized figure in the silver-grey of the Bengal Light Cavalry clicked to attention. He was bareheaded, his grey hair cropped short in the fashion common in the army when they had still worn wigs. In one hand he held what looked like a large family Bible and in the other, a whip.

Major Tomkins' face brightened when he saw the soldier, who even though standing rigidly to attention was so bow-legged that his knees refused to touch. 'This is your riding master, Bold. Rum and Fornication Jones – Sergeant Shadrach Elihu Jones, renowned for his bible-thumping throughout the Army of Madras,' Tomkins smirked and then snapped, 'All right, Sergeant Jones, stand at ease. This is your new officer, Lieutenant

Bold. He will be in command of the half squadron. Give him every possible assistance.'

Jones mustered the young man with his keen dark Welsh eyes, his tough old face searching, before he answered, 'You can trust me, sir. I know my duty to God, the King – and the Company.'

'Good for you, Sergeant Jones. All right, off you go now,' Tomkins rapped, and the bandy-legged riding master moved away, while Tomkins stopped and said sotto voce, 'Rum and Fornication, you no doubt ask, Bold? I'll tell you. Because Sergeant Jones is one of those damned Welsh Methodists who is always preaching fire and brimstone when he's sober. But when he's drunk Methodism goes out of the window and it's all rum and fornication. Then Jones is like the rest of the common soldiers, interested only in whores and grog.' His smile vanished and just like Jones he looked at John searchingly. 'Remember, Bold, you are to train your men hard and fast. That is urgent. But do make sure that they can fight, *your* life might depend upon it.'

The emphasis caught John's attention. 'Why *my* life only, sir?'

Suddenly Major Tomkins looked uneasy, as if he wished to say more but dare not. 'This is a strange land, Bold, a strange violent land, full of deceit, treachery and betrayal. It is fitting and wise that in such a place, an officer is supported by men he can trust. Now good luck, John Bold.'

They shook hands firmly. Then Major Tomkins was gone, his shoulders slightly hunched as if to ward off a half-expected blow, leaving a puzzled young lieutenant squinting after him in the glare of the sun.

2

Sergeant Jones commenced with the remounts sent over to the new half squadron's lines. The bandy-legged riding master, who could have been any age between forty and sixty, certainly knew his horseflesh. 'You've got to watch 'em all the time,' he whispered to a half-amused John, nodding towards the sergeants who had brought the horses from the Remount Depot. 'They'll try to palm off any old nag on yer, if yer don't. They're corkscrews and screwdrivers the whole lot of 'em!' He indicated a big tough sergeant with the florid, good-humoured face of a drinking Irishman. 'One-Eyed Reilly we call him.'

'*One-Eyed* Reilly? But he's got both his eyes!'

'That he has. But once he palmed off a

horse on a riding master which had one eye, riding it round and round the circle with its good eye showing. That's the kind of men in that godless pack.'

John grinned and told himself that the godless pack would have to get up very early in the morning to fool Sergeant Shadrach Elihu Jones; and he was right. Jones went to work with a will, despite the boiling morning. He examined the remounts' teeth to detect their age, felt the carotid artery for the pulse rate, and vetted the legs for lumps and strains before riding each horse at a gallop, leaning far over the flying mane to listen for a whistle in the animal's lungs or a roaring in the nostrils.

In selecting the eighty-odd animals the new half squadron would need he rejected a good score of the remounts. Once he queried a mare, asking O'Reilly whether she was in foal.

'On my honour as a free-born Irishman,' One-Eyed Reilly boomed, 'I do declare to God that that mare is a virgin, pure and wholesome as the driven snow, Sergeant Jones.'

Jones tut-tutted at the use of God's name but he accepted the big Irishman's word, though the Welshman kept looking at the mare suspiciously as if he half expected one of the stallions might mount her the moment his back was turned.

When they had the required number of horses John sent the sergeants on their way with a shilling to buy a pail of beer by way of a reward, leaving Jones, honour satisfied, but shaking his head at the thought of his fellow NCOs indulging in the demon drink. 'Well, sir,' he said finally, 'we've got our remounts. Now we'd best be starting on the men.'

They did so at dawn. John, Sergeant Jones and *rissaldar* Ram Gupta, a white-haired old cavalry veteran, trained their men in a fashion unheard of in India in those days. Ignoring the usual breaks for the midday heat, they kept at it, packing in a month's training in a week.

Jones in his shirtsleeves, cropped head bare despite the sun, stood for hours in the riding circle, exercising the budding cavalrymen and their mounts. With their feet tied under the slippery bellies of their horses and without saddles and reins, he rode the peasant boys – most of whom had never even *seen* a horse before they had enlisted – round and round until they began to feel confidence in their ability to master the strange animal. Then came the jumps, when they sprang over ever higher fences with their hands tied behind their backs, the reins hanging loose, using only their spurs to guide their mounts.

John trained them in the elements of the manual of arms, using the ancient *rissaldar* to translate. He showed them how to use the

193

straight British cavalry sword, making them grind the weapons to a razor sharp finish which was superior to the hatchet effect normally achieved by British cavalry. He spent hours training them in the use of the new Paget short carbine, which was again superior to the Eliott due to its small stock and the permanent, attached ramrod which could not be lost in the confusion of battle.

As the days passed in hot succession, the three trainers packed in drill, the care of horses and a hundred and one other things that a cavalryman needed to know, making soldiers out of peasant boys who had fled the poverty of the villages for adventure – and loot!

'Aye,' Jones had commented one weary evening after they had finally stood down the exhausted men, 'them black heathens are just as bad as our British soldiers when there's a prospect of booty – especially when they have looked on the wine when it is red!' He raised his grizzled head to the darkening sky, as if appealing to heaven itself. 'What transgression has our poor Lord to suffer with his creation, mankind!' Then he spotted one of his black recruits hurrying his sweating mount to the stable and roared in red-faced, artificial rage, 'Will you *walk* that poor wet beast, you blistering black heathen! *Samalo.* Or I'll take my whip to you, I swear I will, you Hindoo devil!'

John grinned and Jones stumped back to his quarters calling down Welsh curses upon the head of the unfortunate trooper, the 'poor Lord' momentarily forgotten.

But while he trained his new command, often falling into bed at night absolutely exhausted, John thought about Georgina. Since he had received his commission he had heard no more of her. Desperate for news of her, he managed to stay awake one evening and rode over to the Collector's residence.

But the majestic black butler said Georgina was not at home. Angry, John persisted until finally the Collector himself appeared at a window and frowned down at him in ponderous silence. Then John realized it was no use. No purpose would be served by irritating that important personage. He rode back to the fort, his mind in a whirl...

So the days and weeks passed in unrelenting work, with John being thrown more and more into the company of Rum and Fornication Jones. The sergeant was a mine of information on the Company's soldiers and the handling of native troops.

'You can't flog one of them heathens, sir,' he explained. 'But yer white soldier, the John Company can sentence to a thousand lashes, if they like.' And he pulled off his shirt to display his back.

Next to the deep gouge made by some musket ball in a half-forgotten battle the skin was whipped into lumps of calloused flesh and hideous permanent weals. 'There's five hundred lashes, sir, there. But in them days, sir, I was full of the Devil, rum and the wenches. It was my downfall, the follies of youth. Now I am a reformed man.' And he touched the Bible, which he kept by him the whole day. Sometimes John suspected that he slept with it in his hands.

But despite his piety Sergeant Jones was a good man to have with him, John told himself. He was experienced, obviously brave and very definitely loyal, the kind of subordinate he needed for whatever was soon to come. For twice Major Tomkins had urged him to ever more speed with his training; Lord Hastings could not wait much longer for the intelligence on the Ranee of Burrapore. The war with the Mahrattas, according to Major Tomkins, was not very far off now.

So was Christmas, and despite Lord Hastings' pressure his European officers and soldiers were beginning to slacken the pace of training. Celebrations were in the air and there was much talk of the *potage à la Julienne,* the York hams, the special curries, the varied bordeaux and clarets that would be consumed on Christmas Day.

John felt out of it. He sensed no special joy at the approach of the winter festival. Nor did he fancy the mess high jinks which would undoubtedly go with it: the coarse jokes, the smashing of furniture and the usual drunken firing of pistols, often levelled at terrified green-faced bearers. Still he knew that he must give Sergeant Jones the day off and stand down the men.

'We will have a parade that morning – their first parade. Then we'll stand the men down,' he told the sergeant.

'Yessir. Heathen they are, but they deserve to have some benefit of the Christian faith.'

Thus it was that at dawn on Christmas Day 1815, Sergeant Jones came bustling down the line of busy *sowars*, putting the finishing touches to their horses, crying, 'Look to your girths and stirrups, lads! We want nobody falling off this day,' while the troopers in high good humour at the prospect of a holiday yelled back, '*Sab thik hai, sahib!*'

Listening to them, John smiled softly and felt pride in his own achievement. He was a soldier again with his own command, more than his poor dead father had ever achieved. *Bugles at dawn!* Well, there they were – the shrill sweetness sailing across the still cool air, summoning him. He pulled his sword belt a notch tighter, gave himself a quick look of appraisal in the mirror and stepped out into the open.

The bearer in the livery of the Collector's household waiting there salaamed and held out a note. Hurriedly John slipped a few pice into the outstretched palm and broke the seal, his heart pumping. Was it from Georgina at last? It wasn't. The note, written in the green ink which the Collector affected and which no other Company person in his district was allowed to use, invited John to 'attend this Christmas Day evening ... for Dinner and an Assembly'. John's face lit up. He would see Georgina again after all. Whistling tonelessly, feeling strong, confident and happy, he strode to where the *syce* was holding his horse in readiness...

'The half squadron will march past!' The ancient *rissaldar's* reedy voice rapped out the commands in his strangely accented English. 'Half squadron will advance in column from the right... *Walk – march!*'

Sitting proudly erect under the limp Union flag next to John, Sergeant Jones hissed out of the corner of his mouth, 'Here they come, sir ... and they don't look half bad.'

John scrutinized his men. The troopers had filled out in the last weeks. The hollows had gone from their dark faces, and their shoulders, once bowed by the constant toil of the fields, were straight, erect and proud. Admittedly their dressing was not altogether perfect, but normally it took years to train a cavalryman.

The *rissaldar,* bringing up his sword straight above his head, cried, 'Half squadron – *halt!*'

The eighty-odd riders reined their horses, dark faces expressionless, swords lodged across right shoulders.

John looked along the length of their stern young faces, beneath dark grey turbans with a gold spray fan rising from the left side, which contrasted with the silver-grey of their uniforms. They looked a splendid sight. He nodded to the *rissaldar*.

'Half squadron will march past!'

John and Sergeant Jones tensed. The *rissaldar* came level. He circled his sword round and turning his head slowly and stiffly in John's direction, cried, 'Half Squadron, eyes – *right!*'

As one they turned their heads like automatons, and John raised his hand to his turban in salute. He tried to impress each and every face on his mind's eye, and then the *rissaldar* had finished counting off to ten and was commanding, 'Half squadron, eyes – *front! Trot!*'

John lowered his hand. It was already beginning to grow hot and he could smell his sweating armpit.

For a space his half squadron trotted towards the stables before the *rissaldar* commanded, '*Walk – march … form troop column,*' and it was all over.

Jones relaxed. 'Well, sir, what do you think?'

'You did a good job, Jones.'

Jones admitted grudgingly, 'Might not yet be good enough for Horse Guards Parade, but it'll do – for the time being…'

'But Sergeant Jones, we ought to have a name. Every other native formation has. We simply cannot remain a half squadron, Bengal Light Cavalry. That title has no ring about it.'

'Agreed, sir,' Jones said, black button eyes disappearing into his wrinkles as he considered. Then he smiled. 'Sir, if I may be so bold – *haw, haw* – may I baptize the babbee for you?'

'Please,' John answered, wondering what was coming.

'Bold they look – the men, I mean, sir – and Bold is the name of their commander, ain't it, sir?'

'Yes, go on.'

'So why not, sir – *Bold's Horse?*'

Thus on the morning of Christmas Day 1815 on a deserted paradeground, a name was created which would go down in the history of British India – BOLD'S HORSE.

3

John Bold entered the central hall of the Collector's house, handed his sword and turban to the large black butler and passed on inside, to where coloured paper loops hung from the walls in an attempt to give the big, typically bare Indian house some kind of festive appearance. He strolled on, feeling a little nervous at the sight of so many people eddying back and forth, while white-robed, red-sashed Indian servants glided in and out with their silver trays. He was a mere lieutenant of native cavalry, and they were important people, high Company officials and field-grade officers, together with their ladies dressed in the height of fashion.

Major Tomkins nodded in a friendly manner, otherwise he recognized none of the guests. He watched the memsahibs and their menfolk dancing to the music of a half-breed band, mostly French by-blows by the look of them, scraping away at their fiddles. The dancers sweated prodigiously, the men carefully holding the naked shoulders of their partners with lace handkerchiefs – the sweat had already soaked through their white gloves. Others had already found the dancing too much of a strain and contented themselves with 'making a leg', as it was called, and carrying out lazy conversation with the local charmers.

'Enjoying yourself, Lieutenant Bold?' Lanham's voice cut into his musings.

He turned hurriedly. 'Yes, thank you, Mr Lanham and by the way, many thanks for your kind invitation.'

The Collector smiled coldly, his eyes as calculating as ever. 'Not at all, dear boy.' He waved a pudgy hand airily. 'I thought that on your first Christmas away from home an invitation to the assembly might cheer you up.'

'Oh yes, undoubtedly,' John heard himself saying, though in truth he had never felt less cheered in all his life. If only he could talk to Georgina.

'Besides rumour hath it that you will not tarry here much longer to enjoy whatever – er – fleshpots the garrison can offer.' He touched his hand to his mouth, as if he had just uttered an obscenity.

Fleshpots! John thought indignantly. Raddled, poxed old black whores – those were the garrison's fleshpots.

'How do you mean, sir?'

'Well my boy, I must not give military secrets away, but the intelligence coming from Nagpore is not of the best, at least for the Company's affairs. Mr Jenkins – the Resident up there, you remember – is reporting trouble with the local ruler.' He tugged his pasty jowl. 'There is bound to be trouble sooner or later.'

'But pray, sir,' John asked, 'what concern of this is mine?'

But before the Collector could answer, Georgina came into view, attended by the polite, slightly bored clapping of the guests. She was dancing with Major Rathbone, who wore his hair long and crimped in the

French fashion and his sidechats long which gave his face a thin cruel look, which many women thought attractive.

John frowned. Rathbone was of private means and didn't give a damn about anything, save his own pleasure. Black or white, married or unmarried, he took women as it pleased him, and in the garrison it was rumoured that he had twice duelled with married men this year on 'a matter of honour', as it was put delicately behind a raised hand. In other words some poor cuckolded husband had been forced into a shooting match with the best pistol shot in the Army of the Deccan.

But if John was worried the Collector seemed delighted. His face broke into a smile as the two of them swirled by, Georgina looked voluptuous in light green, her blonde ringlets flying. Evidently the Collector actually approved of this well-known skirt-chaser paying his attentions to Georgina.

Suddenly John's jaw jutted angrily and his eyes blazed. A look crossed his face – a legacy of his hot-tempered Gallic-Celtic ancestors – which, in years to come, would be feared by his enemies – and subordinates. You make your own destiny, John Bold, a hard voice inside him snapped. Don't feel sorry for yourself, man. Just don't accept tamely, react to events – *act, man!* He bowed to the Collector and said hurriedly, 'Excuse me, sir.'

Marching straight through the sweating dancers to where Major Rathbone and Georgina were politely applauding the orchestra, he said, 'Good evening, Miss Lanham.'

Her face flushed pleasantly, she answered, 'Oh, good evening, Lieutenant Bold.'

'Would you allow me, Major Rathbone, sir?'

Rathbone looked at him with a kind of vague cynical amusement, though underneath it John could definitely sense a moment of annoyance. '*Nomen est omen*, eh? *Bold* by name and *bold* by action,' he said in the soft drawl which so many cuckolded husbands had underestimated the first time. He bowed and stepped back as the fiddlers started to scrape once more.

Red-faced but determined, John took Georgina in his arms and steered her into the already whirling throng. She said nothing. There was a tiny curl of discontent on her pretty red lips, he noted, but still she smiled, as if she, too, was amused – or pleased – at his audacity.

'Georgina,' he said urgently, 'why are you avoiding me again? Have I done anything to displease you?'

'No, John,' she answered, 'and please keep your voice low. You don't want the whole world to hear. There is enough tittle-tattle in this place.'

'But why avoid me?' he persisted.

'It's my father.'

'Your father again!' he snapped.

'Yes, again!' Her cheeks flushed prettily with anger. 'He can't stay here much longer, he is far too old to risk his health in this deadly climate. And, well … he wants to see me safely married before he hands in his resignation to the Company.'

'Then marry me, damn you!' he snarled. He had heard this argument before and it enraged him that she was placing her father before him once again.

Abruptly tears glinted in her eyes. 'I love you, John,' she almost sobbed. 'I sincerely do… But I must think of dear Father, too … and he would never allow me to marry a soldier of no fortune.'

'And what of Major Rathbone?'

She did not seem to hear, but said miserably, the tears brimming, 'We must be sensible, John.'

'Dammit, I don't want to be sensible!' He kept his voice low only with an effort of will. 'One day, soldier or no, I shall be famous, important, perhaps even rich. What do I care about your father's sensible marriage? That is only damned money-grubbing!' He shook his head in irritation, and across the room Major Rathbone took the cigar out of his mouth and looked at him hard, the cynical amusement vanished from his eyes.

'Oh, if that were only true, John – that you will be famous–'

'I will be,' he broke in savagely. 'I shall *make* it happen, you wait and see. I–' He felt a hard tap on his shoulder and turned round startled, breaking his step.

It was Major Rathbone, who said icily, 'I see Miss Lanham is slightly indisposed. Do you not think it better she leaves the floor now, *Lieutenant* Bold?'

The emphasis on the rank was clear enough, and John's face flushed even more angrily. 'If you say so, *sir!*' he snapped. 'Naturally, *sir!*'

Now it was Rathbone's turn to flush as the three of them left the floor, followed by curious stares. But he maintained his calm, though he was notorious among his cronies for the shortness of his fuse. In silence they gained the outer room, where it was somewhat quieter, Georgina dabbing softly at her eyes while the two men flanked her, their faces hard and set.

Major Rathbone could not hide a telltale ticking of his jaw muscle – always a sign that he was very angry. Indeed that muscular twitching had been one of the last things that a good half dozen of his opponents had had time to note about him before he had shot them dead in one of his clandestine duels.

They halted out of earshot of the other guests and Rathbone, the sword scar that ran from the corner of his mouth to his chin suddenly livid, growled, 'I am not pleased by your conduct, sir.'

'And what does not please you about my conduct, sir?'

'Your behaviour to Miss Lanham, sir!'

John controlled himself. He was not afraid of the Major, but at this moment he did not want to jeopardize his new career by being involved in some scandal, perhaps even a duel, which would only reflect badly on Georgina. 'And what is wrong with my behaviour?' he asked coldly.

'Miss Lanham has been brought to cry in her own house, sir,' Rathbone replied, eyeing Bold carefully and realizing that this was not one of those cowards who would back down at the first sign of a threat. 'That is not conduct becoming to an officer and gentleman.'

John measured him from foot to face, taking his time about it, knowing that now he would fight – and *damn* the consequences! Rathbone's intentions were obvious. If he frightened John off, he would take and use Georgina as he wished. Some women were impressed by the physical threat that men could present, and Georgina was one of them.

'With all due respect, sir,' he said coldly, 'I submit that Miss Lanham herself is the best judge of my conduct, not you, sir. If she wishes to criticize my behaviour, I think it is up to her, don't you, *sir?*'

Rathbone flushed crimson. 'Why, you damned impertinent puppy!' he hissed, hand falling automatically to where his sword normally dangled from his belt, 'How dare a griff like you talk in such a way to me. Why, I should have you whipped by my bullies.'

John faced him calmly. 'Out here, sir, there is no questions of bullies.'

Georgina looked from one flushed, hard male face to the other and breathed, 'But gentlemen!' Yet to John it was clear she didn't really mean it. There was a sudden thrill in her green eyes which told him that she was enjoying this clash – a clash that was really about her and *who* should have her! The danger and tension brought excitement into the boredom of her recent life as the Collector's daughter.

'There may be no bullies, Bold,' Rathbone hissed softly, voice full of naked malice, eyes fixed on John's face. 'But there are other ways in which a gentleman can find satisfaction.'

'You mean the field of honour, sir?'

'Yes, I do – if you are not afraid of naked steel, sir,' Rathbone added with a sneer.

'I am not afraid of steel – or powder, sir, for that matter,' John answered, meeting that dark, threatening gaze evenly. 'It is up to you, sir, to make the arrangements, if you so desire.'

But there would be no duel in Musuli-patan this day, or many days afterwards for that matter. By the time that John would be in a position to meet Major Rathbone on the 'field of honour', the latter would be long dead, a Mahratta spear skewered through his reckless philanderer's heart. For in the very moment that Rathbone drew back his right hand to slap the young man across the face and issue his challenge, the Collector's big black butler announced, 'Lieutenant Bold, sahib. Man at the door for you, sahib... Say orders for you ... *from Lord Hastings sahib himself...!'*

Rathbone said something under his breath and dropped his hand hastily. Georgina breathed out hard, as if she might have been holding her breath.

John hesitated, wondering what he should do.

'Very important, sahib,' the butler said urgently. 'Very important indeedy... *Lord Hastings* sahib!' He rolled his dark eyes.

That did it. He turned and hurried after the butler, conscious of the eyes boring into his back. There would be plenty of gossip and backbiting at the Collector's dinner table this night, he thought sardonically.

Even before the butler flung open the door John could hear the drunken mumbling: *'Righteousness ... exalted a nation ... but sin is a reproach to any ... people...'*

The door opened and there was Jones, swaying wildly, his stock ripped open, his turban replaced by a bright scarlet garter with a cupid's arrow bearing the legend '*amour*'.

John pushed the pop-eyed butler aside. 'Now, Jones, what is this?'

'Let he that is without sin among ye,' Jones quavered thickly, 'let him first cast a stone…'

'*Jones!*' John thundered, though he was tempted to burst out laughing. Sergeant Jones was living up to his reputation. 'Make your report, man – at once!'

With an effort the NCO pulled himself together. 'From Major Tomkins, straight from Me Lord Hastings,' he slurred, 'one hour ago.' His eyes went suddenly blank.

'Go on, man!'

'There is trouble … at Nagpore, sir,' Jones stuttered. 'We march … at … dawn…' Slowly, very slowly, Rum and Fornication Jones sank to the ground, out to the world…

4

At dawn on 26 December 1815, Bold's Horse set off on the long march north. The half squadron left without ceremony. No bugles sounded farewell. India, or most of it, was still fast asleep. Even the sentries at the fort's great gate were drowsy as John commanded, 'Right wheel – trot!' and his riders dug in their stirrups and took the wide, unmetalled road to Nagpore.

If his *sowars* were still drowsy, being barked at now and again by the *rissaldar* to keep alert and watch their dressing, John was wide awake, his mind buzzing with the details of his unexpected mission.

Mr Jenkins, the Resident in Nagpore, had drawn his six battalions of the Company's native infantry to a high ridge on the Nag River, opposite the capital. The Rajah of Berar, Apa Sahib, had begun making warlike noises, assembling a huge force of Arab mercenaries in the capital, only two miles from the place where Jenkins had positioned his own forces, which were clearly out-numbered.

According to a wounded galloper from Nagpore, who had brought Jenkins' urgent message, the Resident was expecting an all-out attack momentarily. He needed cavalry *urgently* to ascertain the whereabouts of twenty white women and children seized during Jenkins' hurried evacuation of Nagpore. He feared a second Black Hole of Calcutta, which had so inflamed opinion in London a century before. The East India Company did not want adverse publicity back home; it was bad for their shares.

Once the hostages were liberated – *If!* a little hard voice at the back of John's mind challenged – he was ordered to continue his original mission into Burrapore to obtain the intelligence Lord Hastings needed before he commenced his large-scale campaign against the Mahratta princes.

It was a tall order, and John knew it. Even the Collector had shaken his hand and wished him good luck the previous evening, and Georgina had actually embraced him in full view of everyone, including a glowering Major Rathbone. That had pleased him, but not the Collector. Now the memory of that embrace warmed him and made his mission seem less hazardous. 'I'll come back, Georgina,' he had whispered into her ear. 'Don't fret, my sweet. I *will* come back!'

For a moment, in the manner of young men eager for some desperate glory, he savoured the prospect of returning to his beloved – a hero! Then he dismissed the little bit of self-indulgence and turned to Sergeant Jones, who was riding in morose silence, his face wan and his head under the turban wrapped in a large handkerchief soaked in vinegar – his cure for a severe headache.

'Well, Jones, can you talk to me now?' he asked.

'Yes sir, just,' Jones answered a little weakly. 'Oh in the Lord's good name why did I look upon the wine when it was red?'

John smirked. 'And several other things as well. There has been comment about two dusky maidens seen leaving your quarters, stark naked.'

'Please, please, sir, you shame me! In what deep pit of iniquity have I fallen! What a weak vessel I am!'

John's grin disappeared. 'Now Jones,' he said briskly, 'you know I'm a griff out here, and I haven't much time to find out things which I urgently need to know.'

'Yessir.'

'You were once in Berar, is that correct?'

'Yessir, with the Company's expedition of ninety-five, sir. The Residency, sir,' Jones commenced, 'is located to the south of the River Nag. It's on the ridge above Nagpore – built down in the swampy area. Them heathens ain't got the sense they was born with.

'The Residency ain't exactly a fortress, sir, just an ordinary big heathen house, but it does have a good field of fire.'

'What about the roads leading north, Jones? My guess is that this Apa Sahib fellow might have them moved north, to prevent their recapture.'

Jones considered for a moment. 'I recollect of only one road, if you could call it a road, heading north to Burrapore. If that's what you was thinking of, sir?'

John nodded his thanks. Apa Sahib would need transport to move white women and children, who wouldn't be able to go far on foot in this terrible heat – and transport needed roads. He licked his dry lips and began to lay his plans.

At midday he called a halt and while the men warmed their chapattis, he, the *rissaldar* and Jones, who was still suffering from last night's debauch, enjoyed 'sudden death', the usual fare of travellers in that region. A wretched skinny chicken, bought by the *rissaldar* in the last village for a few pice, was now decapitated, gutted and grilled over the fire within twenty minutes, whereupon the *rissaldar* poured a stingingly sharp curry sauce over the meat. Jones looked a the steaming yellow mix, clutched his skinny vitals, and declined. He could barely find the strength to say the grace for John – something which he did even when they were faced with nothing more than hardtack.

John laughed and winked at the grave-faced *rissaldar* who, surprisingly for such a serious man, grown old and white in the John Company's service, winked back. Chewing a scrawny chicken leg, John felt happy to be with such men. Major Tomkins' fears had been groundless. With such as these under his command, he had nothing to fear...

Days passed on that long ride in the blazing sun, the maddening song of the brainfever birds – reputed to turn men crazy with their persistent, high-pitched chirping – accompanying them interminably. But the men stood the strain well. They rode without complaint about the heat, the dust, the poor food, like seasoned soldiers, though the *rissaldar* chided them for slackness, calling them *yotis*, which Jones translated circumspectly as 'the thing with which the ladies make water, sir...'

As they approached the Company's border with Berar, the villages they encountered had been hurriedly evacuated. In some cases the villagers' poor food was still on the crude bamboo tables and the chickens in their roosts.

As they finally crossed into Berar itself, John was assailed by the uncanny feeling of being watched.

Sergeant Jones confirmed his suspicions. 'They're out there all right, sir. I know a Hindoo by his smell, whether I can see 'im or not.'

The weary troopers of Bold's Horse, their mounts lathered in dust and sweat, rode into the lines held by the Company's native infantry above the River Nag on the morning of 7 January 1816.

Vultures circled above the dead who sprawled everywhere on the ridge slopes. It was obvious that the Resident had already beaten off several attacks from the direction of Nagpore.

There was death, too, on the ridge itself: death of a horrible kind that John Bold would become all too familiar with in India. For it was the traditional punishment for those natives whom the Company felt had betrayed it. Prisoners, barefoot for the most part, their clothes in rags and stained with blood, were being led to a central place, shuffling along wearily, resigned to their fate. The *feringhees'* savage retribution had been going on for three days now, ever since the defenders of the ridge had begun taking prisoners.

Suddenly there was a muffled boom of a cannon firing close by. As one, the brow-beaten prisoners jerked up their heads. John gasped with horror. To his right there was a star of exploding blood and flesh. Ragged bits and pieces of a shattered body flew through the air. For a moment it seemed to rain blood, the ground all about them was splattered red.

In a solemn voice, Jones intoned, 'May their God rest their poor souls!' while the prisoners who had seemed so resigned to their fate began to wail and moan piteously, going on their knees and raising up their thin chained hands in the classic pose of supplication.

'My God, what happened?' John cried as a round ball of flesh, once a human head, rolled to a stop only yards away.

'They're blowing the heathen off the end

of a cannon, sir,' Jones said tonelessly. 'Breaks 'em up altogether ... then they can't go to their niggah heaven, see.'

John did. He told himself that Britain had brought civilization to these poor benighted natives, but the price their white masters exacted when they felt betrayed was exceedingly high. They went on their way thoughtfully.

Mr Jenkins was being bled by his surgeon and assistant when John was ushered into the room which served as his HQ. The fat, tall Resident, with the red choleric face that all these old Company officials seemed to have, was clad only in his trousers, his white breasts like those of a woman dangling down his naked chest. Impatiently he held up his right arm to the harassed surgeon and snapped, 'Hurry up, man, I haven't all the time in the world. I want to see some more of those damned insurgents blown to kingdom come.'

The surgeon was obviously finding it difficult to discover an area of the Resident's skin not already scarred by regular bleedings, hovering over the arm with the newfangled scarification-box. Finally he found a relatively clear spot. He pressed a catch and a series of gleaming razor-sharp blades sprang into view.

Jenkins looked exceedingly pleased at the sight and snapped at John, standing at the

217

door rigidly to attention, 'Do you bleed, sir?'

'No sir,' John replied as the surgeon retracted the blades before placing the box on Jenkins' arm and pressing the catch. Jenkins gave a little intake of breath as the bright blood started to trickle down the white skin to where the surgeon's black assistant waited with an enamel kidney dish to catch it.

'You should, young man,' Jenkins said. 'Relieves the strains and pressures of life. After this morning's attack by that traitor over there' – with a nod he indicated Nagpore on the other side of the river – 'I feel the need to indulge myself a little.' He beamed with pleasure as more of his blood trickled down his arm into the dish.

'Now, sir' – he raised his voice above the shrieks of yet another victim and the boom of the cannon – 'to business. The hostages those damned rebels have seized are not really important people, Lieutenant Bold. Counter-jumpers for the most part. Wives of clerks and NCOs, though I do believe there is the wife of a schoolmaster among them – and oh, yes, that of an officer. No-account people on the whole. But they are *white*, mark you ... and under no circumstances can we allow white women and children to remain in the hands of black heathens. No telling what those niggahs might do to the women, doesn't bear thinking about. You understand?'

'Yessir, I understand,' John answered, telling himself that with children the pace of the kidnappers would probably be even slower.

'Now – oh, all right, Surgeon, that'll do. Stop the bleeding now and let me get dressed. I feel considerably lightened.'

While the surgeon and his assistant went to work with towels and ointment, the Resident continued, 'They are clearly taking those wretches north by now and it is your task to apprehend the abductors, punish them and free their captives. If you don't, we'll have the devil's own job, not only dealing with the Rajah of Berar, but with the Pindarees and that trollop up in Burrapore.'

'You mean the Ranee, sir?' John queried.

'Yes, exactly. I met her once. A cunning jade with more tricks up her sleeve than a dozen monkeys. She's more than a match for most men, I can tell you.' He shook his head, as if in admiration.

John absorbed the information. Once again this mysterious woman in her remote mountain fortress had been praised for her deviousness and cunning by a high-ranking Company official.

'Now sir,' Jenkins went on, 'we have intelligence that Apa Sahib's Arabs will attack at noon tomorrow. He thinks he knows our habits and that we'll be resting during the heat of the day.' He grinned maliciously. 'He will be mistaken! We'll be waiting for him, ready to give him a taste of fine English steel. Now, sir, while the battle rages, you will take your cavalry through the usual confusion, ford the River Nag, skirt the city and take the road north with all urgency. You understand that I want the captives returned to our lines as speedily as possible. Their return will strengthen my hand considerably. When the time comes to deal with that princely niggah,' he sneered, 'I need not then make any concessions.' He brushed by John and stared out to where the cannon glowed dull red and smoking, the paint on its barrel blistered. Still the executions had not finished and the sweating white gunners were lashing another screaming wretch to the muzzle.

'If I had my way,' Jenkins said, 'I'd strap the whole damned lot of them, including the Rajah, to the end of that cannon and blow them apart. Then I pledge you, sir, we'd have no more trouble with the damned niggahs. It's an unfailing remedy.' He sniffed and turned to John. 'Well, sir, make your dispositions and then sleep. You have a lot of work before you.' He waved a hand in dismissal.

'Sir.' John clicked to attention, saluted and turned, glad to be dismissed from the Resident's presence. To senior Company officials there were only two kinds of people – masters and servants. The Jenkins of this world were meant to command and prosper;

the others would live their short span and then disappear into the wretched obscurity from whence they had come. He strode over to Jones, waiting with their horses, and told him their orders.

Jones accepted the news calmly and said, 'The *rissaldar* has got the men quarters for the night, food for them and fodder for the horses.'

'Good,' John said, mind buzzing with his new task. Then he saw the look on Jones' wizened face and stopped short. 'Well, Sergeant Jones, what is it *now?*'

Jones grunted. 'You know that mare One-Eyed Reilly of the Remount Depot palmed off on us?'

Puzzled, John nodded, recalling the cheerful Irish rogue with his mare that was as 'pure and wholesome as the driven snow'.

'Well, sir,' Jones said bitterly, 'yon virgin of his is with foal, damnit!... God forgive me.'

The look of self-disgust on Jones' face did it. John broke out into a great laugh, the tears beginning to trickle down his face.

'The virgin's to be a mother! ... ha ... ha,' he chortled uproariously, the tears streaming down his face now. Thus the young man laughed and laughed. It would be the last time he ever did so.

5

Georgina lay on her bed, staring at the ceiling. It was still stifling hot and beneath the lace peignoir she was naked, her white body slightly damp.

The house was settling down for the night. The Collector had returned from an 'assembly' still drunk on iced claret and gone to his chamber almost immediately. Now the rattle of dishes from below, accompanied by the acrid smell of curry, had vanished, indicating that the servants had returned to their miserable hovels in the grounds. Only the guards would be around and they would probably be dozing. The house was hers.

She lay perfectly still, her breast moving softly, her hands tucked between her legs, thinking of men. It was something she often did when she was alone in her bedroom.

She rolled over and stared at herself in the long mirror of the *armoire*. She felt her lips go dry suddenly as she eyed herself. Her hands smoothed her firm breasts, caressing their nipples for a moment. A delicious shudder ran through her body. Abruptly she felt very hot, as if with fever. Her legs parted slightly. She closed her eyes and let her hands caress her belly slowly, languorously, the fingers already seeking that warm secret part as her heart started to drum more quickly.

She smiled, her eyes tightly pressed closed, stroking herself at regular intervals, savouring the pleasure, making it last, her middle finger working with a cunning that seemed inborn.

She thought of naked men. De Courcy, big, hairy, his magnetism so great that even his touch on her hand had sent a burning heat surging through her body. But the fool – hadn't he drawn back at the very last minute when she had longed for that penetration? What had it mattered that she was only fifteen?

In the end it had not been the high-principled Captain de Courcy who had taken her virginity, but a lout of a gardener's boy at her school in England, a boy so chuckleheaded that he had been unable to read.

But what he lacked in his head, he had made up for in his breeches – amply so! How they had played with him in that smelly little shed at the end of the grounds, sneaking down the ivy when the good misses who ran the school had been fast asleep, tucked in their narrow virginal beds.

Seth had been his name – a huge rambling fellow of eighteen with sloping shoulders and lazy gait, as if he were carrying a weight. In a way he had. How delightfully shocked they had been – Vicky, Bettina, Dot and all the rest of those gawping teenage girls crowding inside the shed – when they had seen it the first time! Vicky, who came from the Colony of the Cape of Good Hope, had gasped, clutching her cheeks in amazement at the sight. 'I've never seen a thing like that, even on a Zulu!'

What games they had played with it, tickling it with feathers, fondling it longingly, once even taking turns to write their names on it with a pencil, while Seth stared at them – and it – in stupid bumpkin pride…

Cunningly her fingers flicked in and out of that delightful warm hole, her mouth gaping, her breath coming in hectic little gasps, as she remembered and enjoyed the heady perverseness of those memories. Once again she remembered that first time for her, after the others had allowed themselves to be taken one by one. He had watched as she had accepted the whole length, wriggling with pain and delight, making little grunts as she took yet more, a strange perverse laxity about his face, his teeth bared like those of an animal, grunting all the time, 'You like it, don' e? … you like it, don' e, missy?'

And she had – and all those snakes of flesh which had followed. How she did! The men with their erect, exposed meat, holding it in front of them like a club. *Men … men … men…!*

She moaned at the thought, waiting for the rapturous explosion, breath crazy, eyes screwed tightly together, spine arched, her naked body glazed with sweat now, imagining John Bold thrusting it into her, her nostrils full of his scent yet again, the raunchy meaty odour of men in rut. She was convulsed. She had–

Something struck the window softly. She started and sat up, eyes blinking open, heart thudding. There it was again. Hastily she pulled her wet fingers from that dripping secret place and gathered the gown about her nakedness. *What was it?*

'*Georgina!*' the voice came in a soft whisper from below. 'Georgina, can you hear me?'

Major Rathbone!

She bit her bottom lip, her nerves still jangling electrically, and shivered with excitement. Instinctively she knew why he was there. What should she do? If she were discovered there would be a scandal – and even as she posed the question she knew the answer; what she would do.

'Georgina.' There it came again, the voice a little stronger now and more insistent. 'May I come up?'

She lay trembling for a moment, then like a dreamwalker, her legs strangely weak, her surroundings seeming so unreal, she crossed to the window.

Rathbone stood against a tree, his cheroot

a cherry-red glimmer in the purple light.

'Yes.' Her voice seemed miles away. 'What do … do you want, sir?'

'*You!*'

'Sir, you can't–'

'Your niggahs are all sleeping fast,' he interrupted calmly, 'and your father is undoubtedly doing the same. He must have sunk at least two bottles of iced claret tonight.' He took a last puff at his cheroot and dropped it to the ground carelessly. 'Well?'

'I cannot,' she faltered, but then, her mind still hazed by what had been happening only moments before, 'You may come up, but only for a few minutes, sir.'

'Yes, *for a few minutes.*' The irony was only too obvious in Rathbone's voice. Then he was clambering up the thatch that protected the walls during the monsoon, as easily as any barefoot Jack Tar climbing the rigging of a man o' war.

Lightly he sprang through the window as she stepped back, clutching the gown tightly, knowing her exquisite body would be clearly outlined beneath the lace by the light of the candle.

Gallantly Rathbone bowed and proffered her the flower he had just picked below. 'A rose for a rose,' he said, 'even if it is stolen from your father's garden.'

She accepted it and noted his finger was bleeding where he had pricked it on a thorn.

'Why, you're bleeding, Major Rathbone.' Without thinking, she took the finger and kissed the blood away, as her mother had done to her when she was a small child.

He watched her through half-closed eyes, the gallantry gone now, face set, handsome – and cruel – as she softly licked away his blood. She saw and recognized the look, and hastily dropped his hand – and he sniggered.

She swallowed hard. 'Now, sir, what is the reason for your call at this time of night – and in this manner?' She tried to put conviction and firmness in her voice, but failed lamentably.

He laughed softly. 'I would never make love to a woman if she did not want me,' he said quietly. 'Georgina, you will have many love affairs. For all I know you might have had some already – that insolent fellow Bold.' He shrugged and dismissed the matter, while she went red. All the same she could not deny the fatal attraction that the rakish cavalry officer exuded. She could feel her heart beginning to beat faster.

'I am sure that the Collector will want you to protect your – er – *assets* until you are safely married. There is a school of thought which maintains that a man who takes his wife's virginity on their wedding night will keep complete control over her ever afterwards.' He touched the ends of his sweeping moustache, a mocking look on his dark face.

'My experience has taught me otherwise. If a man can arouse a woman, she will be attracted to him and continue to be so, as long as he can arouse her. Virginity, one way or another, is not worth a fig!' He snapped his fingers contemptuously.

She knew he had talked in this bold, outrageous way to many a woman, yet it was still effective, better than all the mealy-mouthed simperings of those three-hundred-a-year men who talked about love and honour and kept a string of native whores on the side. 'What do you want of me?' she repeated, already weakening rapidly, her legs barely able to support her.

'This!' Rathbone hesitated no longer. He took her in his arms. Her nostrils were assailed by the odour of man – tobacco, unperfumed soap, sweat – and against her nearly naked loins she felt the brutal hardness that she had been longing for. Next moment his lips descended upon hers, taking a kiss with cruel relentlessness as he swung her effortlessly into his arms and bore her to the bed.

He flung her upon it, his face suffused and very angry-looking now, and pulled off his shirt, revealing a hard muscular chest matted with black hair, followed by his breeches. His male flesh sprang free and towered over her like a threatening club as she lay mesmerized.

'No,' she breathed, *'please no!'*

He laughed softly. Next moment she felt his hard masculinity swamp her, and it was too late...

He had gone when she awoke. It was still dark and tranquil outside, but the cavalry were to ride north at dawn, an advance party of Lord Hastings' campaign to come, and Rathbone would soon be leaving at the head of his squadron.

'A short life, but a gay one,' he had told her somewhere in the middle of that confused hectic night after he had made love to her for the third time, 'and make a handsome corpse – that's the motto of the cavalry, my pretty pigeon.'

She lay there, head cradled in her hands, feeling sore and bruised but tremendously relaxed, wondering about men like Rathbone, who took what they wanted and didn't give a damn about anyone, seizing their pleasures swiftly and ruthlessly because they were aware they would not live to grow old. *'And make a handsome corpse,'* she repeated in a whisper.

Somewhere a cock crowed. Already the sky was beginning to flush the blood red which heralded yet another burning day. She was reminded that she had to face the world again this new day; she couldn't live in her fantasies all the time. She had to deal with reality.

But what was that reality? Her father's with his concern with position, wealth and stability? Or Rathbone's, living for the day? Or was it John's.

Yet what was John Bold's world? He was young, determined, brave, but what did he want out of life? Was soldiering, pure and simple, his world? If so, she could be no part of it... It was all so very perplexing.

Outside there came the first hawking and spitting which signalled the arrival of the first of the servants.

She buried her head deeper in the pillow and continued to think, while it was still cool enough. She heard the rattle of a servant preparing her *chota hazri*, a pot of tea and biscuits. Soon life would seize her up once more and she would be forced to act her part again, say the right things, make decisions, however minor. But what was her part to be?

The first rays of the new sun dappled her naked body. 'Who is the real me?' she whispered to the ceiling. '*Who?*'

But there was no answer forthcoming. She yawned, stretching out her long limbs like a fat cat satiated on cream. A rich whore? She mused. A dutiful wife, bored to the back teeth by children and a dull husband?... The mistress of an adventurer perhaps, living in a tent in the middle of nowhere?... *Who?*

In the end it was too hot to think any more

and when the *ayah* knocked timidly and whispered, *'Chota hazri, memsahib,'* she responded with alacrity, eager for conversation even with a servant, glad not to think any more.

6

It was glaringly hot. Across the River Nag far below the blue heat haze rippled and the Arabs who would soon lead the assault were standing naked, dousing their bodies and soaking their robes in the cool water. Watching through his glass, John estimated there were at least five thousand of them. Expected or not, the assault would not be that easy for the Resident's six battalions of *sepoys* to repel.

'Sir.' It was Jones accompanied by a captain in the uniform of the native infantry.

John folded his glass and looked at the captain, his coat torn and stained with gunpowder, his face under grizzled hair white and wan. He might well have been forty or more, old even for the Company's service at that rank.

'Elders,' he introduced himself as John saluted, 'Elders of the Sixth Native Infantry. I hear that you are to rescue those poor unfortunates once this battle begins.'

'Yes, Captain Elders?' John answered dutifully wondering what the distraught man wanted of him.

Elders' voice trembled and there were tears glistening suddenly in his red-rimmed eyes. 'I beseech you to do your best, Lieutenant Bold, for me and the rest of the menfolk! You see my Alice–' His voice broke momentarily.

'*Alice*, sir?'

'My wife, Lieutenant. They took her. She is a mere eighteen. She came out with the fishing fleet last autumn and married me within a week, one of the most joyous days of my life.' The words flooded from Captain Elders now, as if he had been bottling all this up too long and wanted to be relieved of it. 'Alice knows nothing of India – and its cruelties.' He looked significantly at John, who knew exactly what he meant. There was no telling what her abductors might do to the woman, what they had *already* done to her. Elders clasped his hands together, eyes wide staring. 'You must save her for me!'

John felt his hand go out to grip the poor fellow's arm and he heard himself say with more confidence than he felt, 'Don't fear, Captain. I shall do my damnedest to ensure that not one hair of your Alice's head is harmed – or that of the others either. You can rest assured of that.'

Elders' response was drowned by the blare

of trumpets and the sudden rattle of kettle drums.

'The alarm!' Sergeant Jones cried, as the *rissaldar* rose in his saddle and yelled at Bold's Horse, waving his sword.

'Goodbye, Lieutenant Bold, and good luck!' Elders bellowed above the first roar of the cannon massed near the Resident's HQ, and doubled back to his lines.

John mounted and jerked at the bit. His horse, nervous and jumpy, pawed the air as he forced it round. Everywhere soldiers ran to their posts, officers and sergeants shouting orders, and from all sides the cry went up: *'They're coming ... they're coming again!'*

The attackers swarmed on the craggy hill-face ascending from the River Nag, yelling, waving their weapons and green banners, firing their muskets into the air purpose-lessly, thousands of them, spread along the length of the line but putting in their main attack on the centre.

With them came a good score of elephants, trumpeting wildly, their fronts heavily armoured with chain-mail. Swaying alarm-ingly on their broad backs were square boxes filled with archers and sharpshooters, whose task was to kill the white officers and NCOs among the defenders. Like most soldiers of the native princes, they expected that with the white men killed, the black soldiers would flee. It was a mistake they often made.

More than once the Company's *sepoys* had fought on long after their commanders had been eliminated.

But John's concern now was to judge how the main attack would go in and avoid it, finding a way off the ridge and across the River Nag with the fewest possible casualties.

An elephant was hit. He had a momentary vision of the beast's vast ears and tiny red eyes as its trunk lashed the air furiously; then the picture vanished as a six-pounder cannonball smashed directly into the creature's face and it disappeared in a welter of gore, through which bone gleamed like polished ivory. It dropped, churning the screaming, panicked men in the *howdah* into pulp as it tossed and writhed in its death agonies.

Its death had the effect the British gunners had hoped for. The other elephants panicked. The *mahouts* ripped at their sensitive ears with their steel hooks to no avail. The beasts turned and lumbered back the way they had come, trampling screaming Arabs under their flying feet.

But still the attackers came on, thousands of them scrambling from rock to rock, as the cannoneers filled the air with grape and chain-shot, cutting great swathes in their ranks.

John nudged Sergeant Jones and pointed to a *nullah* to their immediate right. It was dead ground, but he suspected the Arabs were not using it as cover for their approach; for once out of it they would be faced by a hundred yards of open ground before coming up against Jenkins' second battery of six-pounder swivel guns. 'Do you think the men could get down there without breaking their necks – or their mounts', eh?'

The riding master had confidence in his *sowars*. 'If they take it careful, they could do it, sir. Me and the *rissaldar* could do it first to show them it can be done and to keep them from going at it too fast.'

'Right. Once we're down we'll follow the river bank to that collection of huts. You see them? The ford will be there.'

Jones grinned to himself. John Bold was like all the young officers he had served under. They never had the doubts that came with a lifetime of serving with the colours. Perhaps it was better that way. He touched his hand to his turban. 'I'll tell the *rissaldar*, sir, will I?'

'Yes, do so. We march in exactly five minutes, Sergeant.'

'Sir!'

While he waited, John loosened his pistol in the leather holster to the left of his saddle. It might come in useful in an emergency, but he would rely mainly on his sword. He drew the long heavy blade, with its razor-sharp edge, and without orders from the *rissaldar* his *sowars* did the same, the dark young faces set and determined. This would be their first action, but John knew he could rely upon them. He stood in his stirrups, voice raised above the roar of the cannon and the fanatical shrieks of the advancing Arabs. 'Bold's Horse ... Bold's Horse will advance – *at the trot!*'

As one the half squadron moved off, the men sitting proud in their saddles, contemptuous of danger. John felt a warm glow of pride, then concentrated on the business of getting them safely down the *nullah*.

They breasted the rise in a tight bunch, jostling, digging in their spurs and jerking hard at the bits so that the horses' mouths foamed and their heads quivered with the biting pain. But even the worst riders among them knew that they must maintain control over their mounts now.

Cautiously Jones and the *rissaldar,* keeping a short rein, went over the edge and disappeared. John swung his head to catch the slightest noise coming from the dead ground. Nothing save the clatter of their hooves and the slither of falling shale. He hesitated no longer. 'Forward!' he cried and waved his sword.

They went over. Before them stretched a steep slope littered with boulders and covered with grey shale but clear of sharp-shooters. Heaving back in the saddle, cruelly tightening the bit, he started to descend, his mount's forelegs thrust straight out, the hindlegs half-crouched, acting as a brake. A great cloud of dust rose from the half squadron as the mounts slithered and skidded down the slope, the troopers exerting all their strength on the reins, the rowels of their spurs already tipped with blood where they dug them savagely into the terrified horses.

Yard by yard they advanced, while to their front, Jones and the *rissaldar* boldly turned their horses to left and right to ensure that no one broke the ranks and started a panic which could only lead to self-destruction.

John's shoulder muscles burned with the effort of controlling his panicky horse. But even while he concentrated on getting down, he realized that their luck could not last much longer. The dust they were raising would not go unnoticed by the Arabs.

The roar of the musket came from only twenty yards away. The Arab who fired it could not miss in those packed ranks of sweating horsemen. A *sowar* screamed shrilly, threw up his arms and slipped out of his saddle, to be trampled by the horses coming behind.

John watched helplessly. God willing, the *sowar* was dead already. Instead, as a figure in white loomed up from the cloud of dust, he didn't hesitate. His sword hissed down to cut right through the man's turban and into the bone of his skull.

As musket balls started hissing in from both sides, John made a quick decision. They would be slaughtered in the narrow *nullah* if they didn't move swiftly. *'Gallop!'* he cried shrilly above the noise. 'Bugler sound the gallop ... for God's sake!'

Instantly the shrill urgent notes of the gallop rang out. The men cheered, released their bits and raced pell-mell down the slope.

Then they were down, with only that one man lost, the troopers laughing crazily with relief and the *rissaldar* bellowing his usual sexual insults at them for their slackness. The sound of musketry died away behind but they were not out of danger yet. As they trotted the sweat-lathered, frisky horses alongside the brown, slow-flowing waters of the Nag, it was Jones who first spotted the robed figures where John had planned to ford the river crossing and shouted, 'The heathens are among the huts, sir!'

John flushed angrily. He should have anticipated that they would attempt to defend the ford. But there was no time for self-recrimination now. The Arab mercenaries were setting up a leather-bound cannon in the middle of the track.

Already one of them was ramming down the ball into the muzzle. It wouldn't take a minute before the devils fired. If he ordered his men to ford the river here, it might be deep enough to slow them in mid-stream, sitting ducks. It had to be the ford.

'Bugler, sound the charge!' he cried. The instrument blared. A great cheer went up from Bold's Horse, as if that shrill sweet sound had released them of all tension, all doubts. Bent low over the manes, swords drawn and level with their mounts' necks, they surged forward, crying obscenities.

Their formation fell apart. It was to their advantage, though the *rissaldar* shrieked curses on their misbegotten heads. In the same instant that the cannon thundered and a chain-shot – two cannonballs linked by a length of chain that would slice down any-thing in its path – the split formation streamed to left and right of a group of dusty palms. The chain-shot howled harmlessly into the distance and the *sowars* galloped on madly, laughing crazily like a bunch of silly schoolboys just released after a long day in class.

Again the ancient cannon thundered. The ball hurtled towards them, black and fright-ening. It hit the earth, sod flying high, then reared up and slammed into a chestnut. The horse went down on broken legs, its chest a mess of blood. The rider dropped to his knees, unhurt. The *rissaldar* barely paused as he bent down and scooped up the shocked *sowar* as if he were a feather and then they were riding on again, the trooper clinging on

239

to the *rissaldar's* waist for grim life.

An Arab thrust up the ramrod like a pike. John parried, turned the staff, and his sword came hissing down. The Arab reeled back, blood spurting from a great gaping wound across his face like pulped tomato. Now Bold's Horse were in among the huts, slashing and hacking with primeval fury, carried away by that old unreasoning bloodlust of battle, horses rearing whinnying on their hindlegs as the fight raged all around in a fury of grunting and harsh swearing.

A tall Arab with rapacious features grabbed for Sergeant Jones' boot and tried to tug him from his horse. He had not reckoned with the veteran. Snarling like a rabid dog, Jones bent down and slammed his sword hilt into the man's face. His nose smashed. He went reeling back, blood splattering the dust like great gobs of red rain.

A minute later they were through, gasping like bellows, some of them so exhausted that they fell over the horses' necks, swords bloody to the hilts.

'Sound recall,' John gasped hurriedly, for already the attack on the ridge had failed and the survivors were streaming back down in their hundreds. Bold's Horse had been spotted and insurgents were beginning to point in their direction. It wouldn't be long before they attacked in strength.

The young bugler, now minus his turban,

blood running down his face, needed no urging. Even as he sounded the call, a great roar went up from the Arabs.

The noise was too tremendous for orders to be heard. John waved his sword and jerked his mount round and into the dark brown water, praying desperately that this was really the ford. His men followed, the Arabs closing at their heels, waving their green flags, shouting their war cries.

The cavalry plunged on, the water rising all the time. In a moment, John thought, the horses would be swimming and that would be that. The Arabs would be lining the bank behind them, popping off the stalled troopers at their leisure as if at a turkey shoot.

Suddenly his face broke into a relieved grin. The water was shallowing. Already it was falling from his straining mount's chest to its flanks. It *had* been the ford after all and they were through!

Galloping next to him, throwing up white water to left and right, Sergeant Jones chortled, 'Not bad for a bunch o' heathen niggahs, sir, eh?... Bold's Horse has gorn and won its first battle!' He winked hugely and John winked back.

He was right. Bold's Horse *had* won its first battle. His heathen niggahs, as one day not only Sergeant Jones would call them, had written the first page of their illustrious history – *in blood.*

241

7

On the second day of their march north it had become clear that someone was laying a trail for them. They had spotted the rag Sambo on the afternoon of the first day across the river. It had been lying in the dust of the unmetalled road that led to Burrapore, shabby and worn, with one of the button eyes missing, but still recognizably European.

At the time they had thought little of the find, but on the second day when the *rissaldar*, who had the keen sight of a man half his age, spotted the marbles laid out in a crude arrow pointing north, they knew they were definitely on the track of the hostages. Fortunately no scavengers had come along after the prisoners to remove the signs they had left.

That evening over the dying embers of the campfire, with a tiger barking deep in the heart of the jungle and some mad dog howling at the yellow ball of the moon, the three leaders discussed the matter. Jones was suspicious. Perhaps they were being led into some sort of a trap; the captors couldn't be so lax as to let the hostages drop things behind them. The *rissaldar* did not agree. In his strangely accented *chi-chi* English, he said, 'Hindoo like children, even white children of sahibs. They give them freedom even if prisoner. They think children are good... Not suspicious like Sergeant Jones think.'

'But children are not that clever,' Jones objected. 'There's a grown-up behind it, if you're right, Rissalder Sahib. And everybody knows that women ain't got much sense. Not a lot under their tiles,' he sniffed contemptuously.

John smiled softly and said, 'Well, the proof of the pudding is in the eating.'

The following day Jones was proved wrong. Just before noon they came across the site of an old camp beside the road. The *rissaldar* checked the ashes of the fires and judged they had gone out at least two days before.

Now while John tramped about trying to estimate how many men had made up the party Sergeant Jones made his discovery.

It was on a tree, the letters crudely burned into the trunk and ragged, as if done by someone with hands behind the back, secretly. 'A ... L ... I...' Jones spelled them out slowly, brow wrinkled with concentration. He straightened up, puzzled. 'Now what's that supposed to be, sir?'

John did not have to think long. 'Someone has tried to write a name there – Alice! The wife of Captain Elders – it can only be her!'

Now they quickened their pace, despite

the heat and the weariness of their mounts, sure that they were on the right track. Their discovery of the following morning, ghastly though it was, made it absolutely certain.

A child, a pathetically little bundle, lay huddled beside the road, virtually smothered in a writhing, buzzing, revolting swarm of bluebottles. They were everywhere, crawling over his glazed unseeing eyes, into his nostrils, ears, open gaping mouth. But there was no mistaking the colour of one of the exposed legs.

'A white boy,' the *rissaldar* called as they reined their horses. *'It is them, sahib!'*

John swung down and was about to cross over to the dead child when Jones caught him by the arm and said urgently, 'With respect, sir, but don't go near the poor little fellow!'

'Why not?' John demanded a little angrily.

'Look at that muck over there, sir.' Jones pointed to a heap of drying green slime. 'And over there.' He indicated a patch of green vomit hardened to the side of a tree.

'But what is it?'

Softly, hiding his mouth with his hand so that only John and the *rissaldar* could hear, he said, *'Cholera!'*

'What!' John recoiled, face suddenly blanched, as if he had been struck. Everyone knew that the terrible killing disease was borne by the wind. Hastily he commanded, 'At the trot – advance... Hurry

244

now, *rissaldar*, get them moving!'

The aged veteran needed no urging. He knew that cholera, the scourge of India, could fell a whole regiment in days. It was not wise to linger in any place where it had broken out. At a brisk canter Bold's Horse departed, leaving behind the poor little mite, unburied and without even a cross to mark his passing.

There was little chance of a cure for cholera. Some patients were purged, others were bled. A few desperate wretches were even ready to be blistered all over their pain-racked emaciated bodies with red-hot branding irons to burn out the fever. But in the end, whatever the treatment, most succumbed, sometimes within hours.

John's mind was in a commotion as he considered what to do now. That dead child would be only the first. Both captors and captives could be expected to catch the disease, so to overtake them now would be a grave risk to his men's lives.

But John Bold was already becoming that hard unyielding man with a firm sense of purpose and duty that would mark him in Indian society in his mature years: an officer who would brook no weakness in himself or in others and who never shirked a task, however unpleasant or dangerous. Now he made his decision. They would continue the pursuit...

One day later they came across more cholera victims, abductors abandoned in panic by their comrades in crime, their faces haunted and already sunken, their eyes bulging and too bright, green bile rushing in great body-shaking eruptions from their throats, their tongues swollen and cracked.

Jones nodded as they veered to the other side of the road whenever they came on these dying wretches, as if each new one confirmed his opinion that Lieutenant Bold was mad. For surely the people they sought to rescue would be infected and dying, too, if not already dead, by the time the cavalry caught up.

'But that is the strange thing, Jones,' John said slowly when he raised the point. 'Since we came across that poor dead white boy, there have been no others.'

'You mean whites, sir?'

'Exactly.'

Two hours later they spotted them, perhaps *smelled* them would be a better description, for it was the stench that first attracted their attention – a stench like a cesspit being opened.

Cautiously, his stomach already churning, John led his men round a bend in the road and there they were. Perhaps a half hundred of them, some lying flat in their own filth. Others, squatting sullenly on their haunches, muskets between their knees, watched their dying comrades in the soulless manner of those who live in a country where life is cheap.

One of them staggered to his feet somehow, clutched a tree trunk like a sailor grabbing a spar in a gale, and began retching a bright green bile, his white robe indescribably stained.

Jones nodded glumly. 'It's the plague all right, sir.'

John nodded his understanding whilst his eyes scanned the crude encampment for the captives. But there were no white faces in that crowd of black ones.

The *rissaldar* came up. 'Sahib,' he whispered, 'I have looked around the back... There are no white sahibs anywhere.'

John's bewilderment grew. The abductors were about at the end of their tether, but would they have let their prisoners go without attempting to slaughter them? Or could the whites all have died? That seemed hardly possible. They'd have come across the bodies. *So where were the women and children?* He had to make a decision – and soon. The longer they waited outside the enemy encampment, the more they risked being infected by the airborne disease. He could, of course, simply leave, but then he would never know what had happened to their captives. He had to speak to one of the enemy. But how?

Almost as if he could read the young

officer's mind, Jones said, 'Sir, I must admit that I'm afraid of the plague. A man who doesn't fear it is a fool. But I'm not *that* afraid. I've been around cholera before – *and survived!*'

John forced a wan smile. He could imagine that Jones had survived a lot of things in India, and would probably survive a lot more. 'Go on,' he said encouragingly, while the *rissaldar* edged closer, listening.

'Well, sir, first we need red-hot branding irons.'

'Why?'

'Because any one of the *sowars* who looks funny, gets it applied to his bowels. It works up the intestines. They say it's a cure.'

John winced.

The little Welshman didn't notice. 'Then we all piss in our neck-pieces and use them to cover our mouths. Keeps the plague away. Then we surround the place and shoot the lot of them at a distance – except that cove there.' He pointed a dirty finger at a hulking, black-bearded man who kept a little apart from the rest and was actually eating – a chapatti – in this rural charnel house. 'That one looks all right, *he's* the one we keep alive for questioning...'

Hardly daring to breathe the young troopers crouched in position, surrounding the unsuspecting encampment. Wet smelly masks across their faces, waiting for the order to fire, each man had already selected his target.

At the far side of the glade the *rissaldar* raised his sword to acknowledge that his section was ready. John aimed his pistol at one of the few armed abductors still on his feet, squinted through the sight, controlled his breathing and pulled the trigger carefully. The pistol barked. A cloud of powder. The muzzle jerked slightly. Suddenly the man let his mouth drop open stupidly. He staggered, staring at the spreading patch of scarlet on his dirty tunic. The musket fell from abruptly nerveless fingers. Next instant he pitched face forward to the ground, dead before he hit it.

The single dry pistol shot acted as a signal and John's troopers opened fire. At that distance even the worst shot among them couldn't miss.

That first devastating volley galvanized even the sick into violent, frantic action. The balls slammed into their thin weakened frames, as they tried desperately to bolt for cover. Men went down screaming and cursing everywhere. They grabbed at their shattered bleeding limbs, howling with pain, only to be hit once again. A few attempted to seize their weapons and charge their attackers. To no purpose! They were cut down within a few yards.

The troopers reloaded, working their ramrods frantically, while John, Sergeant Jones and the *rissaldar*, who were prepared for this momentary break in the firing, kept up the killing with their pistols, standing upright and exposed now, as if firing on some barrackground range.

Again a volley of musketballs slammed into the survivors. A dozen men went down thrashing, raising clouds of dust in their death agonies. A man tottered towards the attackers, blinded, his face a ghoulish red mess, feeling his way with his hand like a blind man. John took careful aim and felled him unfeelingly.

Now there were perhaps some dozen left alive on the killing ground, grovelling for the most part, their weapons abandoned, one with his hands clasped about his ears like a frightened child trying to blot out the dead sounds of a nightmare, another clasping the dead body of one of his comrades to him as a kind of primitive shield. It was the black-bearded rogue John had selected for questioning. He lowered his pistol and cried, 'Save the one with the black beard! Kill the rest. *Fire!*'

The troopers' blood was up. That old primeval blood-instinct for slaughter had taken possession of them. Kneeling or standing bolt upright now, they selected their targets, huge grins on their sweating black faces, as if it gave them the greatest of pleasure to kill, and poured a hail of fire into the survivors. Thus it was that they didn't hear the muffled trot of many horses' hooves – until it was too late.

Breast to breast, packed tightly in the road, the cavalry swung round the bend, sabres flashing, silver equipment jingling, horses nervous and frisky, already scenting the danger of the skirmish to come.

The *rissaldar* overcame his surprise first. He dropped his pistol, sprang on to his mount and unsheathed his sword. Digging in his spurs cruelly, he surged forward. Veteran that he was, he didn't have a chance. At twenty yards' range the leader of cavalry, who had sprung this deadly trap on those who had felt masters of their own trap, fired. The old *rissaldar* flew over the neck of his horse, head blown away, dead before he hit the ground.

'*Treachery!*' John cried, raising his own pistol to take aim at that well-remembered face with its great sweeping moustache. There was no mistaking it. It was that of the French *beau Sabreur* – Nom de Dieu!

The blow on the back of his head caught him by complete surprise. A shock wave surged through his body. He felt sick. For a moment he fought to resist the red fog that threatened to overcome him. To no avail. An instant later he pitched face-forward into the white dust, unconscious.

8

In the big echoing room, heavy with the odour of perfume and *bhang,* the women began to dance as John, weighed with chains and flanked by two huge guards, waited in numb bewilderment. There were scores of women, some dancing, some lounging in diaphanous gauze pants – through which could be seen their naked shaven lower bodies – and little brightly coloured waistcoats from which their breasts bulged like melons.

Some were dark – they could have been Nubians – others were almost white, their faces heavily powdered. One with rosy cheeks, who wore only a veil, bracelets and gold sandals and was pouring water into a large brass basin for a Nubian lounging on silken pillows on the floor, was definitely white. Even in his numbed state John could see that. Dully, his head still aching from that fearful blow of two days before, he wondered how she had come to this remote fortress in the mountains.

He swallowed with difficulty; he was parched. Since Nom de Dieu had delivered him and the survivors of Bold's Horse to this place, he had neither drunk nor eaten.

He licked his cracked lips as the opulent Nubian, all breasts and black belly, began to prepare coffee on the little table which stood next to her pile of cushions. His guards were totally uninterested, however. Neither the opulent charms of the Nubian nor the nearly naked whirling dancers seemed to attract their attention. They stared rigidly to their front, swords balanced over their right shoulders at either side of their prisoner, as if these women flaunting their charms so openly were an everyday occurrence, totally commonplace...

For Frenchmen, Nom de Dieu and the rest of his hard-riders, now dressed in a strange powder-blue uniform and turbans like those of Bold's Horse, were strangely uncommunicative. All that the fifty-odd survivors of that surprise charge could learn was that the white captives were safe. They had been removed from their captors when the cholera broke out, apparently too precious to Nom de Dieu's boss to continued exposure to the dread disease. But their captors had been left behind to bait the trap into which John had fallen.

He sucked his teeth bitterly at the memory. What an overconfident fool he had been! On account of his youthful pride and impetuosity, thirty good men had died.

Though his head had ached miserably once he had recovered consciousness, John had kept his ears pricked for information but had heard only veiled references to the *'chateau'* ... *'otages'* ... *and 'la princesse'*, the title uttered with a degree of reverence that seemed foreign to these hard-bitten mercenaries...

Opposite him, one of the near-naked women arched herself on her bed of silken pillows, her thighs slack and inviting. John, feeling a faint stirring of lust, caught a mocking look in the dark eyes contemplating him over the veil. If this were some sultan's or rajah's seraglio, why were the three men allowed to see the charms of his women displayed so openly? Surely the harem was always kept hidden from prying male eyes, save those of the master himself?

A bell tinkling gently attracted John's attention. The girls hastily returned to their cushions, some of them holding hands, or with arms around others' waists like lovers.

A small dark woman was standing in the shadows to the left of the great room, clad in a flimsy bodice which the big heavy-nippled breasts nudged through, a bell in her heavily bangled hand. She rang it once more and nodded to John's guards.

He stumbled awkwardly, his gait restricted by the leg irons, pushed along by the guards. The girls on their cushions giggled at his plight, though some were looking at him in pity.

He sensed, too, that the dark woman leading the way felt some pity for him. Once he tripped and one of the guards snapped a curse at him. She retorted in the same language and now the guards supported him down the dark, roughly flagged corridor.

They entered a large chamber, dimly lit by flickering tapers. The woman gave a command and John was dragged to a halt, in the centre.

A soft stifled moan, like someone waking up to discover himself in pain, attracted his attention. He searched the shadows noting that his guide was frowning in disapproval.

Then he saw a woman – a white woman – lying trussed on a low *charpoy*, hands outstretched behind, legs spread wide apart, revealing her plump naked body in all its totality.

John realized who the woman was, as her tormentor bent over the bed like a spider gloating over the fly it had just trapped in its web – Alice Elders, the captain's wife. Bending over her, the little man clad in European clothes, complete with beaver hat, cut an oddly feminine figure, his full soft buttocks enclosed in tight buckskins. But there was nothing feminine in what he was doing.

With a riding crop he lifted first the one and then the other of poor Alice's large breasts, chuckling softly, like some cattle-dealer examining stock. As she strained at her bonds, he touched each nipple lightly with his crop, seemingly pleased when they both grew erect. Alice clenched her teeth and shuddered, closing her eyes as if she wished to blot out the scene.

Suddenly the tormentor ran the crop down the length of her full figure, whispering, 'A body made for love.' A whimper escaped Alice's clenched teeth as the crop lingered over her pelvis and began probing deeper.

'Goddammit, you filthy black swine!' John exploded in revulsion, 'have you no shame!'

He aimed to throw himself forward, but the bigger guard jerked at the chain on his wrists and he came to a sudden stop as the steel cut cruelly into his skin. The guide flashed a look of warning.

But the man had heard. Slowly he turned and doffed the beaver, and long tresses of dark hair tumbled over his shoulders, glistening with palm oil. 'Ah, Mr Jean-Paul O'Hara,' the creature said in perfect English, 'or now I hear you prefer John Bold. Welcome to Burrapore!'

John reeled back a pace, gasping with shock, confronted with the dark smiling face of the woman he had seen through a gap in the *Gasthaus* curtain in Aachen, totally naked while a girl stroked her body. He knew now who she was – that princess whom Hastings had likened to a 'blend of whore, tigress and Machiavellian prince – the Ranee of Burrapore!

FOUR: DEATH AT BURRAPORE

1

By the spring of 1816 the situation in Nagpore had reached a crisis. In February Apa Sahib launched an all-out attack on Jenkins' position on the ridge.

At one point a British battery ceased firing. No one ever found out why, for none of its gunners survived. The Arab attackers stormed the position in their hundreds, yelling in triumph, swinging their scimitars, and put everyone to sword.

They then turned the battery round and began bombarding the British positions, slaying several high-ranking officials and officers, including Sotheby, the Assistant Resident. In a nearby building the white women and children set up a piteous wailing, for undoubtedly they would be slaughtered by the Arabs advancing, confidently under cover of their own cannonade.

At that moment reinforcements, the first to be sent north by Lord Hastings, arrived in the shape of a Captain Fitzgerald with three troops of the Sixth Bengal Cavalry. His troopers numbered less than a hundred, but the gallant Irishman did not hesitate. Leading the charge, Fitzgerald breasted a *nullah* at the gallop and raced for the guns. The Arabs panicked and threw down their arms in surrender. But Fitzgerald and his *sowars* showed no mercy. They slaughtered the Arabs to the man, turned the cannon on other Arabs further away and drove them off before retiring to the Residency with the recaptured cannon, to the ecstatic cheering of Jenkins' infantry.

Emboldened by this surprising success, Jenkins ordered his infantry to charge and as the London *Times* reported some months later:

The *sepoys* on the Ridge set up a joyous cheer and a party at once attacked the Arabs whom the fugitives should have supported. Totally unable to withstand a bayonet charge made in the European Fashion, they gave way and were driven from their ground. In leading this charge Captain Lloyd and Lieutenant Grant distinguished themselves greatly. Grant was thrice wounded, the last time mortally.

The troops of Apa Sahib now gave way on every side and by noon they had abandoned the Field, and fled in panic, leaving all the remainder of their Artillery with the Conquerors; and so ended a conflict more desperate than any that had taken place in India since the days of Clive.

While Apa Sahib now temporarily withdrew from the fight, sending *vakeels* to Jenkins to express his regret at what had happened and, as *The Times* phrased it, 'with true Indian cunning disavowed that he had authorized the attack', Lord Hastings poured troops into Berar. The Governor General had decided to deal with the treacherous Rajah of Berar once and for all before he commenced his great war against the Mahrattas. There was still the problem of the Pindarees, but for the time being the clever, calculating Governor General decided to ignore that nagging old sore.

That April General Doveton, commanding the British force which consisted mainly of native troops but did include one of Scotland's most famous regiments – the Royal Scots, a formation of so ancient a lineage that it was nicknamed throughout the British Army as Pontius Pilate's Bodyguard – launched his attack on Nagpore.

The British force was massively outnumbered, with the Rajah having twenty-one thousand men and seventy guns. Still, Apa Sahib surrendered himself at the sight of the British advancing bravely towards his walled capital, flags unfurled, drums beating the pace. Taking a horse he fled to the British Residency. Still General Doveton suspected treachery, with so many armed Arab mercenaries to his front, and he decided to act against them. As *The Times* would record:

On the morning of 24th April, while darkness enveloped the city, the marshy plain, the river and its wooded banks, the Signal was given. With loud cheers, the stormers rushed from their trenches towards the breach, into which they made passage. But were immediately assailed by a heavy fire of matchlocks from the strong and lofty adjacent buildings – a fire which they were totally unable to return with effect, or to evade by coming to close quarters. Sheltered thus behind walls, windows and terraces, the Arabs, in the grey dawn, marked with fatal aim and entire immunity their destined victims and their fire proved most destructive.

But the Arabs had not reckoned with the gallantry of the Royal Scots, mostly veterans of Wellington's campaigns in the Peninsula. Time and again they attempted to storm the Arab positions, losing nearly a third of that gallant battalion. In the end the Scots failed, but the Arabs had had enough. They offered to surrender. They were allowed to do so, and, after giving up their arms, left the country. With that all resistance collapsed in Nagpore, and Berar was British.

The news was received with great rejoicing throughout British India in the presidencies of Bombay, Madras and Calcutta. Victory bonfires were lit. There were public celebrations and great balls. Everywhere the victorious Battle of Nagpore was heralded as the prelude to Lord Hastings' defeat of the Mahratta princes.

Collector Lanham in his remote up-country outpost was not to be outdone by Madras. He ordered a full-scale assembly, inviting not only the Company's men and their ladies but also those officers of the Regular Army now passing through on their way to join Hastings' army massing on the frontier with the Mahratta states.

As he told Georgina, clad only in her sheer silk shift (for it was damnably hot again), while he dressed for the victory assembly, 'Money is pouring into India. Supplies, victuals, gunpowder, cannon, it's all coming in, bringing with it – *money!*' He beamed at her as he fiddled with his cravat. 'In London the shares of the Company are rising tremendously. Shipbuilding is running mad as well. My dear Georgina, we senior officials stand to make a fortune out of this war.'

Georgina was not impressed. Her face bore the sulky look he knew of old. Her mother's face had had a similar look often enough when she had the monthly vapours, or her weekly sulk when she had exceeded her allowance and he had refused to give her any more cash.

'What is it, my dear?' he asked, gazing at her pouting lips and feeling an unpaternal stirring of his blood. Why did she reveal so much of her body now that she was a full-grown woman? 'You look sad.'

'And why not, Papa? This war *is* a bore, you know. All the young men are going to the battle and the ones who remain behind are so ungallant. Counter-jumpers the lot of them!'

He patted her knee with a 'now, now, Georgina', staring at her full breasts nudging through the thin material and removing his gaze only with difficulty. God, it was only the other day that she had pleaded to come and snuggle up in bed with him after poor Mama had died! He swallowed with difficulty and said, 'tonight I shall introduce you to a really delightful young man – no less than a colonel of *British* cavalry, my dear.'

'Some frightful bore,' she said in a melancholic tone, 'with a wig and dyed moustache and nothing to talk about except his damned horses!'

'On the contrary, Georgina. He is no more than six or seven years older than you. He has bought his own regiment to come out here. Why, his papa is a crony of no less than the Prince of Wales himself – *and* the Duke of York!'

Georgina Lanham yawned, completely unimpressed...

264

But while the cities of British India rejoiced, Lord Hastings' forces did not meet up to his initial expectations. Under his command were some 130,000 men, of whom less than a tenth were white. The Mahratta Confederacy could field 130,000 horse and 8,000 foot, *plus* some 15,000 Pindarees.

Of course his army was a great force, but he had always estimated that the attacker should outnumber the defender by three to one. Besides, he was almost destitute of sappers and miners, battering trains, scaling ladders and entrenching tools – things he would need to attack entrenched positions. And even now after some four months of skirmishing in Berar and other places with his erstwhile enemies, he did not really know who might prove friend and who enemy, once he marched.

In particular he was virtually in the dark about the Ranee of Burrapore and her Pindaree allies. 'If the Pindarees attack my flank once I have crossed the River Jumna and move north up country, gentlemen,' he announced gravely to his staff, 'we are in serious difficulties. Let us say, for instance, that our forces are held at the powerful fortress at Gwalior, and we are compelled to carry out a protracted siege, they can easily cut us off from our main bases of supply in the Presidency of Madras. If only that young Lieutenant Bold could have supported me with intelligence about that she-devil up there at Burrapore, I would be a much happier man this day.'

But on that stifling April day Lieutenant John Bold was in no position to supply intelligence to anyone. For he himself was completely in the dark, desperately trying to find out what his own fate would be – and that of his men.

'And now this,' Hastings continued, looking grim. He nodded to Major Tomkins, who produced an object and laid it on the table – a gold-embossed leather sabre sheath.

Hastings let them stare at it for a moment before explaining, face grim, 'A sabretache of the Seventh Chasseurs d'Alsace, a French cavalry regiment which fought with Napoleon.' He paused significantly. 'And it was *found last week by General Doveton's men at Nagpore!*'

There was a sharp intake of breath from some of his listeners, though Major Rathbone, standing to the rear, continued to puff at his cheroot in bored cynicism.

'Do you mean, My Lord,' General Sir John Malcolm asked in his broad Dumfries accent, 'that it was taken from the body of a Frenchman?'

'No, that was the irritating thing. There was no body, just this and other pieces of military equipment, including a pistol engraved with the regimental number of the

Chasseurs d'Alsace.'

Casually Major Rathbone took the cheroot from his thin lips. 'Perhaps some niggah bought the stuff in the native bazaar, my Lord?'

Hastings looked hard at Rathbone. He did not like the man, though he was brave enough. 'Hardly likely, Rathbone,' he snapped. 'There is this, too.' He opened the sabretache and pulled out a somewhat ragged sheet of paper. 'A French *carte d'identité*, issued in the spring of Waterloo.' He let his words sink in. 'It is unlikely that such a thing would have found its way on to some Indian bazaar so swiftly.'

There was a murmur of agreement and Rathbone shrugged slightly, as if the whole subject was a bore anyway. 'I concede, My Lord, that you are probably right.'

Hastings ignored the comment. 'You see the problem, gentlemen?'

They did. 'You mean, My Lord,' Sir John Malcolm said, face brick red with anger, 'that the Indian princes are recruiting French officers to lead their armies?'

'That seems so,' Hastings agreed. 'Before they returned to France to fight with Napoleon, there were French officers who were bought by the native princes for gold. In virtually every case they were highly regarded fighters, who put some stiffening into the natives' levies, just as do our own

267

Company officers give their black troops. Now, it appears, they're back.'

The room was silent as the officers considered this new threat, until Sir John Malcolm ventured, 'If they are here, then, My Lord, the less time they have to train the native troops of the Mahrattas in European battlefield practice, the better. I suggest that the Grand Army marches against the Mahrattas as soon as Your Lordship finds it convenient.'

There was a rumble of 'hear-hears'.

'Time is of the essence. Let us break those damned princes once and for all!'

'Agreed ... agreed,' a worried Hastings said, raising his hands for silence. 'I agree fully with your desires and it shall be done as speedily as possible. But if I only knew what those damned Pindarees would do when we march into Gwalior... *Oh, where in the devil's name is Lieutenant John Bold...?*'

2

Later when it was finally assaulted and captured, the Ranee of Burrapore's *'chateau'* turned out to be a very tough, almost impregnable fortress. 'The Gibraltar of the East', *The Times* would say in its dispatch on the storming of the place.

Atop a small mountain not overlooked by any other of the Burrapore Range, it consisted of an upper and lower fort. Around the upper fort, with one exception, were sheer precipices of eighty to a hundred feet, surmounted by a wall closely loopholed for musketry. The lower fort was protected by strong gateways towering thirty feet and by flanking earthworks manned by cannoneers whose artillery was ancient yet would be devastating at close quarters. For any storming party would have to get within two hundred feet before they could assault the earthworks.

Staring out of their quarters on the top floor of the upper fort at the silver snake of the Burra River far below, John Bold told himself any rescue force the Company might send would have a devil of a job on their hands.

It was now over four months since they had been captured. He had long recovered from that tremendous blow over the head and his cellmate Sergeant Jones had finally regained the use of his right arm, which had been badly wounded by a French sabre. So far their imprisonment had not been severe. After that first surprising meeting with the Ranee of Burrapore he and Jones had not been placed in the vast underground dungeons of the lower fort, where his *sowars* were languishing. Instead, they had been lodged in this great bare echoing stone chamber, from whose slit-like windows they could see for miles.

Their cell, locked, bolted and permanently guarded, was dirty and lousy, the dust of centuries cushioning the floor. Devoid of furniture save a table and two *charpoys*, its centre was a hole in the floor through which they could gaze down a dizzy drop. This hole was their only means of sanitation and when it was not in use they placed their bamboo table across it for fear that in the darkness of the long nights they might fall through it.

Their food was adequate, but limited – the bitingly hot curries of the region, washed down with well-water and occasionally a kind of lemonade, but as the Ranee's subjects were vegetarians there was never any meat. Even fish, save for an overripe, smelly fish paste, was absent from their diet.

'If the Good Lord in His everlasting mercy,' Sergeant Jones had exclaimed more than once at the sight of yet another vegetable curry, 'could just let us have a piece of beef, only a very *small* piece, I'd be a happy man, Mr Bold!'

But the Good Lord refused to grant that favour and they continued to lose weight steadily.

At times John paced the chamber like a caged beast, racking his brains for some way of escape. The chance of Lord Hastings sending a rescue force was remote; they would have to save themselves.

For a while he and Jones studied the possibility of tackling the guards when they brought their daily curry. The one, a tall dark sullen fellow with a great beak nose and jet-black beard, who they nicknamed Hawk-Face, was always accompanied by two armed guards. The other, Pudding-Face, a permanently frightened creature who might well have been a eunuch – his face was totally devoid of hair – never entered the cell but pushed their food through a flap in the great oaken door, not caring whether it slopped on the floor. In the end they decided it wouldn't work. There were always other guards in the corridor when the food came.

Sergeant Jones turned his attention to the slit-like windows. With a rusty nail he had found in the dust and sharpened laboriously on the stone flags, he finally prised out a section of the leaded glass and squeezed himself through to crouch in the slit like a cat. 'See, sir, on the kind of vittles we get in this place, it ain't difficult.'

John tried the opening and had to agree. He could squeeze his six foot body through the gap just as easily as the undersized sergeant. But as he peered down the dizzying drop, along the sheer grey wall of the fortress, he knew that without ropes they didn't stand a chance of escaping that way.

Of course, the fortress was centuries old and the stone should be weathered and holed by winds and the passage of time. But as far as he could see, there were no gaps for toes and fingers to grip.

Then, one February evening, John was dragged out of their prison and told he was to see the Ranee. The guards insisted he had to wash and then forced him to hold out his hands while they poured some highly scented fragrance on them.

The Ranee of Burrapore, he surmised, liked him. Perhaps in standing up to those Prussian louts back in Aachen, in what now seemed another world, he had impressed her. At all events, she received him gracefully, insisted his chains should be removed, and even offered him a *chota peg*, a whisky and soda, although all alcohol was forbidden in Burrapore.

Apart from the guards who were everywhere in the large hall, there were three women present: the Ranee herself, in European clothes complete with beaver hat, wearing it indoors as if she might be Lord Hastings himself; the Indian who had guided him to his first 'audience' with the Ranee and seemed some kind of chamberlain; and poor foolish Alice Elders, who simpered and pouted and pawed the Ranee, looking fat and awkward in the native dress, and whom the chamberlain eyed with undisguised ani-

mosity whenever she believed herself unobserved.

Little was said while he drank his *chota
peg*, hoping his face would not flush red
with the unaccustomed alcohol. The Ranee
asked if the food was sufficient and whether
he wished for something to read. He did,
and she offered him a battered copy of
Robinson Crusoe and the third book of
Richardson's *Clarissa* in French. He thought
of asking her for a Bible for Sergeant Jones,
but decided against it. So far the Ranee was
friendly and accommodating; he didn't
want to antagonize her.

The Ranee of Burrapore, despite her male
pretensions and undoubtedly perverse
nature, exuded wilful purpose and intelligence. Her dark eyes shone with animal
energy, even ferocity, and now John knew
why Lord Hastings had called her 'tigress'.
There was something of that magnificent
beast about her, ready to strike at any
moment, whenever she thought the moment
suitable. In comparison with her chamberlain and the stupid fat Alice, who was obviously completely besotted, the Ranee was a
paragon.

She was a beauty, too. Beneath that silly
male clothing was a wonderful body
designed to give pleasure to the male. She
uncrossed her legs in the tight-fitting buckskins and he saw for a moment the tight

cleft between her thighs and remembered that dawn in Aachen. He swallowed hard with sudden longing, and shivered.

The Ranee looked at him with her infinitely mysterious eyes and said softly, 'You feel faint, Mr Bold?... Some sudden fever ails you?'

He could have answered, 'Yes, the fever of desire, even lust.' Instead he forced himself to reply, 'No, it is nothing, madame.'

She smiled softly, as if she knew well what ailed him, and said, 'Apa Sahib has been defeated.'

His heart leapt with joy at the news, but he felt it was wiser not to comment.

'Soon, he will try once more with his Arabs and then he will suffer – undoubtedly – his final defeat. Then he will go whining to you English for forgiveness. He is a fool.'

Again she waited for his comment. Again he said nothing.

'Then Lord Hastings will march against the Mahratta princes.' She looked at him, as if this time she expected an answer. At his side the chamberlain nudged him covertly, so he said, 'I would think that would be My Lord Hastings' intention, madame. But I am merely a junior officer, I know nothing of these great affairs of state.'

Again she gave a soft knowing smile. 'By now you know India a little, Lieutenant Bold, and realize that we weak women are regarded as chattels whose main function is to please their lords and masters in bed.' She raised her voice and quoted, 'Embrace your Master's waist with your legs. While suspended your Master will insert his Jade Stem into your Flowery Path!'

Suddenly her face hardened and she clenched her fist. 'What male rubbish!' she snorted, nostrils flared, eyes flashing fire. 'I shall show those man-dogs of Mahratta princes what a *weak* woman can really do! Without me they will be utterly defeated and swept from the pages of history, their lands stolen by the English.' She stopped, her chest heaving prettily, as if too angry to go on.

John was intrigued. Despite the fact that the little chamberlain was now softly gripping his arm, he ventured, 'And how will you do that, madame?' She did not reply and he went on, ignoring the fingers now dug into his arm in warning, 'You mean you and the Pindarees? Is that what you are intending, madame?'

She looked at him coldly, in full control of herself once more. 'Lieutenant Bold, I called you here to see for myself that you were keeping well. I am now assured you are. You may also rest assured that my other white captives are also being well looked after. They lack little.' Suddenly she patted Alice's hand possessively. 'Though perhaps they are not as well fed as Mrs Elders.'

John gave a sigh of relief. 'And my *sowars*, how are they being looked after? You know–'

She clapped her hands, cutting him off. The chamberlain tugged at his sleeve, the guards surrounded him, and he was dragged from the chamber. But on the way back to his cell, mystified by it all, he saw another strange sight. Padmini (for that was the name of the chamberlain, as he learned later) halted the procession in a dark corridor and called softly through an open door.

A woman with a baby appeared. Perhaps she was one of the Ranee's favourites who had fallen from grace through having become pregnant; her robes were shabby and she looked undernourished and harassed. Hesitantly she looked at the guards, the prisoner, and then at Padmini. The latter gave her a reassuring smile, said something, and passed over a small leather bag of coins. The woman bowed low, touching her forehead in thanks, and stammered something as she attempted to kiss Padmini's hand.

Gently Padmini released herself and held out her arms. The gesture was all too obvious. She wanted to hold the baby.

Hurriedly the woman passed over the naked brown child while Padmini fumbled with her bodice to reveal one small, perfectly shaped breast. The baby took it unhesitatingly and began to suck lustily.

John saw the sweet, overwhelming yearning that crossed the chamberlain's face; it was that of frustrated motherhood. A few moments later the infant rejected the milkless breast and began to squall. Still smiling gently, her eyes far away and unfocused, Padmini handed the writhing child back to its mother, fastened her bodice, and without another word set off again, followed by John and the wooden-faced guards...

Now, two months later, all that the two captives knew of the outside world was what they gathered from their perch high above the fortress. One day they heard the telltale jingling of horses' equipment which signalled European riders, not Indian; and although, strain as they might, they could not see the riders, the cries which floated up to their eyrie were in French. Nom de Dieu and his gang of mercenaries had returned. John wondered why.

Two days later he found out.

But before then, he was surprised by a visit from Padmini, who slipped into their cell at the same time that Pudding-Face brought their midday curry. Entering without fear, she indicated that the moon-faced guard should close and watch the door behind her.

She spoke English. 'There is danger, Mr Bold.' Her eyes were worried and her face seemed thinner than before. 'The men from the north have arrived. They bring danger for the Ranee – and you.' And she looked up at him, as she said 'you', lingering over the word as if it were of some significance for her. John could have sworn that she was 'smitten', as his father would have put it, and was bewildered. Surely she wasn't interested in men?

'But who are these men from the north?–'

'*Pssh!*' the warning hiss broke into his puzzled question. Hastily she backed to the door and scuttled off with Pudding-Face, who had uttered that warning, leaving John and Sergeant Jones to stare at their cooling pot of curry.

3

Two days later when the guards forced him into the Ranee's presence her male outfit had been replaced by the traditional *saree* and her face had been rouged heavily in the Indian fashion. She sat demurely on an ornate thronelike chair listening to a tall majestic Indian, who, John guessed, was the reason she had changed her attire and banished her females from the place.

He was an imposing man, lean and hard-looking, with one of the great hook noses seen in the north, who lectured at attentive Ranee as if she were some innocent slip of a girl. There was a grave, un-Indian dignity about him, too. This was a man who knew exactly what he wanted and how to achieve those wants. Not even the Ranee of Burrapore could awe him.

The rattle of John's chains as he was thrust forward by his guards caused them to break apart like disturbed conspirators. The Ranee straightened up in her chair and the tall man walked swiftly into the shadow of the wall, but not before John recognized him. Last time, John and Georgina had seen him from hiding as he led a bunch of Pindaree bandits – whose trophies included the severed head of poor Captain de Courcy.

The Ranee of Burrapore wasted no time, while the tall Pindaree leader stood brooding, face set in a look of noble savagery. 'I have intelligence from Nagpore,' she said. 'That fool Apa Sahib has been deposed and his land annexed by the Company. Now your Lord Hastings has crossed the River Spira and engaged the army of the first of the Mahratta princes, Holkar.'

At last rescue was at hand! The forces of Lord Hastings were coming ever closer to Burrapore!

He must have smiled, for she said severely, 'Do not rejoice too soon, Lieutenant Bold! My Lord Hastings has not reached Burrapore yet. Indeed, you may yet regret his victories over those fools, the Mahrattas. You know the original reason why Apa Sahib took the white captives – and why my gallant French officers did not kill you and your soldiers on the spot?'

Something clicked in John's mind at the mention of '*my* gallant French officers' and with the total recall of a vision he remembered the rat of a German in Aachen who had offered him a great deal of money if he were prepared to fight – for whom, he didn't know *then*. That had been the reason for the Ranee's visit to Europe. *She had been recruiting officers for her own army!*

'You mean we are hostages too, not prisoners of war?' he blustered, feeling he must now put up a brave front at all costs. 'I rather think that My Lord Hastings will not be greatly concerned with the fate of a handful of white women and children – nor for a junior officer and his men, madame.' He stared back at her bravely.

She regarded him with her usual cynical, good-humoured guile. 'I think you are mistaken, Lieutenant Bold,' she replied softly. 'Your home country is in the midst of a great boom caused by this war with the Mahrattas. Your merchants are paying tremendous prices for a passage to India. Several colonels have volunteered whole regiments to come and fight against the – *heathen* – here, and naturally to line their own pockets.' She chuckled cynically. 'London is in a furore. Shares are rising at a great rate.

Tremendous profits are being made. Once the *heathen* has been defeated, what spoils in territory and gold will fall to the Company?'

He listened as the words poured from her pretty mouth, realizing for the first time just how very much she hated the English and perhaps all men. But she hated herself, too, for being neither. 'But what has all this to do with me?' he asked calmly. 'What do I know of London, shares, the Exchange?'

She took a deep breath, forcing herself to be calm, while the tall Pindaree turned to look at them, his face calm and passive, like a gambler assessing the chances of two prize-fighters before placing his wager.

'Then I shall tell you, John Bold,' she said. 'Imagine what would happen in London if I had you English put to death in Burrapore. Imagine the indignation! Imagine the Company's embarrassment. A second Black Hole of Calcutta would not help their shares.' She wagged a finger at him. 'And there are those in your Parliament who would seize upon the discomfiture of the Company like hawks. The Company is not liked in certain quarters–'

'*Madame!*' John knew he was in for a penny as well as a pound. 'What are you trying to say?'

The tall man smiled for the first time, and held up his hand for her to be quiet. Such was his commanding presence that even the Ranee of Burrapore fell silent. 'My name is

Cheethoo,' he said simply in English. 'I command the Pindarees.'

Bold gasped with shock. So the rumours were true. There *was* a supreme leader of those cruel marauders.

'I see you have heard of me, Mr Bold?' Cheethoo said. 'Come, let me show you something.' He beckoned, and like a sleep-walker, the young Englishman advanced to the window and looked down into the crowded courtyard of the upper fort. He uttered a low moan, face suddenly contorted, at what he saw.

It was Titch, the undersized youngest *sowar* in Bold's Horse, a skinny ever-smiling boy who couldn't have been a day over sixteen. Now Titch was no longer smiling. Instead his thin young face was contorted by agony as he writhed and wriggled his naked, sweat-lathered body to escape his torturers.

But there was no escape. Tied to a crude wooden cross like some black Jesus, he struggled in vain as his torturers hammered in yet another nail. His right hand, already nailed, dripped thick red blood on to the white dust. While he screamed, tossing his head from side to side in pain, the long nail was hammered through his left wrist and deep into the wood.

Furiously John swung his fist at the Pindaree leader. The chain jerked his arm back in mid-punch and the nearest guard raised his sword ready to cleave the Englishman's skull. Hastily Cheethoo held up his hand and the guard lowered his arm.

'My God, what … what…' John stuttered, so shocked that he could hardly think coherently.

Below, Titch was racked with loud sobs, his body heaving, each of his thin ribs marked on his black chest, as if his rib cage might burst forth at any moment. Stolidly his torturers selected another nail and prepared to drive it through his feet.

'Why … *why?*' John finally found the words. *'Why do … that?'*

Cheethoo clapped his hands and the guards thrust John away from the window. He prayed that those laboured sobs and moans would cease; that poor tortured Titch would fall unconscious, *die* – anything that would put him out of his dreadful misery.

Cheethoo took his time, while the Ranee looked at him impatiently with dark flashing eyes. Even as he agonized, trying to drown out those sobs, John could see that her fate was inextricably bound up with that of the Pindaree leader. Beneath the surface, although they seemed so disparate, they were both animals – savages who would fight tooth and claw to protect their lairs.

Finally the tall Indian spoke. 'That wretch is an example of our power. Just as your Company shoots us off the end of cannon and thus condemns us to perdition, it amused some of my followers to condemn your hireling to die in the fashion of your Lord Jesus – a little joke. And you English are renowned for your little jokes, are you not?'

John's face turned an angry crimson. 'Why, you goddamn murdering swine, let me get my hands free and I'll rip your black heathen heart out, if it is the last thing I ever do!' he shrieked, spittle flying from his lips.

Cheethoo remained unmoved. 'But your hands are not free, Mr Bold.' His smile vanished. 'You have seen then what *we* are capable of. Now hear this. The day that your Lord Hastings marches on Burrapore, we shall commence executing our captives. We shall start with your soldiers. That will not move Lord Hastings, but it will serve as a warning of our intentions. When they are finished with, we begin on your whites.' His eyes bored into John's, and the latter knew that Cheethoo was not bluffing one bit. 'We shall erect a cross at every ten of your miles and nail one of you to it. *Every ten miles,* Mr Bold! Imagine what your Parliament will say to that? How valuable will your Company's shares be then, eh?'

The Ranee sneered, 'Those Mahratta fools do not know how to deal with you English. *We do!*' Her voice rose and now John could see the tremendous arrogance and pride that motivated her when she said, as if addressing a great assembly, 'Then all India will know that the Ranee of Burrapore and her loyal friend Cheethoo, Chief of the Pindarees, have beaten the infernal English. They will rally to us. We will rule all India, as once did the old Emperors from the north. Once again the wind of change will come from the north, *and we will sweep the English back into the ocean from whence they came!...*'

Sergeant Jones was silent for a long time after John had finished his account of that meeting. 'Then, sir,' he said finally, 'we must escape.'

'Escape?'

'Yes, and take all the prisoners with us. White – *and black* – they cannot remain here to suffer like that. There will be no more crucifixions, sir.' It was not a wish just a simple statement of fact.

John was in full agreement. But: 'How can we do it, Jones? We've already looked, and found no way.'

'Then we must look again, sir.'

John sat slumped in thought. Ignoring the problems of releasing themselves and the others, once out the white women and children, without the aid of bearers and transport, would be dead of heatstroke within twenty-four hours. The only possible way to get them out was by boat along the Burra River, which flowed due south and into the much bigger Nag. There were boats aplenty on the Burra, ranging from Arablike dhows, complete with sails, to primitive hollowed-out logs.

By now, he knew where the women and children were lodged. While his *sowars* languished in the dungeons of the low fort, the white captives were housed in its upper chambers. More than once the noise of children had been carried up by the wind and once they had actually spotted a white woman on the flat roof of their dwelling. Somehow she had managed to clamber out of a window and was enjoying the pleasant cool of the breeze from the mountains until the guards dragged her back...

'Once we've released the *sowars*, Jones,' he whispered that night as they lay in their *charpoys*, 'they could take care of the boat. With either sail or oars, we would manage.'

'I agree, sir,' Jones whispered back. 'Most of them grew up along the coast, they'll know a bit about boats. But it would have to be done at night.'

'Yes, that it would. But first, how do we get out?'

Jones dropped his voice even lower, as if Hawk-Face might be listening behind the door (by now they had concluded that Pudding-Face was in the pay of the chamberlain, Padmini, and she certainly meant them no harm). 'I've been thinking of that, sir. The cropping-ken. Come and have a look.'

Noiselessly they moved in the moonlight to the sanitation hole and removed the bamboo table. A faint stirring of cooler air came up from the hole.

Jones knelt and extended his arms to indicate that it was big enough for a skinny man to pass through and John nodded.

'Look *there*, sir,' Jones whispered into his right ear. 'Down below that big grey rock.'

For a moment John could not make it out, then he saw it. The hole dropped sheer at first, but then changed direction, and at that point there was something…

He concentrated on the spot while Jones waited in silence. 'A gun port perhaps,' John said.

'That's what I think,' Jones agreed. 'There's a big hole in the wall, where there might have been a cannon. There ain't one now,' he concluded cheerfully, 'and that hole is big enough for a man to climb through.'

Down below them there was a way back into the fortress underneath the floor of their room; and it was very probably unguarded.

'Well, what do you think, sir?' Jones whispered excitedly.

'Yes, yes,' John answered impatiently. 'You've got something there.' But the distance from their hole to the other one had to be at least twenty feet. He frowned and said with a note of sad finality, 'But where are we going to get a rope from, Jones?'

4

The very next day brought an answer to that question. When Pudding-Face came with their midday meal he opened the door to reveal Padmini standing in the shadows.

A finger to her lips, she beckoned John into the corridor. This time Pudding-Face did not attempt to chain John, and he followed, bewildered, to the little room where they had met the woman and baby. The place was bare save for a *charpoy* and a couple of rickety chairs. Padmini nodded to Pudding-Face, who closed the door and posted himself outside so that they would not be surprised.

Now in the dusty sunshine John could see that she had been crying and there were dark circles under her eyes. Without any hesitation she blurted out, face desperate, 'I must save her! She must not challenge the English. It would be fatal for her, Lieutenant Bold, but the Ranee...' She faltered and shook her head, fighting back the tears, and John realized that Padmini was just as besotted with the Ranee as was Alice Elders. How could a woman hold such sway over others?

'If the English march on Burrapore,' she continued, 'and she carries out her plan to kill all of you, the English will not just depose her, they will *execute* her! She thinks she possesses power, but the real power lies with Cheethoo and if he finds he is losing, he will disappear back into the mountains. Cheethoo is not a conqueror – he is a brigand who cares solely for adventure and loot. You must tell Lord Hastings that.' She held up her clasped hands, begging him to help her.

John was touched. Gently he took her hands and unclenched them. 'Padmini,' he said quietly, soothingly, feeling for her, 'I understand well what you mean and you are right. Let the Ranee do what she likes with us, but she will not deflect Lord Hastings from his purpose. But what can I do?'

'Escape,' she whispered huskily.

He forced himself to remain calm. 'But how can I – all of us – escape?'

'I shall help you. The guards – they can be bought. I have money.' She made that cynical Indian gesture of counting coins. 'Gold opens all doors, they say.'

He shook his head firmly, though he longed to say yes. 'Listen,' he said urgently, 'we *shall* escape and we will tell Lord Hastings what you have just told me. But none of your people must be involved. It would be too dangerous for you.'

'Yes, yes, I understand … but how *will* you

do it, John?'

'That is my concern. All that I require from you is a rope, Padmini.'

'It will be done, John,' she answered and then she did something that took him completely by surprise. Her hands dropped and before he could stop her, she had unbuttoned the front flap of his ragged trousers.

The vegetarian diet had not stilled his youthful fire. For the very instant her cunning little fingers touched his manhood, it stood erect. He willed himself to pull out of her grasp, but the ecstasy was too great and he submitted to her caressing. 'How strong you are!' she whispered softly and pressed her wet tongue to his ear momentarily. 'How proud!'

He shivered with delight. Georgina's urgent, demanding lovemaking had not been like this. Padmini was seducing him in a way that was soft, yet thrillingly exotic, with promises of delights that a man could not even put a name to.

Her lips parted. They were wet and sensual. She licked her little pink tongue along her pearl-like teeth slowly and significantly, keeping her dark eyes on his face. Slowly, very slowly, she started to sink to her knees in front of him.

'*Auparishtaka*, we say in our language,' she whispered, her voice throbbing with suppressed passion. Suddenly her warm wet lips took hold of his manhood and he gasped...

That evening she entered their cell, leaving Pudding-Face outside. John sprang from his *charpoy*, where he spent most of the afternoon dwelling on the exquisite pleasure she had given him. Again she held her finger to her lips. She seemed strangely bulky, and a moment later the two startled prisoners saw the reason why as she lifted her *saree* to reveal a great length of rope wound round her slim body.

Jones' jaw dropped and he gawped. Then as she began to unwind the rope, he hissed, 'God bless you, Missy!'

Urgently John indicated that he should be quiet, while he helped her to free the rope. Finally it was done, and after re-fastening her *saree* produced her second surprise – an ornately wrought great key.

'To the dungeons where the *sowars* are held,' she said. 'I stole it. There is no need of a key where the women are kept. The Ranee is not afraid that they may escape, so there is no key – and no *guard* on their quarters.'

Jones' eyes lit up. 'Then that makes it a lot easier, sir,' he said, even as John was deciding that they would go this evening. But he must not tell Padmini that.

'What about Alice Elders, Padmini? She's not with the other white women.'

Those dark eyes, which could look so loving and concerned, flashed fire and hate.

'Never fear about *her!*' she spat venomously, '*I* shall take care of Alice Elders.' There was sheer naked murder in her face now and John thought it better not to pursue the matter.

Instead, he said, 'Now all I can do is to thank you. Ensure that for the next few days,' he lied to her glibly for her own safety, 'you stay as much as possible in the Ranee's presence, so when we escape, you must not be suspected. You understand?'

'I understand and I obey, John.' She raised her clasped hands to her forehead in the Indian manner, her eyes now holding a look almost of love. 'God be with you.'

He took her in his arms, while Sergeant Jones gawped again and then looked oddly embarrassed for such an old veteran. Gently he kissed her forehead. 'Thank you – thank you with all my heart, Padmini. One day I shall repay the debt I owe you.'

A moment later she was gone, leaving the two of them brooding on only one thing – *escape...*

Midnight. No sound came from Burrapore. One by one the little yellow lights had vanished in the houses near the river.

Jones crossed the cell in his bare feet and opened the flap in the door gingerly, praying that the hinges would not squeak. He waited a moment and then placed a sliver of mirror glass, wedged in a stick, through the opening, while John held his breath. Carefully

Jones turned it and surveyed the corridor in one direction. Satisfied, he reversed the primitive gadget and checked in the other direction. Finally he squirmed round and breathed, *'Nothing!'*

John didn't hesitate. Swiftly he removed the table over the hole. In the last of the real light, hours ago, they had attached Padmini's rope to it and dangled it in space. They had breathed a sigh of heartfelt relief when they saw it extended to the level of the gunport hole. It would do. They had also tested its strength.

Jones scuttled across. 'Sir, don't you think–'

John cut him short. 'We've had that argument before, Sergeant,' he hissed. 'It is my duty as an officer to go first.'

'Yessir,' Jones said, face a little crestfallen.

'Now, this is what we are going to do – or at least what *I* am going to do, Jones,' Bold lectured the sergeant in a low voice. 'Once I'm level with the gunport, I'm going to swing at the end of the rope.' He forced a grin, to which Jones, however, did not respond – the matter was too serious. 'That was an unfortunate phrase, I must admit. Well, put it like this. I'm going to work my body back and forth like a clock pendulum. Once I let go, I'm diving for that port.'

'God with ye, sir...' Sergeant Jones stammered, 'and if you pull this off, sir, why, you'll be a hero.'

For a moment John savoured the word. He imagined himself returning to the British lines to receive a hero's welcome, with the Collector beaming all over his face and Georgina waiting for him with outstretched arms, a look of adulation on her beautiful face. Then he dismissed that little bit of wishful thinking and got on with the task at hand.

Next instant he had swung himself lightly through the hole and was clutching the rope, the wind already tugging at his legs. Now he started to go down hand over hand, feeling the rope taking the strain, with the wind increasing its force by the moment. *Ten feet ... fifteen ... twenty.* Now he was climbing down along a naked rock face, with below him a sheer drop. *Twenty-five.* His hand grasped the knot they had made in the rope at the depth that should bring him face to face with the gunport. He peered through the silver gloom of the spectral sickle moon.

Yes! There it was. A hole in the man-made wall of about two by three foot. Thank God, it was big enough for him to squeeze through. He took a deep breath, feeling red-hot pain already beginning to shoot through his shoulder muscles; he couldn't hang here above the abyss much longer. Now come on, Bold, a hard little voice at the back of his mind snapped coldly, live up to your name. Get on with it, man!

'All right, you bastard, I'm going to do it!' he muttered, and started to swing.

Slowly, almost imperceptibly at first, the rope started to move back and forth along the face of the precipice, creaking and groaning under the strain. He started to gain momentum. The rope creaked even more. The pain in his back and shoulders was murderous, like a burning poker thrust into his flesh.

His body swung back and forth, breath escaping his lungs in harsh gasps, vision blurred. He struck the rock and gasped with pain. Next moment he was swinging out into that frightening void. Above Jones had begun to gabble the Lord's Prayer.

He hit the rock again, and clenched his lips just in time. Otherwise he would have screamed out loud with the pain of it. Once more he swung in a great arc, the cold wind howling against his battered body, threatening to tug him from the rope at any moment and send him hurtling to his death. The dark hole loomed up in front of him. He felt his strength ebbing rapidly. *It was now or never!*

He let go. With both hands held in front, he hurtled towards the gunport, so temptingly near, yet so far. He slammed against the stone. Blindly his fingers grabbed for a hold.

Somehow he held on and with the last of his strength climbed up into the lip of the hole and slumped there like a sack, staring at the silver snake of the River Burra far below...

Two hundred miles to the south at Musulipatan at that very same moment Georgina Lanham squatted in the middle of her father's changing room, directly under the punkah. She had removed her dress. Now clad in her silken shift, which clung to her every contour with perspiration, she moaned, 'Oh, but Papa, Rodney is so fat – and a terrible bore! All he talks about is Prinny' – she mimicked his accent cruelly – 'and the regiment. Those damned toy soldiers of his!' She mopped her glistening face with a lace handkerchief, while the Collector, clad in his dressing gown, watched her from his chair. Ever since she had come back from England, he told himself, trying not to look at her breasts straining at the thin material of her shift, she had become more and more outrageous. The sooner she was married, the better for everyone concerned, including himself.

'Rodney is a very rich and well-connected young man,' he lectured her. 'Count yourself very lucky that this war with the Mahrattas has brought a man of his calibre to India.'

The war! she snorted. 'This boring war – that's all men talk about, especially those who have stayed behind here, while the others have gone to fight.' She sighed and dabbed her handkerchief with cologne. 'When will the really amusing men come back?' Her question was rhetorical, but the Collector thought she required an answer.

With mock solemnity, he said, 'Major Rathbone is definitely dead. A gallant officer, dying at the head of his squadron like that! And that other young fellow, Lieutenant Bold.' He flashed her a look, but she didn't respond to the name. 'He has been long considered dead by Lord Hastings' staff, Georgina.'

Her expression remained petulant and bored. The Collector frowned. Her mother had looked like that often before she had become the evil-tempered, lazy shrew who had been – fortunately – carried off by fever. Women in India, who had nothing better to do but flirt and gossip, often became like that, taking out their unreasoning rages on their long-suffering husbands and servants. 'Georgina, the time for you to get wed has arrived. If Rodney asks me for your hand in marriage, then I think it is your duty to accept, do you hear? The Colonel is rich and is in society with absolutely the best connections.' He lowered his voice in case the servants were still up and listening. He did not want *gup* in the bazaar on the morrow. 'What matters it that he is fat and a bore, Georgina? You will be in England and in the finest society. There will be opportunities to meet…' he hesitated, wondering how to put it, 'well, to meet other – er – *people!*'

For a few moments Georgina thought of Rathbone and Bold, and compared them with Rodney. She knew instinctively he would be no good in bed, all panting and puffing and no performance. But her father was right. There would be 'other people'. She yawned, those dead young men already slipping back into the furthest recesses of her mind, and said lazily, 'I suppose you're right, Papa'…

And on that dark cliff face John Bold sweated for his life.

5

Twice they had passed rooms occupied by their enemies. But with their feet bare, they had glided by noiselessly and unobserved. Once a dark shape had shot out in front of them, magnified enormously by the light of a pitch torch fixed in a bracket high on the wall. But whoever it was, he had not noticed them. A moment later they had heard the hiss of water rattling into an empty pot and Jones had grinned.

Now they were almost out of the upper fort and John was still amazed at how easy it had been so far. The huge place, which housed the Ranee herself, seemed virtually unguarded. He could only surmise that some of the Ranee's troops had been sent to the border to prepare for Hastings' invasion. He prayed that whatever cavalry she had under the command of Nom de Dieu's Frenchmen had gone too. For once they had a boat, only cavalry could stop them.

Sergeant Jones stopped abruptly. To their immediate front a guard was lounging, and there was no mistaking the outline of the long musket which he had cradled to his chest. For a moment John was mesmerized. The man had his back to them, but if he had his forefinger crooked around the trigger and they attacked him, it would go off and the alarm would be sounded.

Then Jones picked up a pebble. Carefully, like a bowlsman in the newfangled game of cricket, he measured the distance to the lounging guard, and lobbed the pebble forward, as the bowlsman did with the wooden ball.

It struck the ground to the immediate front of the guard. As Jones had anticipated, the man bent down to see what it was, using his musket as a support. Jones dived forward. The two of them slammed to the ground. The native opened his mouth to scream a warning but Jones didn't give him the chance. His clubbed right fist came down with all his strength on the back of the man's thin neck. He went out like a light, the scream stifled.

A minute later they were outside, John armed with the ancient musket, Jones with the sentry's sword. Silently, like grey ghosts in the night they made their way down the slope to the lower fort, slinking in the shadows, darting swiftly through patches of moonlight, hearts thumping madly, bodies tense for the first shot, the first cry of alarm. But none came. The whole of Burrapore had seemingly gone to sleep.

They entered a kind of tunnel, an ancient, covered structure which in time of siege would protect the defenders moving from one fort to the other. It dripped with moisture, the floor treacherous and slippery. More than once they heard the horrid scurrying of fleeing rats.

The escape plan John had formulated was straight-forward. He and Jones would first release the *sowars,* half of whom would be sent direct to the river to secure a boat. The rest would help to free and evacuate the women and children.

To the immediate left of the entrance to the lower fort, there was an area of dead ground, both inside and outside the defensive wall. With a bit of luck, if fate smiled kindly upon them, the first group of *sowars* would be over the wall and away undetected. The real danger would come when getting the women and children over the wall. Even as he hurried through the slimy tunnel John worried at this difficulty. Then he had it. The diversion. Hastily, he told Jones what he wanted the first party of *sowars* to do once they'd secured a boat.

Jones nodded his understanding and hissed, 'It'll be risky, sir. But it's the only thing we can do. I'll do my best, sir,' he added loyally.

'I know you will, Sergeant Jones,' John said warmly. 'You have always done so. In our adversity, I could not have wished for a better subordinate – *and friend!*'

Thankful for the cover of darkness, Jones blushed.

Moments later the tunnel ended. They crouched in the shadows, eyeing the entrance to the lower fort. Two *flambeaux* flickered fitfully by the unguarded door.

John tugged the end of his nose in a mixture of irritation and disbelief. It was all too easy. Here were half a hundred prisoners or more, on whom the Ranee of Burrapore was pinning her hopes of coercing Lord Hastings into doing her will – and they were unguarded! It hardly seemed possible. But as he tensed there, ear cocked to catch even the slightest sound, he could hear nothing. Perhaps the Indians in their usual sloppy careless way were really all sleeping?

Anyway, asleep or not, there was no time to waste. He nudged Sergeant Jones, who nodded and indicated the door with his sword.

They stole forward into the light. Nothing stirred, although they were in full view of any observer now. John crouched, matchlock at the ready, as Jones swung open the great door carefully.

It squeaked rustily and John's hands on the ancient weapon broke out into a sweat. God, he thought, everyone in Burrapore must hear the damned sound!

No one did.

Jones went in first and found nothing save the stench of unwashed bodies, animal droppings and ancient cruelties. Cautiously John followed the crouched sergeant and closed the door behind him, praying that it would not squeak so much. It did.

To either side now in the dim light were set small barred doors, one every few feet or so. They were the doors of cells in which, John guessed, a man could neither stand up nor stretch. The prisoner would be condemned to crouch in the tight box in a way that some Irish Paddy might keep a pig for fattening, not allowing it to move more than was necessary. But each cell as they crept by was empty. The *sowars* were elsewhere.

They passed a bamboo chair, bench and European-style desk. They, too, were unattended, but someone, perhaps the guards, had occupied them recently, for there was a half-eaten chappati on the desk and when Jones touched it, it was still warm. They weren't all alone in the cell block after all.

They pressed on deeper into the building, and from the increasing stench it was obvious that they were close to a large number of unwashed humanity. Now they could hear the occasional muffled cough – the sort of cough John remembered from school when the cougher is afraid of making too much noise in case he brought trouble on himself. Once they heard a soft fart.

He paused and whispered in Jones' ear, 'It's them, I'm sure.'

Jones had raised his head and was sniffing the warm air like a game dog. 'Natives, sir,' he hissed. 'Can smell 'em. No mistaking that niggah smell.'

'Where?'

'To our front.' Jones gripped the curved sword more firmly and they turned a corner cautiously. To their front was a room lit by flickering pitch torches and there, around a rough table in the centre, were a good half dozen guards, some dozing with their heads slumped on the uneven boards, others half awake, stolidly chewing on betel nut, pausing only to spit a lazy stream of red juice on to the already filthy floor.

John knew immediately that they could

not outwit the guards. They'd have to fight, and their only chance of success was to take them by surprise. Hastily he whispered his orders and Jones nodded, the gleam of battle in his eyes. Under his breath, as he raised the matchlock and took aim, John started to count off three seconds.

'*THREE!*' In that same instant, John fired. A blast of fire. Gunpowder. A tremendous deafening echo in the tight confines of that underground chamber, and as Jones leapt forward, the nearest guard was lifted from his perch by the impact of the close-range ball and slammed against the wall to crumple like a broken doll.

A cry of rage. The alarmed chatter of the awakened *sowars.* Jones' sword hissed savagely. A guard trying to rise from the bench reeled back screaming, trying frantically to hold the two halves of his face together, as the bright blood seeped through his fingers.

John darted in, swinging the matchlock like a club. A guard reeled back spitting out his teeth. Another swung his sword. John countered just in time. The killing blow belted against the butt of the matchlock. The impact nearly knocked the weapon out of his hands. But he recovered more quickly than the swordsman. He upturned the matchlock and smashed the butt cruelly into the swordsman's chin and the man howled with pain and staggered back like some drunken dancer doing a complicated *paso doble*.

At John's shoulder Sergeant Jones, slashing his sabre to left and right with crazed energy, cursing fluently, his face streaming with great beads of sweat, flung the key neatly through the bars of the cell, directly into the outstretched hands of the gleeful, half-naked *sowars*. Next instant he parried a great swing by one of the guards and diving in underneath his sword, cried as if at a fencing academy, *'Have that, sir!'* The point sliced right into the guard's belly. His entrails fell out like a steaming grey snake.

Now the *sowars* were fumbling madly with the key, while the guards, their surprise overcome now, were steadily pushing the two assailants back against the opposite wall. In the flickering blood-red light their swords flashed silver time and time again as they dealt out wild slashes and swipes, raising sparks on Jones' sword as he parried them and cutting chunks of wood from the butt of John's matchlock. But the pressure was mounting, a desperate John knew, and time was running out. Sooner or later the noise of this wild scuffle would penetrate to the outside and then the fat would be in the fire. Fervently he wished the *sowars* would get that damned door open and come to their aid. The two of them couldn't hold off the guards much longer, damnit!

He slipped on a patch of blood and went

down on one knee. Opposite, a guard, face pocked and bearded, yelled in triumph and raised his two-handed sword high above his head. His intention was all too clear – to cleave John's skull in two!

That wasn't to be.

With a great roar the half-starved *sowars* burst out of the cell, surging forward, fists and arms flailing. The guards, screaming and shrieking for mercy, which didn't come, disappeared beneath a pile of skinny, half-naked bodies. Feet stamped down hard on upturned faces. Cruel fingers gouged out eyes. Hands sought and found throats to stifle the lives of those who had tormented them savagely over long hard months of imprisonment.

Minutes later it was all over. The floor was strewn with broken bodies as the jubilant prisoners grabbed the weapons available from those lifeless figures and began to form up into two groups under the command of their two white superiors. The final stage of the break-out was coming...

'*Jhanto!*' – one pubic hair – the *sowar* cursed softly as he slipped in the water and fell to his knees.

'*Yoti!*' Jones cursed back, more to please the *sowars*, who enjoyed such sexual banter, than because he was angry. 'Do you want to wake up the whole garrison?'

They had secured the boat by now, a dhow,

which was also equipped with oars. It was small, but they would all fit into it. Besides it was not too big for them to handle. Now all that was to be done, Jones told himself, was to plant the diversion and hope it would work long enough for Lieutenant Bold and the other *sowars* to get the women and children over the wall and dead ground and down to the Burra.

He detailed two men to guard the boat while the rest hastened to gather the *bhoosa*, chopped straw and cattle fodder, which lay in great piles near the dhow.

'Enough,' he commanded *sotto voce*, when each trooper had a great armful of bone-dry stuff. '*Chalo...*'

Bent low, they hastened forward to where the entrance of the lower fort was outlined a stark black against the faint silver of the moon. Here and there an anxious, tense Jones glimpsed the head and shoulders of a silent sentry between the crenellations of the battlements. He prayed that no one would spot his troopers before they got into position.

Now like hurrying ghosts, the *sowars* spread the straw and fodder before the great oaken gate, glancing up constantly to see if they had been spotted. But they hadn't. Twenty feet above them the sentries paced their beat, apparently completely unaware of the frantic activity below.

Five minutes later all was ready. The *sowars* stole back to where Jones was waiting with his matchlock, trying to work out where Lieutenant Bold might be with the women. Suddenly, startlingly, there came the hoot of an English barn owl.

It was the signal! The rescue had reached the wall. It was now or never. Jones raised the matchlock, aimed at the centre base of the gate where his troopers had piled a great heap of *bhoosa,* and prayed as he pulled the trigger.

The darkness was split by a slash of scarlet flame. The ancient weapon slammed against Jones' shoulder, and from above a startled voice cried, '*Khon hy?*' The red-hot musket ball sliced into the fodder, hit the gate and dropped back into the pile, which started to glow immediately. The *sowars* cheered. Already the first greedy little blue flames were beginning to lick upwards.

'*Yih Angrezi hy?*' another angry-startled voice demanded from above, as dark faces under turbans peered down at the flames.

'Of course, we're damned English!' Jones cried angrily, ramming home another charge, hoping that Bold was now heaving the women and nippers over the wall. 'When I give the order,' he commanded at the top of his voice, as if leading a whole battalion to the assault, 'open fire... *Fire!*'

He squeezed off a shot at a sentry poised

above the gate, clearly outlined by the leaping flames. The man screamed, flung up his arms as if climbing an invisible ladder, then disappeared backwards into the courtyard.

That did it. In an instant all was confusion along the wall overlooking the great gate. Sentries ran back and forth crying in panic, *'The English attack ... sound the alarm ... the English attack!'* A wild fire fight broke out. Scarlet flame stabbed the darkness on all sides. Musket balls hissed through the night, as the whole length of the gate was engulfed by flames. Somewhere a bugle blared. There came the sound of running feet – many running feet. Jones knew he could not wait any longer. Firing one last shot, he yelled above the angry snap-and-crackle of the small arms battle, *'Charge!!...'* and with a cheeky grin on his wizened face, indicated that his men should run not forward but *back* – for the river.

6

Much later, three months after those dramatic events in Central India, in fact, the *Old Thunderer* would report in its issue of 6 September 1816:

As our Troops were crossing an Arm of the River Sipra, the Enemy's left was brought forward in anticipation of an attack and a destructive fire of grape and shell was opened upon the British. Encouraged, however, by the gallant example of Sir John Malcolm and Lieutenant-Colonel McGregor Murray, the Royal Scots rushed forward in the face of this tremendous fire and the Village and the Batteries were carried at the point of the Bayonet. The enemy's artillerymen were resolute and stood their ground until they were finally bayoneted.

While the British were victorious at this point, the enemy's Right was overpowered and his Centre gave way upon the appearance of Sepoy Brigade ascending confidently from the margin of the Sipra. While the Rest of his troops occupying a position where their camp stood also fled on the gradual advance of the British forces, who came on firing, with a Cloud of smoke rolling before them. In taking the guns the Royals had Lieutenant McCleod killed and Lieutenants McGregor and Campbell wounded. Their other losses were only Forty men.

The remnants of Holkar's forces fled to Ramporra, a large Walled town in the heart of the Province of Malwa, one of the innumerable places called after Ram, the Hindoo demigod. In the pursuit which was continued along both banks of the Sipra by

Sir John Campbell and Captain Grant immense Booty was taken, including many elephants and hundreds of camels.

These Holkar Mahrattas now agreed to, and hastily concluded a Treaty of Peace, placing their territories under British Protection and surrendering in Perpetuity to the Company various Districts, Forts and Ghauts.

It was here that the *Times'* writer expressed some surprise at Lord Hastings' next action:

It is of some concern that the Governor General did not then proceed to invade further the Territory of these Mahratta Princelings so as to ensure that the newly concluded Treaty was accorded to. Instead, for reasons which are still not known here in the Capital, My Lord Hastings has now ventured into the mountain fastnesses of the tiny and remote state of Burrapore. New Intelligence from India will undoubtedly explain this startling and surprising new Manoeuvre in due course.

By the time the news correspondent discovered the reasons for 'this startling and surprising new Manoeuvre', the state of Burrapore would have been long passed into British control.

After his victory on the Sipra and the surrender of the Mahratta princes, Lord

Hastings decided on a calculated risk. The monsoon period, which would hamper large-scale military operations, was not far off. Daily the air was stifling hot with never a wisp of breeze to stir the steamy air. In the grey sky the sun was a dull copper ball like a penny glimpsed at the bottom of a green-scummed village pond. These were the signs that the great rains were approaching.

That was the first reason for his change of strategy. The second was the surprise appearance of a battered little dhow on the Sipra, its sail ragged with the holes made by hundreds of musket balls, carrying half a hundred people who had been long thought dead. John Bold and his party had finally reached the British lines; and with him he brought the news that there was a great chief of the Pindarees, thought to be still with the Ranee in the Fort of Burrapore.

As an excited Lord Hastings told an emaciated, bronzed John on that first afternoon of his arrival, 'If we can smash Cheethoo and his Pindarees *now*' – his dark eyes gleamed in his monkeylike face – 'we can deal with Central India at our leisure. The threat that the Pindarees pose to our flank and to the Presidency of Madras will be banished for ever!'

Now, one week later, Hastings met together with his staff to finalize his plans for the surprise march on Burrapore. But first he met Captain John Bold (promoted on the spot for his bravery in rescuing the hostages), immaculate in a new uniform, the commander of a reconstituted Bold's Horse which had been brought up to the strength of a full squadron with recruits from other native cavalry regiments. Hastings eyed the young captain and nodded his approval. Whatever puppy fat Bold had once possessed had vanished in those months of imprisonment. Now his face, burned almost black by a week's voyage down the Burra, was lean and hard, the blue eyes seeming almost too large. Captain Bold looked like an officer who had gone through hell – and was prepared to do it again.

'Bold,' Hastings said, as outside the troops toiled by in the midday heat, sweating and cursing, and gallopers came and went bearing their dispatches, 'I would dearly have loved to send you back to Madras for a rest. You richly deserve it. But your presence in the van of my army is vital to its success. Only *you* know the terrain, the conditions pertaining in the entourage of that she-devil in Burrapore. You understand?' His simian features softened into a momentary smile.

'I understand, sir,' John replied dutifully, and dismissed his daydream of returning to Musulipatan to a hero's welcome and Georgina's arms. It would be many a weary month of campaigning before he could do that.

Enthusiastically Hastings slammed his hairy fist down on the table. 'If we can capture or kill this Cheethoo fellah of yours, then the power of the Pindaree is broken for good! And you, John Bold, will identify him for me. It is vital. Now, I have great matters of strategy to discuss and you must go.'

Then, surprisingly, instead of accepting John's salute, the Governor General shook his hand. 'You will go far in the Company's service, John Bold. Destiny has put its mark upon you. Disappointments,' he added enigmatically, 'you will undoubtedly suffer. But always remember, however much adversity attacks you, *destiny has put its mark upon you!*'

With that John left, stepping out into the cloying heat of the pre-monsoon period, brow set in a puzzled frown. What had Lord Hastings meant?

His bewilderment was compounded by Major Tomkins, who arrived in the middle of Hastings' last conference, his horse lathered in sweat, he himself covered in white dust so that his red-rimmed eyes seemed to be peering out of a mask. John caught him after he had delivered his dispatches from the Presidency of Madras and asked, 'Sir, did your route take you through Musulipatan, if I may ask?'

Wearily Major Tomkins nodded. 'Yes, it did, Bold.'

'Sir, may I venture to ask if you saw the

Collector and Miss Lanham?' John hardly could contain himself.

But Major Tomkins was oddly evasive and, later, when the great betrayal had taken place, John knew why. 'I did chance upon him for a moment or two, Bold,' he answered, avoiding John's gaze. 'I saw Miss Lanham, too, for an equally short period.'

'And how was she, sir?'

Tomkins waved his hands in an airy manner, trying to cover his embarrassment. 'Oh well, I suppose, well... And now, my dear Bold, you must excuse me. I must really try to get a bath and clear myself of this wretched dust.' And he tugged at the head of his weary mount and departed, leaving John in even more bewilderment...

One day later the march on Burrapore commenced. Line after line of *sepoys* marched stolidly through the dust and heat, followed by six-pounders drawn by lumbering oxen; *tongas* jolted up and down in the ruts, laden with supplies; then came the rumbling, ponderous elephants weighted down with water; while to right and left flank the cavalry probed, sending picquets to every hilltop to warn against any surprise attack by the Pindarees.

Mile after mile, hour after hour, the long columns plodded under the dull glare of a murderous sun, their agony broken only by a few minutes' stop where they could seek the blessing of shade and the boon of a gulp of tepid water. Men cursed; men sobbed; men fell to their knees in ankle-deep white dust and sand and were beaten mercilessly to their feet by red-faced NCOs; men collapsed, as if poleaxed, from heat stroke, never to rise again; men went mad.

At the end of each day the swaying columns moved at snail's pace, each man's mesmerized gaze on the feet of the man in front; and every night those who had survived the day's terrible march collapsed on the unyielding earth, too tired even to eat, seeking only oblivious sleep before the march commenced again.

It grew even hotter, the grass a parched yellow, the mangoes brown and dry of juice. The water in the wells of the abandoned villages was lukewarm and tasted of cinders.

Now the wind burned. Men, even the *sepoys*, marched with rags wrapped round their scorched faces. The wind brought clouds of dust particles that stung faces like a myriad tiny cuts from a sharp razor. It coated everything with a fine white powder that burrowed into their throats, eyes, ears.

When the winds eased, the coppery sun hovered, shimmering in an incandescent, merciless sky where vultures circled slowly, ominously, *waiting...* There was prey enough for them now. Behind the toiling columns the trail was littered with men struck down by the cholera, dying in their own filth and muck and vomit; men felled by sun stroke, turning black within minutes; men stricken with a dozen different fevers, their faces moving writhing masks of loathsome blue-black flies. Lord Hastings was paying the price for his bold manoeuvre – one that could only be counted in blood.

In the van, Bold's Horse fared better than the rest. The *sowars* did not have to suffer dust raised by marchers in front. Too, they had the first pick of the water in the abandoned villages lining their route, gauging its suitability by its smell – and whether or not the fleeing villages had deposited dead dogs in it.

Thus it was that while the rest of the invading army marched like automatons, John's troopers kept alert, scouring the rugged, barren countryside for the first sign of Cheethoo's followers. But there were none. In the whole of the first week, they saw not a single person. The whole of Burrapore seemed completely deserted.

Sergeant Jones, the veteran of so many campaigns in India, was not fooled. 'They're there all right, sir,' he remarked more than once, tapping the end of his long, peeling red nose sagely, 'I can smell 'em. They're right on to us, never you do fear, sir.'

Late in the afternoon on the eighth day the shrill tones of a bugler rang out a mile ahead of the main body of Bold's Horse from a small forward patrol.

Hastily John swung up his glass. Dark figures on the ridge to the right sprang into focus – riders, dressed in the native fashion. The enemy.

'Pindarees, sir?' Jones asked at his side.

Suddenly there was the glint of silver accoutrements and John grunted, 'No, their equipment is burnished. They're European.'

'The frog-eaters, sir?' Jones ventured grimly as the distant watchers turned their mounts and disappeared down the far slope of the ridge.

'Yes, it's the French all right, Sergeant.' Nom de Dieu's hard-bitten professionals.'

Now as they pushed ever further north, the heat easing a little as they entered the Burra mountains, the watchers appeared time and again. Like stark black phantoms they hovered on the high ground, their mounts motionless, observing the invaders. There was something eerie about their strange brooding observation. More than once red-faced staff officers exclaimed angrily, 'Why don't the damned froggies attack?... What are they waiting for?... It's damned ungentle-manlike to stare at us like that!'

Twice Bold was ordered by Hastings him-self to send out a patrol to apprehend some of the French observers. The first patrol, commanded by a relatively inexperienced *rissaldar,* did not come within a mile before the French took to their heels and with their fine thoroughbred Arabs easily outdistanced the *sowars.*

The second patrol at dawn next day was equally a failure, but a disastrous one. It was commanded by a sixteen-year-old cornet, a dark-eyed eager boy named da Costa, who said he was a Portuguese, but who John guessed was probably a half-breed. Like many of his kind, neither Indian nor European, he had volunteered for the Company's services, John surmised, in order to find a place where he could belong.

That dawn da Costa sallied forth in great style after a couple of riders were seen on a height about two miles away. This time the riders stood their ground and fired their carbines, though out of range, at the patrol.

Da Costa's enthusiasm at the prospect of action knew no bounds. He stood upright in his stirrups, dark eyes flashing, and waving his sword yelled, *'Charge!'* Like a dark V, as John observed through his glass, the dozen riders shot forward, swords held straight out in front, carried away by the wild excitement of the charge – all flying hooves, wild yells, wind whistling by the face, the rattle of equipment.

Exhilarated by the crazy primeval madness of the impending clash, the British did not see the large body of cavalry hiding in the *nullah* to the left of their quarry.

'Look out!' John cried as he spotted them in his glass.

But da Costa and his men were too far away to hear. Too late they saw the trap as, with shouts of *'Vive la France ... salauds ... à l'attaque, mes braves'* the French horse surged out of the canyon, sabres flashing, knees and spurs digging deep into the flanks of their mounts.

John's men hadn't a chance. Here and there swords clashed. For a moment or two the young *sowars* parried the brutal thrusts and slashes of Napoleon's veterans. But only for a moment. They were cut down mercilessly, until finally the sorely wounded da Costa cried, *'Withdraw ... withdraw immediately...'*

Ten minutes later as Cornet da Costa died in his arms, John Bold knew with the absolute certainty of a vision that the Ranee of Burrapore and Cheethoo, chief of the Pindarees, were going to make their stand at Burrapore. Lord Hastings had to be prepared for a prolonged siege of the Gibraltar of the East – and it was only a matter of days now before the monsoon broke.

This cruel dawn, which had cost Bold's Horse seven lives, Hastings' strength had been tested and found wanting. Now with torrential rains due at any moment, rains that could bog down his whole army, Lord

Hastings had to discover some stratagem to capture Burrapore swiftly. The alternative was a long siege, with the possibility that the Mahratta princes to his rear would revolt once more. It seemed that the she-devil of Burrapore had the upper hand once again...

7

On the horizon lightning stabbed the grey brooding sky in jagged scarlet slashes. Thunder rumbled ominously. They waited, as if inside a bakehouse oven. The very air was heavy with the approaching storm.

But the eyes of the watchers on the hilltop were fixed exclusively on what was happening to their front, before the fortress of Burrapore. Now as the massed bands of the army played 'The Downfall of Paris' and back and forth across the valley the bugles echoed and re-echoed their urgent warnings, a brigade of *sepoys* was advancing stolidly.

They had abandoned their packs and other heavy equipment. Now in four lines, with their officers in front and the flags unfurled, they moved forward, bayonets fixed, keeping perfect step, moving in to the assault.

Lord Hastings removed his hat and waving it three times about his head, cried,

'Pray, let the artillery commence!'

Swiftly his order was relayed and in a moment some sixty artillery pieces opened fire. Black balls of sudden death hurtled through the air as the sweating, half-naked gunners sponged, loaded and rammed, and those four lines of rigid infantry approached ever closer to the main gate of the lower fort.

Standing on the hillock behind Lord Hastings, awaiting whatever orders might come, John felt a shiver run down his spine, and the hairs at the back of his skull stood erect.

To his front the high walls of the fortress were already pockmarked and slashed by the British cannonade. Timber, splintered into matchwood, vomited upwards. Stone and smoking debris came slithering down as shot after shot slammed against the ramparts. But not a single shot had yet been fired by the defenders.

John strained his ears and just caught the urgent rattle of the brigade's kettle drums. Faintly he heard the cries of its officers as they waved their swords, and the pace of the advancing men quickened noticeably. They were getting very close now. It would not be long before they charged, aiming to reach the dead ground immediately beneath those terrible high, crenellated walls.

A rocket hissed spluttering, red and angry into the leaden sky. For a moment it hung there, colouring their upturned faces an unnatural hue, before hissing down spent. It was the signal to the horse artillery.

There was a furious blare of trumpets. At the gallop, horses stretched unnaturally long in their traces, gunwheels bucking over the uneven ground, gunners on their caissons hanging on grimly, a battery of light guns raced after the infantry. They would give the final support for the assault.

'*Capital ... capital!*' Lord Hastings said in high delight, slapping his raised knee. 'Did you ever see such a splendid sight?... *Capital!*'

Still not a single shot came from the fort. It was as if they had already abandoned it. But John had spied their heads behind the ramparts. They were waiting for the right moment.

Thunder rumbled and echoed across the valley in ever-increasing strength. The storm would not be long coming now.

To the front of the *sepoy* brigade their general raised himself high in his stirrups to take one last look at his men, stretched as far as the eye could see to left and right. He tugged at the bit and his beautiful white stallion reared up, pawing the air. It was sheer drama, like one of those portraits romanticizing the bloody reality of the Battle of Waterloo. The general called out, and with great deliberation pointed his sword at the fort. In a sudden flash of lightning the weapon gleamed bright silver. A great bass cheer rose from the *sepoys* and they surged forward in a kind of shambling run. *The final assault had commenced!*

On the hilltop, Hastings' staff responded with a cheer of their own and again the Governor General slapped his knee exultantly. Everything was going according to plan. Victory over the she-devil of Burrapore was just around the corner.

The defenders let them come on, pelting towards the great ditch which ran to the front of the lower fort. Now the covering artillery had ceased firing. It was too dangerous for their own men. Soon the *sepoys* would be down in the ditch. Sappers would be thrusting scaling ladders against the walls and the *sepoys* would be clambering up and over the top. John felt himself sweating with tension and praying fervently that they would make it.

The defenders' reaction came with startling abruptness. Little cheery-red lights winked suddenly the whole length of the ramparts. From inside the courtyard came the deep throaty thud-thud of mortars. Rockets shrilled over the walls, red, angry, vindictive.

Suddenly great gaps appeared in the ranks of the attackers. *Sepoys* were going down everywhere, piling up in heaps as their officers and NCOs slashed furiously at them with the flats of their blades, urging them on. What now happened was no longer war, but mass murder. Caught out in the open, without artillery support, the *sepoys* were easy targets even for the worst marksmen. Cannonballs, grape and chain-shot hurtled into them. Within five minutes, it was calculated, the brigade lost half its effectives.

But still the attackers did not break. The years of iron-hard brutal discipline, and loyalty to their officers and regiments, paid off. They stood their ground. But John, peering dismayed through his glass, could see that the steam had gone out of the attack. The men were milling, trying not to step on their dead and dying fellows who littered the shattered, steaming ground everywhere, obviously confused and knowing not what to do.

'Take a hold of them, man!' Hastings roared, face brick red with fury, 'Get a grip on 'em! Come on now, be stout fellahs ... *keep on moving!*'

The general leading tried, he really did. John saw him momentarily through drifting gunsmoke, as he reared up his horse and waved his sword towards the battlements. Here and there more determined groups of *sepoys* surged forward once more. But the impetus had gone. Most of the survivors simply stood dazed or crouched miserably under the lethal hail of fire like lost children. And already from within the fortress came the clatter of hooves indicating a new danger.

Hastings was always quick to make decisions; it had been the saving of him and the Company's arms on many a bloody battle-field. 'Bold ... Captain Bold,' he cried urgently. 'Take your squadron and see what you can do!'

'Sir!'

John doubled to his waiting horse. 'Bugler, sound the alarm!'

The young *sowar* raised the silver instrument to his lips. Without even spitting, he sounded the urgent call. Within seconds, or so it seemed, Bold's Horse was surging over the battle-littered ground at a fine lick, heading for the smoke and confusion of battle.

The first stragglers from the decimated *sepoy* brigade were already running to the rear, weapons cast aside, eyes wild and staring in contorted, glistening brown faces. Unseeingly they brushed by the cavalry, stopped neither by taunts, threats nor blows until Jones called in the native language, 'Let those sons of a serpent run!'

A group of four *sepoys* came towards him. They had made a stretcher of their muskets on which they bore the general. Half the side of his head had been blown off. John swallowed hard at the great gaping scarlet wound through which he could see the white shattered bone and the grey mass of the general's brain still pulsating. Next to the makeshift stretcher, clutching the general's hand like a distraught child leading an injured parent home, was a cornet, bloody bandage round his head, sobbing heartbrokenly.

'What news, Cornet?' John gasped.

But all he got from the youth, uttered in an eerie unreal little voice, was, 'Calamity... There has been a great calamity ... *calamity...*'

Even as they galloped on, shells now bursting to left and right, John seemed to still hear that uncanny voice: *'Calamity!'*

Now the *sepoys* were streaming back in total defeat, officers and sergeants among them attempting to cover their retreat, turning at regular intervals and firing their pistols into the fog of war at their heels.

John knew he had to protect the rear of the fleeing survivors. If Pindaree cavalry got among the *sepoys* they'd slaughter the lot. Raising himself so that all his men could see, he yelled at the top of his voice, 'Form a skirmish line ... extend the column... Sergeant Jones ... *rissaldar* ... form a skirmish line – *at once!*'

Despite the noise, they understood. Urging their horses through the retreating *sepoys,* some of them now dragging their wounded, they formed up in extended order; while above them the drum-roll of thunder grew ever louder.

Now they were almost through the *sepoy* brigade. Everywhere in the churned-up earth, scattered in the unreal poses of those who had been violently done to death, lay their comrades in arms.

The battlements loomed out of the smoke. The firing had almost ceased – the defenders were not going to fire on their own cavalry, which would soon emerge; the clatter of their horses in the courtyard was all too obvious.

With a loud huzzah, skidding and fighting to keep upright, jostling and crowded together in a great sweating mass of horseflesh, white and black men cursing each other, kicking out with their spurs to gain space from the other riders, the Pindarees' cavalry burst into the open.

Immediately they fanned out, faces wild with excitement, swinging their swords, digging their spurs cruelly into their panicked mounts. Here and there brave little groups of *sepoys* stood and fought. But after the first burst of musket fire, which felled a good half dozen of the riders, the cavalry were upon them, slicing and cutting mercilessly, hacking them to the ground in moments.

Now the enemy cavalry surged forward, crouched low over their horses, carried away by the mad lust of the chase. *Sepoys* went down everywhere, sliced from behind, howling with absolute agony as they fell, skulls cleaved, arms severed, great gaping scarlet holes skewered in their backs.

'Halt! ... *fire!*' John commanded his bugler

as the enemy horse streamed to his right, seeing nothing but the fleeing *sepoys* and exposing the whole of their flank. His troopers needed no urging. Hardly had the second bugle call ceased than they began firing right into the whirling ranks of the unsuspecting enemy. Riders went down everywhere, slammed from their saddles or slumped on their horses' necks and carried away from the battle – dead already. Others fell with foot trapped in a stirrup and were thrashed screaming along the uneven ground, bumping and jolting, mouths vomiting blood until they collapsed like boneless dummies.

But the rest reacted quickly enough. Now more and more of them were reining their sweat-lathered steeds to a skidding halt and were pointing in the direction of the motionless line of troopers firing into their flank. For what seemed a long time, though it could only have been a matter of moments, they remained motionless thus, taking fire and casualties and not even seeming to notice until finally an order was shouted. The whole mass began to wheel round to face the *sowars*, the manoeuvre accompanied by cursing and much shouing.

John raised his sword in warning as his troopers worked feverishly to reload before the enemy charged. Even as he did so, he heard the first soft hiss as a raindrop splattered on the parched dust at his horse's feet.

'They'll cheer first!' he cried so that all could hear. 'The French always do. Then they'll charge!'

'You heard the officer!' Jones cried loyally. 'And don't let the squadron down. Stand fast when they come.' The little Welshman eyed the massed ranks of white and black cavalry facing them – outnumbering Bold's Horse by at least ten to one – and rattled off a quick prayer. At least, he consoled himself as the enemy formed up in their final attack formation, I'll die on hossback and not in a prison cell!

John tensed. The enemy were almost ready, their officers filing through the massed columns to the front. Flag-bearers followed them, the first drops of the monsoon rain pattering off their ornate silver breastplates. He raised his sword once more. Behind him his troopers, trying to control their skittish horses with pressure from their knees, raised their carbines and took aim. John licked his suddenly parched lips and prepared to shout what could be his final command, for Bold's Horse did not stand a chance against such a mass, especially when it contained Nom de Dieu's hard-bitten rakes.

'Prepare to fire!' he called, hearing his own voice as if it were a long, long way off, at the far end of some great tunnel.

His troopers' fingers curled and whitened on the triggers of their short carbines, one eye closed, the other glued to the sight. It could only be a matter of moments now. The patter of raindrops increased. The air was becoming noticeably cooler, too, and the wind beginning to whip up sand devils which danced and toyed with the silent faces of the dead.

'*HURRAH!*' That great expected cheer startled John all the same. His horse attempted to bolt. Tugging cruelly at the bit, he cried, 'Stand fast, men... Stand fast ... *here they come!*'

'*À l'attaque!*' The French war cry rose from many a hoarse throat. Next moment the enemy cavalrymen were streaming across the plain, eyes narrowed against the sudden rain, sabres stretched outright, parallel to the flying manes. It was a fine, brave sight. But John had no time for the terrible beauty of the battlefield. Above the great thunder of flying hooves, he bellowed, '*FIRE!*'

A hundred and fifty carbines spoke as one. The volley struck the attackers like a solid iron punch. Horses and riders went down on all sides, bowled over in full gallop, men whipped from the saddle as if by magic, flung to one side, screaming in their death agonies. Horses went to their knees, great scarlet patches appearing suddenly on their flanks as their riders cursed and screamed, digging spurs into mounts which were dying under them.

Great gaps appeared in the charging ranks, men and broken horses on the ground everywhere with those coming on behind skidding helplessly into the pile-up. Rapidly John's troopers rammed their carbines into the leather bucket holsters and grabbed for their swords. The attackers – those who had survived that terrible volley – were almost upon them now. The fight to the death was about to commence.

John fired his pistol at a swarthy-faced Frenchman only fifty yards away, and watched him slide from the saddle almost casually, to disappear beneath the flying hooves of the following horsemen.

John threw his now useless pistol to the ground and gripped his sword in a hand wet with sweat, waiting for the great shock of the charge, holding his mount steady between tight knees.

Suddenly he gasped, peering amazed through the falling rain. There was no mistaking that over-large brown beaver hat and those tight-fitting buckskins which revealed the gentler female curve of the thigh.

It was the Ranee – the Ranee of Burrapore – personally leading the charge, a great black dragoon moustache painted on her lip. On another person it would have looked absurd, but not on the Ranee, whose face was set in lethal determination. The she-devil of Burrapore was intent on slaughtering the lot of them.

'Prepare ... prepare to withstand a charge,' he croaked, knowing now that he would never survive this charge.

In that very moment the monsoon broke in all its terrible fury. The wind struck across the plain at a hundred miles an hour, bringing a howling dust through which the tropical rain belted in penny-size missiles. Then solid sheets poured down, deadening every sound bar its own persistent hiss and banshee whine.

Saved by a miracle, John didn't hesitate. Bending his head close to Sergeant Jones' cheek, the wind tearing the words from his mouth, his face dripping with raindrops, lashed by rain, he screamed, *'Retire!'*

John nodded with an exaggerated movement, his turban sodden and limp already.

The squadron turned while scarlet shots seared the howling grey gloom in vain, for the Ranee and her men could no longer see them although they were only yards away. Skidding in the sudden glutinous morass, bent against the storm, Bold's Horse slipped away, saved at the eleventh hour.

8

Outside Hastings' big tent it rained: a steady, never-ending downpour that filled the *nullahs* and creeks with tawny water, swirling the dead, the rotting corpses, the debris of battle into the raging Burra River. For two days the monsoon had held sway and Hastings' camp had turned into a sea of mud.

The monsoon brought the usual fevers and ailments, prickly heat, tick typhus, malaria and dysentery. Day and night men squatted miserably all over the camp, evacuating their bowels, moaning with the pain of their rotten guts, sometimes falling over unconscious to disappear slowly, but surely, into that mucilaginous swamp.

Supplies were failing to come up from the rear. Water was polluted. Even the hardtack was soggy and full of weevils. As Sergeant Jones had moaned to John as he squatted, racked with dysentery, 'Nothing's going in, sir – *and everything's going out!*' And again his skinny bones had been racked by another painful spasm.

These had been two days of doubt and indecision for Lord Hastings. Due to Captain Bold's daring – and good luck – the defeated *sepoy* brigade had not been wiped out altogether, and Lord Hastings treasured every man who was still capable of bearing arms; the army was melting from disease and fevers at an alarming rate. Yet what was he going to do with those men, that was the question uppermost in his mind, as the damned rain thudded down. Should he withdraw to the south while there was still time, or should he attempt one more attack? As long as the fortress of Burrapore was under siege, the Pindarees would be unable to launch an assault on the Presidency of Madras; there was no room for them to manoeuvre in the tight valley of the Burra. That was, at least, one consolation.

But how long could he maintain the siege with his men falling sick? And there was always the danger, while his back was turned, of the treacherous Mahratta princes rising again. It was all damnably irritating and perplexing.

Of course, there were among his staff the 'bookkeepers', as he called them contemptuously, who advised retaining a pretence of a siege at Burrapore, while the bulk of his army marched back to the frontier. But he didn't like to put his forces in penny packets like that. The aim was to concentrate, for in the end, spreading your forces meant you didn't have sufficient strength anywhere.

On the afternoon of the third day after the

attack, while the warm rain still sheeted down, Major Tomkins, himself pale and wan and racked with the 'the thin shits', as the common soldiers called them, reported to the Governor General that Captain Bold was requesting an interview on a matter of some importance. Managing to summon up a feeble smile, Major Tomkins said, 'Our young hot-head has a plan, sir.'

Hastings gave a feeble smile of his own, for he felt the first headache which heralded the onset of malaria. 'Half the damned camp has got plans, Tomkins,' he said. 'But do show him in. Bold deserves the courtesy at least of being listened to. He is a brave young man.'

A few moments later John was ushered in, his uniform as wet and as mud-spattered as everyone else's. But although he looked bedraggled, there was no mistaking his hard determined look, and Hastings thought once again: *Nomen est omen.*

'Well, Bold,' Hastings commenced immediately, 'you have a plan, I hear.'

'Yessir,' John answered eagerly. 'If I could request a chart of the fortifications?'

The Governor General nodded and Tomkins spread out a map of Burrapore and its fort on the rough trestle table.

'You see here, sir, to the right of the main gate?'

'Yes.'

'Well, here – where the wall runs close to

the Burra – is an area of dead ground both *inside* and *outside* the fortifications.'

'What kind of dead ground, Bold?'

'The constructor of the fort must have made some mistake,' John continued, 'for this area – *here* – is out of musket shot to both sides. And only those men on the wall immediately above any attackers would be able to spot them.'

Hastings whistled softly. 'You mean the defenders cannot bring any enfilading fire to bear from left and right of that spot?'

'Correct, sir,' John answered, eyes full of energy and purpose. 'Of course, they could fire, but they would be firing blind, with most of their balls flying above the heads of the attackers.'

Hastings flashed a wild look at Tomkins, and the Major nodded hastily, as if to confirm what Hastings was thinking.

'But how are we to get the men to this dead ground? They would have to cross the whole front of the fort under enemy fire.' Hastings frowned, as if angry with himself for raising such objections.

John licked his lips and pointed to the map again. 'We would not need to do that,' he replied, 'but cross the Burra – here – about a mile away from the fort and out of its sight, take this track on the right bank – again out of sight of the fort. I know, sir, because we used this route when we made our escape. Then we would cross the Burra once more – *here* – directly opposite that area of dead ground – *and attack....!*'

'Don't like it, sir,' Sir John Campbell snorted in his dour downright Scots fashion. 'Don't like it one bit.'

'I agree, sir,' General Doveton, the victor of Nagpore, chipped in equally firmly, 'there are too many imponderables.'

'What?' Hastings snapped.

Outside, the world rocked and shook crazily, lightning shot great burning violet bolts back and forth across the Burra, the whole valley seemed to quiver. The rain continued.

'Well, sir,' Doveton said, 'this plan entails two doubtful river crossings in terrible weather. Supposing the crossings were successful–'

John opened his mouth to object, but a glum Lord Hastings raised his hand for him to desist.

'–Then we will have to storm the fort with' – he shrugged – 'how many men? A battalion at the most, for that is about all we would be able to get twice across the Burra.'

'Aye,' Sir John agreed, 'and the loss of one battalion, which would be insufficient to overwhelm the defenders, would be a serious blow, a very serious blow indeed, My Lord.'

The meeting relapsed into silence while Hastings brooded. He could see what the objectors meant, and, God, how he wished his damned head would stop aching so that he could think straight! In the end the Governor General gave up. 'Gentlemen,' he said wearily, 'let me think the matter over before I make my decision.' He looked pointedly at Bold, who obviously had more to say, indicating by his gaze that the young officer should remain silent.

When they had gone, splashing out into the rain and mud, he lay on his bed, already breaking out into the first sweats of malaria, a sorely troubled man. For he knew that if he made the wrong decision now, he risked the whole presence of the British in Central India. Perhaps the rot might not even stop there. Madras might go, Calcutta perhaps, *even Bombay!* He dabbed his sweat-lathered brow and moaned. *The whole of British India was at risk!*

Miserably he tossed and turned on his narrow camp bed, racked by indecision... But it was not only in the British camp that there was indecision and discord. A mile away from where Lord Hastings tossed and turned on his trestle bed the Ranee of Burrapore and Cheethoo of the Pindarees faced each other, the one flushed and excited, the other hard-faced and glacial.

Ever since that wild exhilarating ride with her cavalry when they had repulsed the English, the Ranee had refused to take off her male attire, even in Cheethoo's presence, and the Chief of the Pindarees didn't like it. He was used to the usual complacent Indian woman, who regarded the male as her lord and master. The sight of this woman, princess as she might be with power of life and death over her subjects, upset him – though, as always, he was careful to conceal his anger.

He said, while the fat stupid white woman, who seemed to be the Ranee's current favourite, sulked on a pile of cushions in the background, eating sweetmeats, 'Ranee, you have had your pleasure.' He looked at her male dress pointedly.

'It was a success, wasn't it, Cheethoo!' she retorted hotly, face flushed.

'The time for such games is over. Now we must make decisions about the future.'

'What decisions?' The Ranee glanced over at Alice, who had just spat out another sweetmeat half eaten – sulking because she was being ignored. The Ranee told herself that Alice was a very stupid person. Still it gave her a secret thrill to know that this white woman was hers totally, more than any other woman would be under the thrall of a husband. She, a brown woman, had made that foolish white woman do things to her that a husband could never dare dream about.

'What are we going to do next, Ranee?' he said coldly, his face revealing nothing of his thoughts.

'We sit the siege out here until either the British leave or the Mahratta princes go to war with them again, and then we seize our own chance.' She opened and closed her hand, a fierce look in her eyes. At that moment he thought of her as a spider waiting for its prey to walk into its trap.

'What if neither takes place?'

'*It will*, rest assured, Cheethoo. Either one or the other. One only needs to have good nerves, doesn't one?'

He flushed a little, knowing what she implied. 'My nerves are exceedingly good, Ranee. But here in Burrapore there is no room for me and my people to manoeuvre. We are the ones who are trapped.'

She hesitated a moment, as if she might be having difficulty in formulating her words, but the fires which burned within her took control and she blurted out, 'You mean really, you wish to ride and *loot?* The cause of India means nothing to you!'

'*India!*' Cheethoo shrugged his broad shoulders cynically. 'What is India?'

Her eyes gleamed dangerously. 'There are too many like you Cheethoo,' she hissed, her voice now full of menace. 'Ever since the Europeans came and destroyed the old Moghul Empire, princes and chiefs have concerned themselves only with their own petty kingdoms. They have forgotten that our great country exists. Now at last we have

341

a chance to redress the balance, drive the British out of our country for ever and begin restoring our ancient glories and power once more.' She stopped for lack of breath, her breasts tied down beneath the man's shirt heaving.

Cheethoo remained unmoved. 'The British came as conquerors and imposed their will on the people. The Moghuls before them did the same. In all our history we have been united only by outsiders.' He sighed, as if it was too much of an effort to continue, but he did so all the same; this foolish perverted woman needed to be taught the harsh facts of life. 'Ranee, we are *not* a people and we are *not* a country. We are a collection of *many* peoples and *many* countries. They can only be *forced* into unity. You and your Mahratta princes will never be able to do that forcing. Why delude yourselves?' Unable to restrain his contempt for her and her foolish woman's ideas, he hawked and spat on the floor at her feet.

On the pile of silken pillows Alice paused in her chewing. She did not understand the words the male pig had uttered; but she recognized the deadly insult well enough. She gawped open-mouthed.

The Ranee's hand fell down to the little jewelled sabre at her waist.

Cheethoo looked down at her haughtily, his hands well away from his own fearsome sword. His look told the Ranee everything. The brigand was contemptuous of her – a woman playing games. She decided then that she would eliminate Cheethoo, Chief of the Pindarees.

It was thus that Padmini came upon them: a scene from a melodramatic Indian play with the actors frozen into their positions for ever; that stupid English whore with her mouth open, dribbling sweetmeats; the tall haughty Pindaree chief staring down at her mistress challengingly; and the Ranee herself, face flushed with rage, hand on sword, eyes flashing murder.

Hastily she raised her hands to her forehead in salute, aware of crisis. For a long time the Chief of the Pindarees had been quietly disgusted by the Ranee's behaviour, but he had tolerated it because he needed her for his attacks south. Now that tolerance had come to an end. The tension and hatred between them was tangible; she could smell it in the air. 'We have intelligence, Ranee,' she said swiftly.

For a moment her words did not seem to register. The actors in this strange little drama remained motionless. Then the Ranee shook her hand, released the hold on her sword and said flatly, not taking her burning gaze off Cheethoo, 'What intelligence? From where?'

'From the English camp. They are preparing something.'

'What?' the Ranee asked in that same toneless voice.

'We know not what, mistress. But our spies tell us the English are planning some move.'

While she spoke Cheethoo made up his mind. He realized now that the Ranee of Burrapore had been using him all along for her own purposes. It was time – for better or worse – to disassociate himself from her. Let that crazy woman face the future, whatever it brought, triumph or tragedy, without him. He raised his hands to forehead in a parting greeting and stalked out.

For what seemed a long time no one stirred. Finally, Alice could stand the brooding silence no longer. She had understood little, only that there had been a break between her beloved mistress and the big, evil-looking brigand. She said, beginning to chew the sweetmeat once more, 'You showed him, my darling... You gave him an earful all right!' She popped another sweetmeat into her slack mouth and began chewing happily.

Padmini shot her a murderous look, but the Ranee ignored her; she had other things on her mind. 'You think that he will abandon us?' she asked sharply.

Padmini nodded, a worried look on her face now.

Like some caricature of an ancient Indian warlord the Ranee paced the chamber, hand on sword.

Padmini waited. Alice waded through the sweetmeats, totally unaware that a world was falling apart all around her. Finally Padmini could stand the tension no longer. 'Mistress,' she quavered, her love for the Ranee filling her soft voice with anxiety, 'will you now declare a truce with the English – while there is still time?'

The Ranee paused in her pacing and stared as if she was seeing her chamberlain for the very first time. '*A truce!*' she echoed, and threw back her head and laughed out loud – and there was something crazy about that laugh now. '*Never*, Padmini. I am a princess of India. A princess of India does not make a truce. No, never! A princess of India dies with her sword in her hand.'

Padmini's head drooped. Slowly great soft tears began to course down her brown cheeks.

9

Ne'er in a score-and-seven years in the King's Service in the Remote East, (wrote Sir John Campbell many years later) did I ever experience a night like that.

The Duplicity of the Eastern Native is well-known to all who have ever served in that clime. That night, however, it was exceeded by good measure. Never could there have been a night of such alarums and excursions, compounded by treachery and counter-treachery, which commenced when those brave fellows of the Army of the Deccan first crossed the raging torrent of the Burra River and set spark to the train of events that resulted in those barbaric savageries carried out by the well-known She-Devil of Burra-pore.

Even now, all these years later, I recall well the words I uttered last to Captain (now General) John Bold, as he commenced that daring undertaking on the banks of the Burra…

'Mark well, My Lord Hastings' orders!' Campbell yelled above the roar of the swollen river as John's little force, slipping and cursing in the thick mud, toiled to position the two pontoon rafts which would carry them across. 'Your objective is the main gate, *nothing else!* Once you have taken it and given the signal, we will storm the lower fort. But the capture of that gate is essential. If you fail…' The dour Scot left the rest unsaid, and despite being soaking wet and his feet freezing in the icy water, John grinned in the darkness. General Sir John Campbell had probably already written them off.

Only three hours ago Lord Hastings had come out of the malaria coma and given his decision, limiting John Bold, using his own men and one single company of native infantry, to the capture of the main gate. And promptly lapsed into unconsciousness again.

Now John hurried about his task, urging on his men, who were looking at the raging white-wild Burra with increasing apprehension. Laden down with equipment, they had little chance of surviving if one of the pontoons overturned.

The infantry were particularly fearful. Unlike Bold's Horse, they were unfamiliar with rivers. In the growing darkness they huddled in frightened groups, grumbling softly, flashing increasingly apprehensive glances at the swollen Burra; while the brawny rivermen who would paddle the pontoons across fought to steady their craft and embark the troops.

It was then that a worried voice called out of the grey gloom, 'Captain Bold ... Captain John Bold!'

He turned and started a little. It was Captain Elders. He was in rags and he smelled, and since John had last seen him his hair had turned completely white.

'Oh, hello, Elders,' he said uneasily, 'are these *sepoys* yours?'

'Yes, Bold. I volunteered my Company. I want in at the kill.' He coughed thickly and

John could see, even in that poor light, that Captain Elders was a dying man. 'Take my revenge on that female swine up there for what she has done to my poor Alice.'

John said nothing. What could he say?

'I've been ill, you see,' Elders continued, taking John's silence for assent. 'The usual fevers – or I would have been to see you earlier. Do you mind my asking ... but did she die quickly, *cleanly*, Bold?'

John wished that the earth would open up and swallow him. His mind's eye flooded with a vision of fat Alice, clad in the transparent gear of a *houri*, pawing the Ranee's hand in that perverse, possessive manner of hers. Somehow he managed to stutter, 'Yes, yes, Elders, it all went very quickly.'

'Thank God, thank God for that!' Elders said, voice choked a little, 'For poor Alice...'

At that very moment Captain Elders' 'poor Alice' was a very frightened woman. Abruptly the little world she had built for herself with the Ranee seemed to be falling apart. It had started when Cheethoo had insulted her lover by spitting at her feet. Now she realized that for the Ranee the gesture was more than an insult; it signified the end of the alliance – and the Ranee was not prepared to allow Cheethoo to leave Burrapore just like that.

As she huddled on her cushions, the

evening plate of fruit and sugar almonds forgotten in her growing fear, Alice listened as the Ranee and that great boor of a Frenchman, who had always looked at her as if he were mentally stripping the clothes off her, plotted. Although they spoke in whispers, the Frenchman's English – English was their lingua franca – was so bad, that the Ranee had repeated herself several times. More than once she heard the word 'kill' and twice she heard the Ranee say, eyes flashing fire, 'He must not escape ... he must die *this night!*'

'But why?' Alice asked when the Frenchman had swaggered out. 'Why must Cheethoo die?' She caressed the Ranee's hand, blue eyes filled with worry.

The Ranee looked at her coldly, as if she were seeing Alice for the fool she was for the first time. 'Not because he insulted me ... but because he insulted India.'

'I don't understand, dearest,' she stuttered, feeling that look like a knife.

'Imbecile!' the Ranee snapped. 'Why do I waste my time on such a fool?'

Alice's eyes filled with tears. 'But I am just a mere woman,' she simpered. 'I do not understand–'

The sudden thunder of cannon from outside the walls brought the Ranee to her feet, hand at sword. 'It seems that you are not the only fool in Burrapore this night,' she said, as outside the great drum began to beat the alarm. 'The English are attacking again. What possessed them? Do they want to fling away their stupid lives for nothing?' and with that she was gone, swaggering just like the Frenchman.

Alice stared after her open-mouthed, heart beating wildly, face white with fear. She had just been party to a planned murder. Worse – now she had lost the Ranee's love. If she had ever had it?

She had been a fool, of course, a blind, lovesick fool who had been taken in by the wealth and trappings, the blandishments of that niggah – that perverted woman! The Ranee had seduced her, there was no doubt about that. That black monster had made her into a monster herself, doing terrible things that a decent man like James Elders would never have expected from her. What a degraded creature she had become!

On impulse, she clawed at the 'niggah finery', as she thought of it, ripping the fine silks, tearing the transparent trousers from her ample thighs until she squatted there completely naked, sobbing with self-pity and rage, murder in her heart...

Cheethoo listened to the thunder of the guns, lying on a humble straw pallet with his hands clasped beneath his head, in his dark, bare chamber. There was not much time to waste. The English would persist in their attacks. One day they would succeed and before then he must be safe inside a Pindaree mountain fastness far to the north.

Cheethoo frowned suddenly. He had caught another noise apart from the boom and crash of cannon – something secretive, furtive. Immediately he was fully awake. Slowly, soundlessly, his right hand slid beneath his pillow and was comforted by the familiar hardness hidden there.

Now the sound was just outside his door. He could hear the rusty handle being tried. He peered through the grey gloom. The door was being opened stealthily. His finger sought and found the trigger of the pistol. He cocked it silently.

Cooler air began to fan his right cheek. From half-closed eyes, as if he were fast asleep, he peered at the figure standing there motionless, watching. He had the impression that there were others in the corridor.

An eternity passed – in reality, a matter of seconds. With great deliberation the figure stepped into the room, gaze fixed on the re-clining figure. Cheethoo tensed. The intruder raised something above his head. Cheethoo caught the faint gleam of silver. A knife?

He waited a moment longer. The killer was almost on to him now. He could wait no more. In one and the same gesture, he pulled the big horse pistol from beneath his head and fired. There was a great ear-splitting roar and bright flame.

The intruder gave a shrill scream, high and hysterical like that of a woman as he was propelled against the wall, to hang there for an instant like a bundle of wet red rags before beginning to slide down it, trailing blood.

Cheethoo was on his feet. There was an angry curse in a language he did not know, the metallic slither of a sword being drawn from its scabbard. Cheethoo grabbed his own great curved blade from the floor. It was always unsheathed at night; that was the way of the Pindaree.

A tall white man with a scarred face sprang at him. It was the *feringhee* who was training the Ranee's cavalry – a killer sent by her, he knew that instantly. He crouched and waited.

The Frenchman came at him in a wild fury, slashing left and right. Cheethoo knew the technique. It was calculated to frighten an opponent, but he remained calm and parried the blows, first one way and then the other, doing so almost mechanically, taking the measure of this great, scar-faced foreigner.

Suddenly he acted. As Nom de Dieu aimed a great slashing blow at his head, Cheethoo parried. Metal struck metal with a sharp clang. They poised there, locked in a test of strength, as Nom De Dieu exerted the full pressure of his brutal shoulder muscles. Then Cheethoo slipped beneath his guard.

His sword plunged home and Nom de Dieu reeled back, blood arcing brightly from a gaping wound in his left side.

Behind him his fellow assailants jockeyed for position in the corridor, urging the wounded Frenchman to get out of the way so that they could attack.

But Nom de Dieu shook his black curly head ponderously like a wounded, savage animal, preparing for another charge, but not wishing to reveal the murder in its heart. Suddenly, startlingly, he rushed Cheethoo again. His bladed hissed furiously from side to side as it cut the air. It sang with the sheer savagery of that wild attack.

Cheethoo kept his nerve. He had faced the fury of the battlefield often enough. Hacking from left to right, he parried with all his strength. Time and again their blades locked. Angry blue sparks flew up. The force of the blows sent fierce pains shooting up his arm. Somehow he held the other man, but slowly he was being forced back. If he allowed himself to be pinned to the wall, he was lost, with no room to manoeuvre. If he dodged beneath that lethal blade and turned his back to the door, the other assassins would cut him down in an instant. Already they were baying for his blood like wild dogs, cheering on Nom de Dieu and yelling encouragement.

Suddenly he had it. It was a wild chance,

a crazy one. But there seemed no other alternative. He measured the distance to the nearest window, an arch-like structure devoid of glass, thank God. He parried another vicious slash. The Frenchman was breathing harshly now. His face was crimson with the effort, but by the look of triumph in his eyes, Cheethoo knew that his opponent felt he was winning. The *coup de grace* wouldn't be long now.

Cheethoo acted. It was a plan of despair, but there was no other way. Parrying another huge lethal slash, he altered the hold on his sword. Taking it like a spear in his sweating hands, he threw it with all his strength at the Frenchman – who screamed as the point sank into his unprotected chest. For a long moment he simply stood there, his weapon still upraised, staring at the vibrating blade protruding from his breast, a slow trickle of blood already beginning to escape. Slowly, very slowly, his sword arm began to fall, as if he had become infinitely weary. His knees started to fold.

A great cry of rage rose from his accomplices. Next moment Nom de Dieu, who had ridden with Murat and had once been the lover of Princess Hortense herself, sank to the floor dying, killed in a sordid attempt to murder a black bandit.

Cheethoo neither knew nor cared about the Frenchman's past. Now he had to save his neck. Without hesitation he sprang to the window arch. For a moment he balanced there, while the Frenchmen still crowded the door as if frozen, unable to act. The cobbled courtyard seemed a long way down. He took a deep breath and launched himself into space, as at the door the spell was broken and the Frenchmen surged into the room, murder in their hearts...

Now the assault party was in the middle of the raging Burra, white-capped waves, blown to a fury by the monsoon wind, lapping against the sides of the low pontoons, heavily laden with frightened men. Standing upright, their black bodies dripping with flying spume, the boatmen paddled and poled with all their strength. Time and again the river seemed about to snatch them away from their course and take them whirling and powerless into darkness and death. But somehow these simple peasants, who would receive a mere handful of annas for their strength and courage, avoided disaster.

Next to John Sergeant Jones seemed resigned. He prayed in Welsh, apparently totally unconcerned by what was going on all around him.

John wished he had the little NCO's calm. But he wasn't afraid. He was too wrapped up in the concerns of his mission. And he did not want to sacrifice the lives of these brave men, white and black, for nothing.

Now the bank of the Burra came even closer. Beyond, through gaps in the waving trees on the shore, he glimpsed the fortress, grim, silent and impressive. Not a light showed, though above the roar of the gunfire now battering its walls further to the right as a feint, he thought he heard the snap and crackle of musket fire. Perhaps some trigger-happy guard firing purposelessly into the night to keep his courage up.

The tug of the current grew less. The boatmen relaxed a little. John could see their strained breathing easing now, as they poled the clumsy pontoons through the floating debris of the river, nudging their way through logs, bundles of thatch and bodies – those of their comrades thrown into the river after death.

The sight increased the urgency of the mission for John. If he didn't succeed this night, God knew how many other unfortunate wretches would succumb to the miseries of that fever-ridden, starving siege camp.

'Captain Bold.' It was Elders, sword already drawn, wan face determined, demented eyes burning like fiery coals – the face of a man committed to death. Instinctively John knew Elders would not survive what was to come.

'What?'

'I crave the honour of taking up the first scaling party. I can see where the dead ground is now. I need no further assistance.'

John hesitated. What would the effect be if he discovered Alice, perhaps in the arms of that perverted she-devil? He dismissed the consideration.

'You shall have that honour, Captain Elders,' he said as the first pontoon grounded on the bank. 'But pray remember, sir, our objective is the main gate – *nothing else!* That was Sir John's express command.'

'I will mark it well, Captain Bold,' Elders lied easily, his mind dwelling on brutal revenge.

'Good, then let us get to it!'

Happily the green-faced infantry and their equally bilious comrades of Bold's Horse streamed ashore, clambering up the bank with a will, glad to be rid of that terrible river, undaunted by the prospect of sudden death. Above them loomed the grim battlements of the lower fort, waiting for them to come. The sight worried them naught; they were on dry land once more. They began to advance. Now the actors were in place. The final act could commence...

10

Cheethoo winced with pain. Red-hot darts of sheer agony seared his left leg. He bit his lip until the blood came, dry and coppery. But the searchers were going now. They had failed to find his hiding place under the ornate horse trough to the right of the courtyard. It was understandable; the area stank of horse droppings. Despite the pain, Cheethoo forced a smile. He had been saved on account of a pile of horseshit, he told himself.

He waited until he saw their burning pitch flares disappearing back in the direction of the *feringhees*' quarters.

Gingerly he felt his leg. Something was sticking out in his lower calf at an awkward angle, trying to break through the stretched flesh. He touched the spot and bit back his cry of pain just in time. There it was; his leg was broken.

For a few moments he lay there among the horse manure. He knew that his most sensible course of action should be to escape from Burrapore, steal a horse and head for the safety of the Vindhya Mountains to the north. There, a whole army would have difficulty in taking him while he recovered.

There, he would be among his own wild, free mountain robbers, dug in to their hillforts.

But Cheethoo, Chief of the Pindarees, was not just a practical man, who had welded a band of robbers and brigands into a military force to be reckoned with; he was also vain and arrogant, a man very conscious of his own honour. And his honour had been assailed by the Ranee of Burrapore: a mere woman, however powerful she might be, who had attempted to have him murdered by her hired foreign killers. No Indian would have dared to lay a hand on him!

As he lay there alone and injured, he considered how he could pay back that perverted woman. In his mind's eye he saw again the whore's apartments, high up on the second storey of the upper fort so that the air in them would not be contaminated by the smell of the great kitchens below.

'*The kitchens!*' he mused, speaking aloud in the manner of lonely men. He visualized them, with great open arches to north and south to draw cooling air through. '*Wood,*' he whispered hoarsely, ignoring the burning pain in his leg as the plan began to uncurl in his mind like some deadly viper preparing to strike. '*There is plenty of wood.*'

There would be no guards. Who would want to guard a kitchen? The men on duty in the upper fort would be posted around the Ranee's apartments.

He grinned evilly in the darkness, as the cannon pounded away and the first drops of the new rainstorm pattered down. It was about time that the Ranee of Burrapore was taught how to act the role of a good Hindu woman, even though she was a princess; and what better way to teach that lesson than – *suttee?*

Still grinning, and despite agonizing pain, Cheethoo began to crawl towards the kitchen...

The assault party rushed forward. Behind them they left the dead sentries, strangled silently, ruthlessly, as they stood at their posts along the dark stretch of wall, caught completely off guard.

To their right the cannon still pounded away, deadening any sound they might make as they doubled through the darkness of the inner courtyard for the main gate. Pistol in hand, heart leaping with joy at how easily the infiltration had gone so far, John told himself now that his only problem at present was keeping his party together in the confusion of low buildings and shacks that masked the approach to the gate. When that final assault came, for which Campbell's men were eagerly waiting outside, he wanted all his strength.

More than once, as they approached ever closer to the gate, he stopped and waved his pistol at little groups of *sepoys* and *sowars* wandering off on their own, obviously eager for loot. After all, that was what they had joined the Company's service for.

They came to a deep ditch filled with sharpened sticks. They were hardly a hindrance, but the ditch was. Its steep and muddy banks sent the soldiers sliding, cursing and falling in the glowing darkness. Anxiously John waited on the far side as they struggled through while Sergeant Jones cursed and chided them in a manner totally foreign to one devoted to 'the good book'.

Now the main gate was a mere fifty yards away and still their presence had not been discovered. Luck, obviously, was still on their side, though despite the artillery bombardment, the Ranee's soldiers seemed to have gone to sleep for the night, save the handful on duty.

The last man emerged from the ditch, hurried along by a well-aimed kick from Sergeant Jones' boot, and they moved on, crouched low and tense, each man wrapped in a cocoon of his own anxious thoughts. The rain was increasing in strength now and for once they were glad of the monsoon, which drowned the sound of their advance on the gate. Now they could hear the howl of cannonballs as they whined off the stout oak of the gate, screeching up into the sky, carrying a trail of angry red sparks behind them. But still the men guarding the entrance to the lower fort did not react. The musket fire John had heard earlier on, must have taken place somewhere else. He dismissed the thought and concentrated on the gate.

With luck they would reach the structure and plant their charges unobserved. If he succeeded in blowing the gate without a fight, he would retire with his men to the group of outhouses to the right, and barricade himself in until Campbell arrived.

'Jones,' he whispered urgently.

The sergeant appeared at his side as if by magic. 'Sir?'

'Where's Captain Elders of the native infantry?' he demanded.

'Don't know, sir, exactly. Back of us somewhere, I think.'

John made up his mind. 'All right. This is what I'm going to do. We're close enough now. I'm taking half a dozen men to plant the charges – no,' he added firmly before Jones could protest, 'I want you to take charge of the *sowars* with the *rissaldar*, just in case. And no arguments.'

'Yessir.'

'Now, see those sheds. Get the men over there and tell Captain Elders to do the same. Now then be off with you. We haven't got all night.' He grinned suddenly and stuck out his hand. 'Thank you for everything, just in case, *Rum and Fornication Jones!*'

Miserably, Jones took it...

Hastily Elders deployed his *sepoys* as Jones had indicated. He took one last look at their positions and was satisfied with what he saw. He peered towards the gate but couldn't make out young Bold and his party, creeping through the darkness to lay their charges. Then he dismissed all of them; he had other things to do...

John, chest heaving with the effort, looked down at the sentry, his throat ripped from ear to ear by one of the *sowar's* knives, the blood still seeping out of the gaping ragged wound. Then as his *sowars*, moving in absolute silence, for there were other sentries on the ramparts, heaped the barrels of gunpowder in position, he began laying the trail. He prayed that the rain wouldn't affect the fuse-line of gunpowder he was dropping on the ground between the barrels and the cover of a stone stable to the left. From within it he could hear the nervous movement of alerted horses and hoped that there were no *syces* with them to raise the alarm.

Nerves tingling and his breath coming in short sharp gasps, he completed the trail and then went back along it, tamping down the powder with his foot. God, he prayed, please keep the full fury of the monsoon rain away till everything is done!

He finished the tamping and beckoned the *sowars,* crouching next to the slaughtered sentry, to follow him. They needed no urging. They could hear the cries and calls of the enemy guards above them quite clearly every time the impact of a fresh cannonball angered them. The sentries had only to look down and spot the furtive shapes flitting back and forth in the grey gloom.

Hurriedly they sheltered behind the stable. The horses shuffled and whinnied nervously. John cupped his hand, cursing the raindrops which were growing more frequent now. He struck the match. It failed to ignite. Twenty yards to his front on the ramparts over the gate, a sentry was waving a pitch torch as if examining the area immediately below with the aid of its flickering, purple flame.

John cursed. In a minute the man would spot the heaped-up barrels of gunpowder. He struck the match again. *Nothing!* He swore. Had the damned rain ruined it? On the battlements, the man swung the torch in the direction of the powder barrels. Desperately John struck the match once more. There was a tiny spurt of blue flame. Hastily John cupped it with his other hand. At that moment it seemed as huge as the beam of Dover lighthouse. He waited a fraction of a second. Now the match was burning brightly. On the rampart the sentry with the torch had ceased moving. *He had spotted the barrels!*

With fingers that were trembling almost uncontrollably now, John applied the flame to the gunpowder trail. It caught immediately. His heart gave a great leap of joy. Angry red flame started to spurt, popping and spluttering, down the gunpowder trail a swift worm heading straight for the barrels. John held his breath. Next to him his *sowars* crouched, fingers in ears, waiting for the explosion.

On the ramparts the sentry with the torch cried out – he had spotted that red, fire-spitting serpent. Almost immediately wild firing broke out. Musket balls whined off the stable walls, showering the men with sharp fragments of stone. In a moment, the guards would be tumbling down the stairs from the ramparts, coming in for the attack! The snaking trail of fire grew ever closer to the barrels. There was the sound of running feet. John prayed as he had never prayed before. Dear Lord, let the gunpowder explode... *Please, dear Lord...!* A musket ball howled off the wall inches above his head. He ducked hastily. The sentries were almost at the bottom of the winding stairs now. After all the effort, they weren't going to make it. In a moment someone would stamp on that deadly red worm and it would be all over. It was too slow ... too visible.

Then it came, surprising, shaking even those who had placed the trail. It seemed to rock the fortress to its very foundations. A crackle of blinding light. A great shocked hush like some primeval monster drawing in a huge breath of air. The ground trembled beneath the crouching observers' feet. Next moment the barrels went up totally. A horrendous gout of purple flame shot into the sky. The gate flew apart. In that blinding furious light, a half-stunned John caught a glimpse of the sentries whirling and twisting like dolls in the crazy maelstrom of shocked air.

For a few moments they could not move. All they could do was to fight for survival as the shock waves slapped them across the face time and time again, whipping their dirty ragged uniforms against their gaunt bodies, ripping the very air from their lungs so that they gasped and choked as if in the death throes of some terrible seizure. Chunks of wood and stone cascaded down all about them. Inside the stable, the horses broke loose and began kicking in complete panic against the doors. The whole world seemed one great moving mass of noise and sudden death.

Then it was over, leaving behind a great echoing silence which seemed to go on for ever until, dimly perceived by the shocked, half-defeated men, still crouching among the falling debris, came the sound of bugles and the urgent rattle of drums. The Army of the Deccan was coming in for the last attack on the Fortress of Burrapore!

Again the bugles outside shrilled their urgent summons, their sweet sound wafting into the fortress. Weakly John Bold sat down, all strength vanished from his young body as if someone had opened a secret tap. 'Bugles at dawn,' he whispered softly to himself, while his men crowded forward to get a first view of their comrades marching through the shattered gate. Slowly he began to laugh. *'Bugles at dawn...'* His laughter rose hysterically, as great tears began to trickle down his wan face. *'Bugles at dawn...'*

Cheethoo hesitated no longer. That great explosion down below and the muted rattle of the drums told him all he needed to know. It was time to be gone, vanishing in the usual confusion of an assault, back to the remote mountain fastnesses of his home. Careful no longer about making noise, he threw the pan of red-hot embers he had taken from an oven in the deserted kitchen. They slammed into the tinder-dry brushwood he had arranged around the logs stacked high against the walls. The kindling caught immediately. In an instant it was sparking and cracking merrily in a cherry-red glare so that he had to back off, dragging his damaged leg painfully behind him. He picked up the jar of *ghee* he had prepared for this moment. The clarified butter smelled rancid, but it would serve his purpose. He scooped out a handful of the stuff and, balancing as best he could on one leg, flung it at the logs just above the kindling. There was a fresh burst of flame. The logs caught immediately. He started back, feeling the heat sear his hawk-like face, the ever-rising flames hollowing his features out to a red death's head.

He hovered, savouring the fire, occasionally throwing another handful of *ghee* at the logs, but knowing now that the flames had caught. His fire wouldn't go out now and already it was beginning to spread, the first of the blackened timbers which supported the kitchen roof was starting to smoulder. In a moment, impregnated as it was with the fat grime of centuries of cooking, it would burst into flames.

Cheethoo thought of that unsuspecting she-devil up above. There was only one set of stairs leading from the Ranee's apartments and they were panelled with ornately carved wood. It should burn like tinder. He grinned evilly. The she-devil would not have a chance. It was highly suitable that she should perish in the flames like the devil she was. The fire leapt higher and higher. He backed off even more, the pain in his leg forgotten for a moment, as he relished his triumph over the would-be murderess.

Abruptly he became aware of running feet, coming from below, where already wild firing had broken out, indicating that the Ranee's men were attempting to resist. Suddenly he realized his own danger. He had to get out of the kitchen, find a horse and vanish in the mêlée. It wouldn't be the first time he had done so when one of his Pindaree raids had gone wrong.

Hobbling, gritting his teeth against the excruciating pain in his leg, he fell back from the flames and staggered out into the glowing darkness. Musket flames stabbed the night, cutting to and fro between attackers and defenders, but Cheethoo was abruptly concerned by those running feet. Did they belong to one of the Ranee's men coming to warn her?

He dropped suddenly, stifling a cry of pain as the broken bone grated. A man in European uniform was running up the rise, a drawn sword in his hand. Cheethoo, crouched, caught a glimpse of a pale, old face and wondered momentarily how a European had survived so long in India. Then the man had passed and Cheethoo knew he could linger no longer. Taking one last look at the rising flames, he awkwardly bent low and gave a ceremonial bow. Voice full of arrogant mockery, he whispered, 'Goodbye, Ranee of Burrapore.' A moment later he had vanished.

Captain Elders raised his arm against the

searing flames, too crazed to realize his own danger, and peered into the burning building. Instinctively he knew that this was the lair of that female fiend who had caused the death of his Alice. He felt the tears flood his eyes. His poor girl, murdered by that black witch even before she had begun to live!

The flames raged higher, tingeing the rafters and walls a blood-red hue. Why not simply let her roast? But that would not be enough. He wanted to see the pain, the fear, the horror on the she-devil's face as he ran his blade through and through her evil guts.

Blindly he staggered up the stairs as the panelling on both sides, adorned with the usual nauseating decoration of these filthy treacherous heathens, began to shiver and crack. A beam came crashing down, scattering sparks. He sprang over it and clambered on, coughing thickly with the smoke. Now he could hear muffled sounds, screams perhaps, cries for help. He grinned crazily. He hoped they came from that bitch. 'Suffer, you black-hearted whore!' he cried above the roar of the fire that now seared the stairwell. He cackled madly and pushed on, shielding his face with his left hand, sword in his right. The stairs ended. He thrust open a great door. Everywhere were the shapes of the vilest creatures of the most perverted imagination, writhing phallic snakes, whores revealed in all their wanton nakedness, fat lecherous-faced gods wielding monstrous organs, mocking the sanctity of womanhood. His demented face contorted. This obscene affront to Christian humanity was her place.

He swung his sword wildly. 'Where are you?' he cried thickly. 'Where are you, great whore of Babylon?'

A slim frightened black woman – Padmini – appeared to his right. She saw the sword in his hand, the wild eyes, and cried, 'Do not strike my mistress... There will be a great reward for you... Gold, pearls...!' She pressed her body against the door, arms outstretched in a vain attempt to bar his progress.

Captain Elders laughed uproariously, as if it was all one great joke. His sword hissed through the air. Padmini screamed as the keen blade sliced through her arm, bone and all. She fell to her knees, moaning piteously, head hanging.

Elders did not spare her. *'Heathen whore!'* he cried, as the flames came racing in behind him. He thrust hard. The blade slid into Padmini's lean brown belly. Her beautiful face contorted with agony.

'Ran–'

Her last cry died as he withdrew the sword with an obscene sucking noise and she fell, her life extinguished.

Elders peered inside the door which Padmini had defended with her life. But the smoke was too thick. Reason should have told him that his own life was in jeopardy, but Captain Elders was past all reason. Perhaps he wanted to die; without Alice life held no meaning for him.

Another timber crashed to the stairs. Nearby a tapestry started to flame. Vaguely he heard voices calling, but whether they were from below or within his own sorely troubled head, he did not know or care. He entered the inner room. 'Blood and fire!' he cried. 'We're going to burn you black heathen bastards … over a slow fire! You're going to pay now … *blood and fire!*' He stopped short, sobbing for breath, chest heaving.

A naked woman crouched in abject fear in a corner. Her fat white limbs trembled violently and she held her hands to her quivering lips from which no sound came. Next to her was an Indian. A man? No, a woman in male clothing, regal, arrogant – and knowing!

'James … *James!*' At last his name escaped those trembling lips in a shrill of relief and fear. 'James … it's me… *It's your Alice!*'

He looked at her, the mad look vanishing from his eyes, though he still held his blood-stained sword raised. 'What…' he stuttered.

'*Captain Elders!* Don't you recognize me … *Alice?*'

Now he was panting. His mouth was slack, yellow teeth bared, spittle dribbling down his chin. A red vision blurred his gaze. The women seemed to be swaying and jerking before his eyes. What did it mean? Why was the black heathen woman dressed as a man ... and why was the white one naked, flaunting herself thus?

Even as the flames grew nearer the Ranee of Burrapore remained unafraid. Neither they nor this mad Englishman could frighten her. She dropped her free hand on Alice's quivering shoulder and kissed the white woman – deliberately – full on the lips – then straightened up to confront the Englishman, dark face full of proud defiance.

Captain Elders saw it all in a flash: the whole perverted obscenity of these two women, one *his wife!* The black woman was *his* wife's lover. He gave a terrible shriek, an anguished mixture of rage and betrayal. *'Jezebels!'* he screamed. *'Jezebels – both!'*

Alice collapsed, squirming hysterically, while the Ranee defiant and proud to the very last, stood boldly waiting for the inevitable.

A crash. A burning timber slammed to the floor, scattering sparks. The thick smoke increased. Elders saw the Ranee as if through a fog, wavering, swaying, yet always mocking. 'Let there be no mercy,' he croaked. 'Let my sweat run and my blood run... Let the wrath of God strike down the heathen...'

He advanced upon her, wreathed in grey

smoke like some vengeful god from a Nordic saga, fire and Alice forgotten.

She stood expectantly, head raised proudly, sword hanging uselessly in her tiny brown hand. All was lost, her dreams of greatness shattered for ever. She welcomed approaching Death.

'*We have sinned against heaven!*' he shrieked, '*and in Thy sight... We are no more worthy to be called Thy children!*' His face writhed as he raised the sword in both hands above his white head. '*It is the wrath of the All Highest...*'

With a great hiss the blade came hurtling down. She raised her bared head proudly to meet its cutting edge. '*IN ... DIA,*' she cried, as that cruel steel exploded inside her head. '*INDIA...*'

That last defiant cry seemed to go on for ever, echoing on and on, as the Fortress of Burrapore fell at last in one great searing mass of tumbling stone and burning timbers, the fiery sparks sailing up to a merciless, unseeing heaven. '*INDIA...*'

Envoi

By sun and rain, disease and debt,
By alien friend and alien foe,
By wives we must perforce forget,
And children we must never know,
By exile, solitude and hate
By these, Lord, let us expiate.

Hilton Brown

Major John Bold yawned luxuriously as he lolled lazily in the jolting *tonga* which had brought him from Burrapore. Now the monsoon was over and the fields around the road to Musulipatan were bright green. Here and there skinny red-bodiced women worked at their crops. Solemn oxen plodded ponderously about their business. All was peace and contentment, reflecting the young major's mood as the red ball of the evening sun touched the horizon.

What a contrast with what he'd left behind. It was now three weeks since the Gibraltar of the East had fallen and Lord Hastings had annexed Burrapore for the Company.

Almost immediately, after searches failed to discover Cheethoo's body in the smoking ruins, Lord Hastings had ordered John to take out a strong patrol after him. Somehow the wounded chieftain – they had found that out from one of their French captives – had escaped them and John had contented himself after a whole week in the saddle, with viewing those far mountain peaks where Cheethoo had taken refuge.

After he had made his report, Hastings had promised to bring up Bold's Horse to a full regiment if he would venture into that remote mountain country and apprehend Cheethoo. He had turned down the tempting offer, pleading the need for leave. It was nine months since he had seen Georgina.

For some reason Major Tomkins had argued against granting him leave. But in the end the Governor General had allowed him to go, though with obvious reluctance.

John straightened up as they moved down Club Drive to the Collector's mansion, patting at the grey dust which covered his regimentals. His heart began to beat a little faster. It wouldn't be long now before he saw Georgina.

At the mansion, Chinese lanterns burned fitfully in the trees, and muted string music came from the windows. He passed under a floral arch, marigolds worked into a wooden portico, and smiled softly. Were they welcoming home the prodigal son, after all? It would be splendid if it were true.

There were carriages everywhere, all gleaming and highly polished unlike his own shabby, dust-covered *tonga*, the waiting *syces* clad in their best livery.

The driver reined his horse and John stepped out, telling him to wait, slapping the dust from his wrinkled uniform while the elegant grooms looked down their noses at this shabby stranger.

John ignored their glances. The music was louder now. Was it the same orchestra which had played that night when Georgina had confessed she loved him, tears in her beautiful green eyes?

He paused at the great entrance. The room seemed full of noise, important noise made by self-important people. Could he burst in on the Collector just like that? Back in the Army of the Deccan they were calling him the Hero of Burrapore. But that was up country. Here he was a nobody. Abruptly he felt shabby and uncertain, and on impulse, moved to the bougainvillaea-fringed verandah. Feeling a little absurd, rather like the beggar at the feast, he edged his way to the nearest tall window.

Elegant people eddied back and forth while white-clad servants proffered sparkling champagne. *Champagne,* that meant a very special assembly. The Collector was a well-known tightwad. He pressed his nose against the glass. Everywhere were happy, well-fed faces, glistening with the evening heat and alcohol, and all staring at the empty centre of the room.

The music stopped and the Collector came into view, clad in one of the newfangled frock coats in a bright bottle green, his fat face more crimson than ever. He held out a pudgy hand like a head waiter expectant of a large tip. The guests clapped. John gasped.

It was Georgina and there was no mistaking that dress of white satin. Georgina, his beloved, who had writhed with such passion on that white beach so long before, who had said she loved him, was wearing a bridal gown! His heart almost stopped beating.

Dazed, feeling a little sick, yet curious all the same, the unseen observer craned forward. A servant placed a glass of champagne in Georgina's gloved hand. She smiled at the guests, showing her pearl-like teeth, obviously very happy. She raised her glass. 'Ladies and gentlemen,' she said, 'please raise your glasses.' Turning her lovely head to one side, she cried, 'To my husband!'

John barely caught himself from crying out loud. There was no mistaking that pudgy figure and pale, self-satisfied, weak face. The regimentals were different – the Guards uniform had been replaced by a fantastic, ornate cavalry uniform, all gold braid and silver epaulettes, adorned with the insignia of a lieutenant colonel – but still they were worn by *him!* Georgina Lanham was married to his greatest enemy, the man who had not only attempted to have him assassinated but who had ruined his career in the British Army and had forced him into exile on the other side of the world. *Georgina had wed Rodney Hartmann!*

For a moment John was too stunned to move, to react, even to think. He simply watched as the assembly drank the toast to the newly married couple, with his arch enemy gazing in lovelorn stupidity at his bride, slack mouth open and gaping like some stupid village idiot.

The spell broke. He was seized by a burning rage, and overwhelming sense of injustice. He flushed hotly, jaw clenched, a nerve ticking at his temple. His hand fell to his sword. In a moment he would kick his way through the window and plunge his blade into the fat guts of the nonentity who had betrayed him twice over.

Slowly Georgina reached up on the tips of her toes. To her new husband's surprise she planted a kiss on his red fleshy lips. His fat face flushed with pleasure and he drew her slim body to his soft weak frame in a possessive embrace, and kissed her.

The guests delighted in the cloying sentimentality of that moment of 'true love'. Led by the Collector, who had found his difficult daughter a rich, safe husband at last, they applauded, and in that instant John knew he had lost her.

Slowly his rage dissipated. His hand dropped from his sword. For a few moments longer he stood watching the two of them. She had been his dream and for an enchanted time he had believed and hoped. Now the dream was dead and a coldness gripped his heart.

Slowly he turned and walked back to his *tonga*. The music and chatter receded. One of the Collector's watchmen spoke to him, but he brushed the man aside without a word.

An officer of the native infantry staggered out of the darkness, flushed and a little drunk. 'I say, it's Major Bold, isn't it?' he cried. 'Aren't you going to the reception? That old bugger, the Collector, is doing himself proud. There's oodles of bubbly, and–' He broke off, puzzled. Bold was walking past him like a sleepwalker.

A couple crossed the path to John's front. 'Isn't it wonderful, darling?' the woman gushed. 'They sail from Madras, this Wednesday week. Imagine *our* Georgina Lanham mixing with high society – the Prince Regent and his circle…'

The coldness was becoming more acute. The chatter, the music, grew ever more distant. Already he had forgotten them. Now he heard another kind of music – the tunes of battle and sudden death. His eyes were set on distant peaks in remote strange lands.

His driver looked at him strangely. John did not seem to notice. He clambered in, gave his orders and then sat, stiff, erect and silent. The driver shrugged. The pay was good, at least. He flicked his whip. The *tonga* moved off, turning north the way it had come. Major John Bold was returning to the wars…

By exile, solitude and hate
By these, Lord, let us expiate.

The publishers hope that this book has given you enjoyable reading. Large Print Books are especially designed to be as easy to see and hold as possible. If you wish a complete list of our books please ask at your local library or write directly to:

Magna Large Print Books
Magna House, Long Preston,
Skipton, North Yorkshire.
BD23 4ND

This Large Print Book, for people
who cannot read normal print,
is published under the auspices of

THE ULVERSCROFT FOUNDATION

... we hope you have enjoyed this book.
Please think for a moment about those
who have worse eyesight than you ...
and are unable to even read or enjoy
Large Print without great difficulty.

You can help them by sending a
donation, large or small, to:

**The Ulverscroft Foundation,
1, The Green, Bradgate Road,
Anstey, Leicestershire, LE7 7FU,
England.**
or request a copy of our brochure for
more details.

The Foundation will use all donations
to assist those people who are visually
impaired and need special attention
with medical research, diagnosis
and treatment.

Thank you very much for your help.